THE
SINISTER SECRETS
OF SINGE

THE
SINISTER SECRETS
OF SINGE

WITHDRAWN

SEAN FERRELL

ILLUSTRATED BY **GRAHAM CARTER**

PIXEL✚INK

PIXEL✚INK

Pixel+Ink is an imprint of TGM Development Corp.
www.pixelandinkbooks.com
Printed and bound in April 2023 at Lake Book Manufacturing, Melrose Park, IL, U.S.A.
Book design by Jay Colvin

Library of Congress Cataloging-in-Publication Data

Names: Ferrell, Sean, author. | Carter, Graham, 1975- illustrator.
Title: The sinister secrets of Singe / Sean Ferrell ; illustrated by Graham Carter.
Description: First edition. | New York : Pixel+Ink, [2023] | Audience: Ages 10 and up.
Audience: Grades 4-6. | Summary: Eleven-year-old Noah, raised in isolation
with only a robot boy for company, embarks on a quest across the sea to find
his exiled father, only to lure trouble back home.
Identifiers: LCCN 2022061804 | ISBN 9781645951834 (hardcover)
ISBN 9781645951841 (ebook)
Subjects: CYAC: Adventure and adventurers—Fiction. | Robots—Fiction. |
Islands—Fiction. | Exiles—Fiction. | Sea stories. | LCGFT: Action and
adventure fiction. | Novels.
Classification: LCC PZ7.1.F468 Si 2023 | DDC [Fic]–dc23
LC record available at https://lccn.loc.gov/2022061804

Hardcover ISBN: 978-1-64595-183-4
E-book ISBN: 978-1-64595-184-1

First Edition

1 3 5 7 9 10 8 6 4 2

For Aidan, as this wouldn't have begun without you.
And for Sarah, as this wouldn't have been completed
without you.

—S.F.

❀ CHAPTER I ❀

Noah lived in a house that grew larger at night. It was the only place he was allowed.

Crashing and hammering and sawing echoed through the spiraling rooms as he slept. During the day, his chores kept him distracted. In his spare time, he daydreamed at the windows about the trees and the hill and the city beyond and wondered if he might ever get to see them up close. He knew he wouldn't. It wasn't allowed.

After dark, the noises let him know the house was growing—that it was a mysterious, living thing.

Most nights, the noises broke into his dreams. He felt the thuds and crashes as if he were dancing with giants. On nights when the noises woke him—an exceptionally large thud, or a ceiling-shaking rattle—he would lie awake for hours, listening. In the dark, he'd imagine what the new rooms and halls would look like. Enough rooms had been added to the house throughout the years that he'd learned what to expect. Each room joined to the previous at a slight angle. Each floor spiraled above the previous, the rooms oddly shaped, the spiral getting wider as the house rose higher.

When the noises woke him, he usually drifted back to sleep slowly, as slowly as the house grew.

At least, that's how it used to be. This night was different. This night, it was the quiet that startled Noah from his sleep. The harder he strained to catch the now-familiar bangs and whirs, the harder his mattress felt.

He sat up slowly to adjust his pillow, careful to make no sound that he was awake.

Almost instantly, heavy robotic footsteps clicked toward the bed.

"You are not sleeping," Elijah said. "It is night, and you are not asleep." The ticking of the robot caretaker's gears and the occasional singing of his springs revealed Elijah's location. "You should sleep at night."

Elijah was always repeating Marie's rules and warnings.

The robot walked to the side of the bed. Noah didn't need light to know Elijah was worried. Light would only show the robot's face—the face of a boy about Noah's age, unmoving and expressionless and cast from iron. Elijah's expressions came from the speed of his clockwork ticking, not the furrow of a brow.

Noah listened to the house he knew so well. Beyond Elijah's ticking, there wasn't a sound. But Noah didn't need to see the house to know it. After all, it was the only place he'd ever been, home only to his mother Marie, Elijah, and himself—three small figures in a giant, spiraling space. Yet until this night, with its unsettling quiet, it had never occurred to Noah how room after room of it was empty.

Now he could think of nothing else.

From the dark came Elijah's quiet suggestion: "It is nighttime. You should be sleeping."

"I know it's night."

"And still, you are not sleeping."

"I *know* I'm not sleeping. It's because of the noise."

Elijah's gears worked in the dark. Noah could tell his caretaker was tilting his head, straining to hear. "Noise? It's so far away I can almost not hear it."

"That's the problem." Noah sighed his frustration into the darkness. Arguing with Elijah was pointless. His programming and clockworks couldn't understand Noah's exasperation. They could only determine that Noah was not doing what was expected. What was expected was routine. Boring routine. Lonely routine.

Noah reached a hand under his mattress, where he'd hidden a stack of yellowed papers. Papers that were not part of the routine. Papers he had found while exploring.

He and Elijah often played hide-and-seek. When he'd been younger it had been his favorite game. Now, it was more for solitude. Elijah counting to three or four thousand gave him hours to look through the rooms filled with crates, to peek inside containers of gears and springs and tools, to riffle through papers covered with notes and drawings—notes in handwriting he'd never seen before and drawings of mechanical plans beyond what he'd ever imagined. Marie had been teaching Noah how to tinker, but the drawings he'd found had taught him how to imagine.

"Elijah," Noah whispered. "What are the noises from?"

Elijah's ticking stayed steady. "From the house growing larger."

"And what makes the house grow larger?" Noah had a theory. His mother had warned him about the danger of the noises. He wasn't to explore a new room until the noises had moved on. But Marie had never told him why. She'd never said *what* was doing the building.

Elijah's ticking sped up in just the way Noah expected. "The house . . . grows larger . . . because . . . a larger house is a larger . . . home. This home is where Marie keeps you safe. Marie wants to keep you safe."

Noah had asked Elijah these questions before. At first, it had been a kind of teasing game he liked to play. Then it had become a frustration.

Questioning Elijah was pointless. His caretaker would only repeat every rule and double-talk response until Noah gave up. Elijah repeated his script because that's how Noah's mother Marie had built him. She had built him that way so that nothing would ever change.

But Noah wanted things to change.

"Elijah, did Marie tell you not to tell me about the house?"

Elijah's gears sped up again, but he gave the same answer Noah had expected: "Lady Marie is only concerned—"

"Concerned that I stay safe," Noah finished. "Yes, I know." He ran a finger along the edge of the crisp, yellowed papers hidden beneath his mattress. He wanted to pull them out and look through them again. He felt a page slice his fingertip. It stung, but he didn't mind.

As a bead of blood rose on his fingertip, the perfect question formed in his mind. "Elijah, who wanted to build the house for us?"

No sounds came from the dark. Elijah's gears didn't spin. Noah could just make out his caretaker's silhouette in a sliver of moonlight. He began to count his own breaths. As he reached ten, he worried he'd broken his only friend.

At last, there was a high-pitched whine and Elijah's gears sped back to normal. "Lady Marie only wants this home to be safe."

This home, Noah thought. Elijah hadn't said *our* home or *her* home. He hadn't even said *your* home.

The paper cut stung as Noah played with the hidden pages. A week earlier, he'd found the stack beneath the false bottom of a metal toolbox. He'd been searching for a small wrench for one of his tinkering chores, and as his assigned tasks had recently become more complex, Marie had encouraged him to search through the dozens of crates and boxes in the attic and spiral rooms. "You'll find everything you need, my brilliant tinkerer," she had said. He was sure the papers weren't what she'd meant, but they were the only thing he'd found that mattered to him now.

The notes were tied together with string that had snapped the moment he tried to untie it. There were some handwritten jottings, and many, many sheets of drawings, diagrams, and mechanical plans. Gear sizes and spring and clockwork designs. Some schematics showed miniature parts in great detail. Others captured the concept of the contraption as whole.

One in particular had caught Noah's eye: a massive spider made of an enormous round body covered in glass bead lenses for eyes, with four long legs and four shorter ones, each equipped with a different tool—a hammer on one, a drill, a screwdriver, and a saw. This was a robot designed to build, and build quickly. Multiple arms ready for a multitude of simultaneous tasks. Walls, floors, and ceilings could fly and form from the tools of this machine.

The diagram was labeled SPIDERATUS.

And beneath that was a name: ALTON PHYSICIAN.

The moment he'd found the papers, Noah had stared at those two words, dumbstruck. *Alton Physician* was his father's name.

In the stolen moments since finding them, Noah looked at those pages and thought about his father. The house. His mother. Even Elijah. His mother had always made the rules and kept him away from the world. It had only ever been Marie, her rules, and Elijah. But she had kept something from him, something that wasn't hers to take.

The house was his father's, and it was something of his father's design that built it. A magnificent machine called a spideratus. A magnificent machine from someone who must have been a magnificent man.

Grinding his teeth—thinking about how he would find that secret machinery built by his father—Noah finally fell asleep.

In the morning, the routine began just as it always did. Noah almost wondered if his time spent laying awake the night before had been a cruel dream, that he didn't really have the papers with his father's designs. But when he'd peeked beneath the mattress, there they were, the edge of one page smeared with blood from the paper cut that still stung. The crashing and slamming sounded even farther away, as it now did every morning. Noah knew there would be a new room at the top of the house, an odd room with odd angles adding to the wandering spiral.

There is only one way the house could grow at night, Noah thought. *It has to be a spideratus.*

He wanted to rush up the swirl of rooms, but just as he stepped toward the staircase, Marie called up to him about the chores she needed done, and Elijah started rattling on about breakfast.

He had to follow the routine. He could sneak upstairs later, when an opportunity presented itself.

He only hoped that opportunity wouldn't wait too long.

"Good morning, Sir Noah. Did you sleep well after not sleeping well?" asked Elijah. His voice was accompanied by the soft *tick-tick-tick*-ing of his gears.

Noah tried to ignore the same dry toast and eggs Elijah always place before him.

Elijah's unmoving face remained focused on Noah's. "The breakfast is eggs. Is there something wrong with the eggs?"

"They're fine." They were always fine.

"Eat up." Elijah's version of cheery always sounded like commands, and Noah hated commands.

Noah said nothing as he watched the mechanical boy move around the kitchen. At one time, he'd thought the robot a marvelous friend—almost like a brother—but now, after eleven years, he looked at Elijah as a toy he'd long out-grown. His unmoving iron face, once as realistic as Marie had been able to manage, was beginning to rust. And while Noah had aged, the robot still looked like a boy barely older than Noah himself. Soon Noah would catch up, and then pass Elijah. One day Noah would be a grown adult followed around by a little robot boy chiding him about chores and asking to play.

"You will need your energy." Elijah tapped the table. "I'm sure Miss Marie has many wonderful chores for us today."

"I do have chores for you." As if synched to the gears of an invisible clock, Marie entered the kitchen. She looked distracted as usual. Her blue coveralls were filthy from weeks without washing and her dark hair was pulled back from her face with what might have been an oily rag. "But I don't know if they should be called 'wonderful.'"

She indifferently watched Noah. *She might not even know who she's looking at,* he thought. *Does she even know the difference between me and Elijah anymore?*

Elijah handed her a cup filled with coffee and a piece of burnt toast, breaking the uneasy tension. "Thank you, Elijah," she said, but her eyes stayed fixed on her son. She always seemed to be studying him; he was never sure why. "Noah, I have a few things for you to work on today."

Just leave already, Noah pleaded silently. The sooner she left, the sooner he might find a way to sneak upstairs.

"I was hoping I could just tinker," he said aloud. "Maybe even go outside?"

Marie shook her head and looked away. "No, Noah. Not yet. Soon, but no going outside today."

"You always say that, Marie."

She set the cup down, spilling a drop onto the table. "For the thousandth time, you know that bothers me. Please call me *Mom.*"

Noah pushed his eggs around his plate. "I don't understand why. Your name is *Marie.*"

"I *am* your mother." She sounded tired. She always did by this point.

Elijah dropped the dirty skillet into the sink with a crash. "You are his mother! *And* your name is Marie!" His gears clicked as he scrubbed at burnt eggs. Elijah always tried to help, even when there was no helping.

Marie swallowed her coffee in one gulp, then waved for Noah to follow her. She'd never convince him to use the odd nickname. As if there was any confusing her for anyone else. There *was* no one else.

Marie held the toast between her teeth as they walked down the hall and toward the stairs. On their way up to the second floor, she gathered tools and gears and springs from the machine parts littering the halls and worktables and benches she'd built into the walls. They only used the first two rings of the spiral. By the third ring, the rooms gaped, empty and waiting.

Noah could clearly hear the noises from above them now, and with the clatter, his impatience grew. He wanted to rush ahead, looping higher and higher, to find the machine he knew was there.

Marie stopped before a workbench, her hands on her hips, toast still clenched in her teeth. Before her was something resembling a giant mechanical glove. On the floor, a large rubber tire with a series of odd springs and gears protruding from the hub waited.

"Two tasks for you today," she said around the toast, which was starting to get soggy, leaving black crumbs plastered to her chin.

The first project was familiar to Noah. He'd built most of the glove himself. "The gauntlet fits well," Marie explained, "but it needs to be stronger. A tighter grip. And please be careful. It needs to be strong, but not like last time."

They both glanced at the table leg that had been crushed to splinters the last time Noah had tested his work.

"I can make it better," he mumbled.

"Not better. Just *right*."

Noah ran his thumb over the paper cut on his finger. Marie was not only keeping him stuck inside, but from exploring what he knew he could do.

She didn't seem to notice his annoyance as she tapped the wheel with her foot. "I'm trying to improve Liberty's transport system. If I can get rid of the large engines, it will be lighter and more efficient. See what you can do with this. I want it to be able to pull at least . . ."

Noah's thoughts drifted. Above the workbench was a window, and beyond that window stood a dark forest.

Even with sunlight striking them, the trees rose black. The forest continued down the mountain toward the sea, down to where the city of Liberty sat at the edge of the water. The inventions Noah built made their way to Liberty. Every few days, Marie would take the machinery he'd completed down the mountain, always returning with new projects for him. Always the same.

"Are you listening?" Marie was staring at him. Her lips disappeared as she pressed them together. The toast wagged limply in her hand as she waved it to get his attention.

"Can I go to the city with you?" Noah asked. Marie had her rules, but she could lift them.

"It's not safe, Sir Noah." Elijah was suddenly beside Marie. For a contraption that ticked like a clock, he could certainly move quietly.

"But why?"

"You know it's not safe, Sir Noah."

"Thank you, Elijah." Marie waved a hand to dismiss him, but the mechanical boy simply stepped to the side and waited. "Noah, you *know* why."

And he did. He regretted asking, because now Marie would list the same reasons he'd heard a thousand, thousand times. Reasons he could repeat himself with no thought. Reasons that didn't make anything better, and, in fact, made everything much, much worse.

"A long time ago," Marie said, her eyes dark and sad, "your father made a terrible mistake, and he and many other people died because of it. And now you and I work to help the city of Liberty recover from that mistake. We pay the city back because your father . . . cannot."

Noah nodded. He wished Marie would reveal the secrets. Even just one. He closed his eyes, resolving that he wouldn't go upstairs if she'd just tell him one little secret.

"Your father was a genius," she said quietly. Her eyes were still closed, and Noah wondered what she saw in her memory. "A curious genius . . . but even the best of us make mistakes, and the one he made was terrible."

Noah knew. He'd heard too many times. Liberty had been in danger and his father had built defenses for the city. But he built them . . . wrong. Great and terrible machines—robots meant to protect—had instead become the attackers, turning against the city and the people they had been built to defend. Marie called it the Uprising.

She opened her eyes and locked her gaze with Noah's. She was impatient, he could tell, as if staying in the house was torture for her. "We have to unmake your father's mistake, my dear."

Noah hated being called *dear*. "It's just so . . ."

It was all so unfair. It was his father's punishment, but he was the one receiving it. He hadn't even been born when the Uprising occurred. Yet Noah didn't blame his father. Marie was the one inflicting the punishment on him. It was Marie who kept the forest and the city and the ocean beyond his reach. It was her burying him in secrets and rules.

If she tells me this one thing, that will be enough, he thought.

"Is everything my father built gone?"

Marie froze. "What do you mean?"

Far above them rumbled the hammering and sawing of the house growing ever larger. It *had* to be the spideratus. The design was too perfectly fitted to the task to be anything else. The last of his father's creations, left behind, like him, in a giant, rambling, empty house.

Noah and Marie were still staring at each other. Finally, he looked down at the workbench. "I mean, is anything my father made still around? Did any of it work like it was supposed to? I'd . . . I'd like to see it."

Marie shook her head. "No." Her voice was quiet, like a whisper. Noah suddenly wondered if this was how she sounded when she lied. Or was a whisper how she revealed secrets? "Your father's work had to be driven off. None of it was safe. None of it remains."

Noah squeezed at the paper cut until it felt as if he'd made it bleed again. A sentence formed in his head—*I don't believe you*—but he bit his lip to keep it from tumbling out.

Downstairs, the stuck-clock rang eight times. The tall grandfather clock with its long pendulum and ornate, black iron hands stood just at the bottom of the stairs. Perpetually stopped at one minute to twelve, the pendulum didn't swing, the hands didn't move, and the clock didn't tick or tock. Still, somehow, it sounded when it was time for Marie to leave, and it sounded when she was almost home. Noah sometimes wondered what made it work without working.

"I have to go," Marie said, dropping the remains of her toast on the workbench.

Elijah immediately swept it up. "No messes, Miss Marie."

"Yes, yes. No messes, Elijah," she replied absently, impatiently, checking her pockets for Noah-couldn't-guess-what, before stomping down the steps toward the front door. A moment later, she returned, and Noah's breath caught. Maybe she would finally tell him some small nugget of the truth. Instead, she went to Elijah, put her lips close to his ear, and whispered to him.

"I understand," Elijah said. Marie disappeared down the stairs again. The door slammed behind her without so much as a goodbye.

"Have a good day, Miss Marie," Elijah called after her. He didn't mean to sound sarcastic, but saying it after she was gone made it seem that way.

Yes, Noah thought as he looked at the work on the bench, and the city by the sea framed in the window. *Have a good day.*

He knew he'd have to find his moment to sneak away from Elijah, but this would be the day he'd find the spideratus—the one and only thing his father had left behind.

❀ CHAPTER 2 ❀

For a while after Marie's departure, Noah and Elijah stared at each other. Noah wondered what Marie had said to his caretaker, but Elijah's expressionless face revealed nothing.

Then there was a clicking as gears shifted and sped up. Elijah took a few steps forward and said, "Frogs are carnivores."

"What?" Noah's mouth dropped open. "Why did you say that?"

Elijah looked around the room, as if someone else would answer for him. "I thought you would be interested."

Noah needed to think. Although he recognized the projects Marie had left him, everything seemed unfamiliar. He was too distracted by his desire to rush upstairs. *I want to go right now,* he thought. *But I can't have Elijah following.*

"Elijah, how about we play hide-and-seek?"

The robot's gears clicked. "But Marie left us these lovely chores."

"*Lovely?*"

"Perhaps *lovely* is the wrong word." Elijah looked at the shattered table leg. "In any event, hide-and-seek must wait. Too much to do!"

She must have told him to keep an eye on me, Noah realized. He'd also keep an eye out, and a plan would form. Marie always told him that solutions could arrive if his mind was focused elsewhere. This was no different from any tinkering project. The problem was how to distract Elijah, and if Noah worked on the projects now, a solution would eventually come to him.

He lifted the glove from the bench and quickly disassembled it. Meanwhile, Elijah continued to rattle off facts about frogs.

"Frogs lay their eggs in water. Typically."

"Why are you talking about frogs?" Noah asked.

"What animal would you prefer?"

Noah almost said *spiders*, but thought better of it.

He could ask Elijah to be quiet, and Elijah would do as asked, but that would only add to the emptiness. The hammering was too far away, and it was better to have a voice in the room, even one rattling out useless facts. Perhaps that was even better than conversation.

The spideratus loomed in Noah's thoughts. His father had taken inspiration from nature, obviously. It was similar to what Noah did with his own secret projects, building little mechanical contraptions that he released out the window. There had been hopping birds and scurrying mice and even a wriggling metal worm. Sometimes he could see them wandering among the trees. And sometimes Marie would angrily arrive home with one she had caught.

"Frogs have skin that produces secretions. Sometimes it is even toxic!" Elijah announced. The robot boy sounded positively enthusiastic about poison frogs.

As Noah tinkered he continued thinking about his father's work and about the frogs with their powerful hind legs and snapping tongues. By the time he'd finished with the glove, he had discarded most of Marie's original design, lightening the weight by several pounds and improving its speed and strength. He'd also destroyed two additional table legs and punched a large hole in the wall between the room they were in and the next, but as both were just workrooms, he didn't much care. He knew Marie wouldn't care, either. *You choose the goal, then the path,* she was fond of saying. *If you keep your eye on where you want to be, you can find the best way get there.*

Noah wasn't sure this was true, but he'd heard it too often to argue.

By the time he'd finished with the glove, he had also heard all there was to know about frogs, and was startled to realize he'd been unconsciously sketching out plans in his head for a frog contraption. Working on one problem unlocked another. *You choose the goal, then the path.* Noah wasn't sure he liked it when Marie was right. He especially didn't like that she'd gotten Elijah to distract him, but it was too late now. He went back to his tinkering.

Focusing on the hind legs, Noah began to piece together a quick frame for the frog. All the while in his head he was shouting, *There must be a way to distract Elijah.* Hours had passed—half the day gone—and he was no closer to the spideratus than when he had awoken.

"It should jump," Elijah suggested.

"It will."

"Frogs can jump several feet."

Noah smiled. "This isn't a real frog. It will jump much farther than a few feet."

"How much farther?"

Noah looked at the shattered bench leg. He'd already

used some of the parts from the mechanical glove to create the frog legs. "Twenty feet. Maybe more."

"That *is* more than a real frog."

Noah laughed.

Elijah's gears whirred with worry. Noah couldn't understand why his caretaker would be worried now; everything was as boring as usual.

"It's not a real frog," Elijah said. His ticking grew louder.

"She's real enough," Noah said. "She's going to jump and sit under the bushes looking for bugs. She'll eat them. I might even make it so she can let them out unharmed." He thought of the mechanical frog having insect droppings and laughed. "It *will* be a real frog, in its own way."

Elijah's nervous gears started to quiet. "Real in its own way. I see."

He's wondering about himself, Noah thought, considering that perhaps Elijah was as trapped inside Marie's rules as he was. Maybe even more so. Noah had to live by rules, but Elijah had to live according to programming.

"You're very kind," Noah said. "To worry after this made-up little frog."

"I do not think I worry." Elijah's inner workings threatened to whir again, but then settled. "I do think I . . .

wonder . . . about what the frog will think and do in the world. How it will . . . be here."

"That's what makes you so much more than this little frog."

Noah was glad to hear the *tick-tick-tick*-ing of his companion slow to its normal pace. He covered the pieces with a cloth. "I shouldn't even be working on it yet. I haven't started on the stupid wheel."

"Miss Marie did ask you to work on the stupid wheel before tinkering on your contraptions."

"Yes, but maybe don't call it a stupid wheel when Marie is home."

He began tinkering again. He understood what Marie wanted, but not why. The wheel would be connected to its own clock-gear engine, able to propel itself and anything attached to it. The problem was it wasn't running. The contraption was *on*, but it didn't even make a sound.

The silence coming from everything—the house, the wheel, even Elijah—made Noah uneasy, but he tried to focus. Taking a deep breath, he thought of all the simple steps that had gone into putting the wheel together. After just a few minutes, he found the problem in the engine. A bolt had come loose and fallen into the gear works. It was stuck tight, but Noah got hold of it with his pliers and started to tug.

"Should have seen this right away," he said to himself. He glanced at his old companion as he pulled at the bolt. The robot was still and silent, as if stuck like the wheel. Normally Elijah would respond to anything—everything—that Noah said. Not now. It was almost worrisome. "Why are you just standing there, Elijah?"

The robot boy looked back at Noah, and despite his face holding the same, unchanged expression, Noah couldn't help but think Elijah looked terribly sad.

"I wonder—" Elijah began.

And then the bolt came loose.

Distracted, Noah had forgotten to disengage the springs, and the engine clicked into gear. The wheel propelled itself at top speed across the room, then ricocheted off the wall, and spun toward the door. It knocked a table into the air, sending springs and gears flying. The tumbled tapping of tools and machine parts echoed around them. The table toppled, and the wheel bounced between it and the wall—back and forth and back again—until the wood shattered with a crash. The wheel sent splinters flying on its path bouncing from one wall to another, tracing a circle around Noah and Elijah before resuming its path toward the door.

"Grab it!" Noah shouted.

Noah had never seen Elijah move so fast. His gears

whirring, he nearly got to the wheel in time—one finger tracing the treads of the tire—but it spun out of reach and zipped through the door, crashing into walls, the gears screeching as it continued down through the spiral.

"It sounds as if it is breaking many things," Elijah said.

They followed a path of destruction through the house. Broken table pieces crunched underfoot. Scattered tools and machine parts clinked as they ran forward. Tire marks marred walls and doorframes. Noah and Elijah hurried to intercept the wheel as it spun through the spiral back toward the stairs, but it was so far ahead they didn't catch sight of it until they scrambled to the first floor.

"Miss Marie's wheel is going to destroy the house," Elijah said as they ran down the hall.

"We'll fix it!" Noah shouted back. He didn't want to think about what she would say when she returned home. Sometimes she didn't seem to notice that anything had been damaged, and somehow that was worse than when she did.

The wheel ran over a chair and flew into the air, landing on the kitchen counter, where it spun every pan and dish onto the floor in a cacophony of clangs and crashes.

Noah stopped short. He no longer wanted to halt the wheel. He was afraid of it. "Maybe we should stay upstairs."

"How can we stop it?" Elijah asked.

The wheel had its own answer. It raced between them, bounced off the front door leaving a black mark on the wood, and then smashed at full speed into the base of the stuck clock. With a tremendous and sickening *crunch*, the panel shattered in a cloud of silver-gray dust and wood chips. The clock's bells rang out all at the same time, and then there was silence. The device was stuck. The only thing it could do now was fill the room with the smell of hot, burning rubber tire. Noah covered his face and stumbled back. When he looked again, Elijah stood beside the unmoving wheel, a thin layer of gray dust coating his shoulders and head. The device vibrated, its gears continuing to sing. Noah hurried forward and hit the switch to turn it off. Warily, he looked around assessing the damage.

"We have broken everything," said Elijah.

Noah heard a strange sound—a ticking—and it seemed to be coming from . . .

"The clock?" Noah asked. "It's . . . unstuck?"

As if answering, the hands moved to twelve and the clock began to chime.

"I see. We have not broken everything," Elijah said, pointing. "We have fixed the clock."

Noah impatiently slapped dust from his clothes. "Help me get it out of there."

As Noah and Elijah worked together to yank the wheel from the hole it had punched into the base of the tall clock, splintering wood raining down around their feet, the chiming stopped, though the ticking from inside the cabinet was unmistakable.

Noah disengaged the engine while Elijah studied the mess. "It is a fast wheel."

"It is," Noah agreed.

"I'm sure Lady Marie will be very pleased by your improvements to it."

From above there came a crash as some something that had only been partly broken became completely so. Noah sighed. "I'm just glad it wasn't even faster or it might have punched right through the door."

That's when Noah realized this problem with the wheel was actually a solution.

Elijah was chattering away, but Noah heard none of it.

All morning, he'd needed a distraction for Elijah. And now he had the wheel.

Elijah commented on how fast the wheel had been going, glanced up the stairs, made calculations based on time and distance, and still Noah said nothing. He opened the front door, turned the wheel to face it, and reengaged the engine.

The device raced out the door, bounced down the front

steps, and screamed across the yard, heading toward the tree line.

Elijah turned and watched as the wheel hit a rock and bounced high into the air. "There goes the wheel."

"We have to get it back!" Noah said. He knew how Elijah thought, and he knew the conclusion the robot boy would reach.

There was the briefest of gear clicks and then Elijah said, "You must stay here. Marie does not want you leaving the house. I will retrieve the wheel." With that, he ran out the door, following after the speeding mechanism.

Noah laughed to himself. He'd done it: he'd focused on one problem, and a solution to another had been discovered, just as Marie had suggested. "I hate it when she's right," he grumbled as he ran up the stairs.

He wound through the spiral of rooms, crossing floors at steep angles and passing through doors that had been built too low or too narrow. As he raced on, he realized no two rooms were at the same angle. Through the crooked windows, he glimpsed the city far below, then the forest, the mountains, and back to the city. Again and again, higher each time, the sky outside getting darker as the sun set. All the while, the building noises were his guide, the sounds of construction growing louder with every step.

I know what's up here, Noah thought as he ran. *The last of my father's creations.*

He felt a stinging in his stomach. If he was right, it was a machine—a secret—Marie and Elijah had kept hidden from him.

From far below, he heard the chiming that announced Marie's return. How the clock knew of his mother's departures and returns had always been a mystery, but now it was a warning. She would try to stop him. He needed to climb faster.

Not long after, Noah stumbled into the last completed room. It was long and narrow, like a hallway, with many windows on either side. Beams of late-afternoon sunlight streaked across the floor, and the ceiling was dappled by distant shimmering off the ocean. Such a brilliant reflection, even at such a distance, was hard to focus on, so Noah covered his eyes, making his way unsteadily toward the banging and clanging, which were now just on the other side of the last doorway. Something was moving there—black streaks blurred past the opening as the din hammered his ears.

It wasn't too late. He could still turn around and go back to the vast, empty house, to the distant sounds, to Elijah, to Marie, to the rules. And to the secrets.

Secrets that may as well have been outright lies.

He stepped through the doorway to face his father's contraption.

The spideratus was far larger than Noah had imagined. He had envisioned a spider contraption as he might have built it, roughly the size of a dinner plate, but what loomed before him was taller than his mother, the legs longer than that. The body alone was half the size of his bed. Noah gasped and pushed himself back against the wall, taking in his surroundings and realizing suddenly how dangerous they were. The walls extended only a few feet, the floor a little farther. With no ceiling, wind seemed to whip from every direction, strong enough that he feared being blown from the house.

At the sound of his approach, the spideratus had spun its body so the eye lenses could take him in. Noah could see his own reflection in the glass beads. The face staring back at him looked terrified. He couldn't move. He could barely breathe.

The machine studied him for a moment, its long legs gripping the boards, maneuvering quickly and easily. The shorter arms brandished their tools, the drill spinning, the saw blade whirring. When Noah didn't move, the machine made a small grinding noise followed by a ticking similar

to Elijah's before turning back to its work, hammering and sawing and drilling at the wood to make the house ever larger.

From behind him came Marie's voice. "Noah! Please, come back!" She was very close. He didn't understand how she could have climbed so quickly.

He needed more time. Now that Marie knew he knew, he might never be this close to one of his father's inventions ever again. She would make more rules, give Elijah more tasks, probably make the machine disappear forever. If he didn't try to understand the spideratus now, he might never get another chance.

Noah pushed away from the wall and walked cautiously to the center of the unfinished room, holding his hands out as if balancing on a rope. Ahead of him, the floor ended, and the drop to the treetops below was a long one. He inched toward the spideratus.

"Let me look at you," Noah said. Elijah could understand him, so he figured this machine might, too.

"Noah!" Marie sounded closer. "What are you doing?" The quiver in her voice almost made Noah stop. Almost.

The machine paused its work again, and the glass eyes turned back to study Noah. He could see himself so clearly. His reflection smiled back at him.

He had never seen a contraption so magnificent. Everything he had worked on, everything Marie had taught him, was small or just a part of something larger. Here was an entire robot: huge, complex, and wonderful.

His father had clearly been a genius. What could possibly have gone wrong with such perfect mechanical creations?

"You're beautiful," he whispered, realizing he was close enough to touch it. He reached out a hand to the black, cast-iron body.

Marie's footsteps stopped in the doorway behind him. She was panting, her voice hoarse as she called out, "Noah, get away from there!"

"Why didn't you ever tell me my father's work was here?" he shouted. When he looked back, Marie's hand was shaking as she reached for him. He was suddenly furious. He didn't want her touching him. She had secrets and lies and nothing more for him. "It's not fair. It was here the whole time! And it's amazing!"

His hand touched the metal body. It was cold, and from inside he felt the vibration of clockworks busily spinning.

The spideratus let out a metallic clang and hopped high into the air, spinning as it rose, before landing in a low crouch. Its four short arms pointed their tools at Noah like weapons.

Marie screamed and tried to step forward, but Elijah had appeared and was holding her back. He said something, but Noah couldn't hear over the sounds coming from the spideratus. There was a rhythmic clanging and then a kind of high-pitched whine, as if the machine was frightened. It took a sudden lunge toward Noah, caging him in with its long legs. Its body was close enough to touch again, and in the black bead eyes, Noah saw himself pinned against the floor, his face a mask of fear.

"*Noah!*" Marie screamed again. "*Get away from it!*"

Though he was terrified, Noah saw how the machine's eyes kept pivoting toward him. But even as it turned, two eyes always stayed fixed on him—two smaller eyes sitting high on the upper part of the body. Noah recalled his father's diagrams, trying to remember some of the detailed drawings of the inner workings. There was something about those eyes. He remembered thinking the way the wiring was connected was odd. They hadn't looked like they'd function as eyes at all.

The spideratus raised its four tools so they all aimed at Noah. He no longer heard the blaring alarm of the robot or the screams from Marie and Elijah. Just the wind, his own breathing, and the calm rhythm of his heart.

Carefully, he leaned out, placed a thumb on each eye,

and pressed. They sank deep into the metal body, followed by a click. It was a small click as far as noises go, but obviously an important one. The spideratus—without warning—turned off.

The air was eerily quiet, except for Marie crying his name as she rushed to him.

"Noah! Noah, are you all right?" She dropped to her knees and grabbed him, her hands running over him as she checked his arms and face for injuries. Suddenly, he felt unbearably tired, too tired to even speak, but he managed a small smile at her. He couldn't remember a time when her only worry was him.

Mother and son turned to look at the frozen machine. The spideratus was still in the same menacing position, but there were no more sounds, no movement. It was a statue.

"It's so amazing."

Marie wiped sweat from her face. "You have no idea how many hours I've spent trying to shut that thing down."

Noah shrugged at her. "Why?"

Marie laughed, though it wasn't a happy sound. "I thought your . . . father might have sent it here for a reason. Maybe to deliver some kind of message. It arrived so suddenly and—"

"This is Alton Physician," a deep voiced boomed.

Marie pulled Noah closer. They slowly turned. Elijah was standing right behind them, his expressionless, iron face peering down at them. "Congratulations," he said in a voice not his own. "You have proven yourself capable of assisting me in my work. This robot, Elijah, shall help you in reaching me. He is my emissary. I do not know how long it will be before you have passed my spideratus test, so I do not know what you will know of me. Let me just say this: I have been lied about and vilified, my work twisted by jealous, inferior minds. My exile is unjust, but it is the work that matters. Not the lies. I will see you soon. Elijah will know how to reach me."

Elijah stopped talking in Alton Physician's voice and stared down at Noah and his mother. His cold eyes made the boy shiver.

Marie clutched Noah tighter. "Elijah," she said. "What was that?"

The robot looked around as if awakening from a dream. He walked around Noah and Marie, resting his own metal hand on the iron body of the spideratus. "I have long wondered if it would be Noah who would pass the test." He glanced back at the others. "I have to go. There are preparations to make."

Marie's voice was low and shaking. "Elijah . . . I command you to stop."

Elijah knelt before her. "I am very sorry, Lady Marie. I cannot. Alton Physician's programming will not allow it." He stood and walked to the edge of the unfinished floor. "Sir Noah, I will see you soon. I think this is going to be very exciting."

And then the caretaker robot stepped off the edge and fell out of sight.

Noah and Marie scrambled on hands and knees to the opening, holding on to the heavy, slender legs of the spideratus to steady themselves, before peering past the last floorboards. Below them, Elijah jumped from ledge to ledge of the misshapen house. His descent was swift. He looked smaller the farther he went, until at last he was just a dot landing on the front yard. And then he ran into the forest, and was gone.

Marie took hold of Noah's hand. Her own was shaking.

"Oh, Noah," she said. "What have you done?"

❀ CHAPTER 3 ❀

Noah had collapsed into a stunned heap. Everything was too bright, despite the sun sinking toward the horizon. Sound came from too far away, and nothing he touched felt solid.

How could any of that be real?

As everything that had just happened swirled in his head, Marie pulled him from the unfinished ledge, leaving the spideratus behind. A couple of rooms away, she led him to a window, but not one of the exterior ones looking toward the forest. It was positioned on the opposite wall, facing the house's interior, and climbing through it, Noah realized how Marie had reached him so quickly. In the center of the spiral, Marie had constructed a series of ropes and ladders. It was like climbing through the center of a frozen tornado. They passed the windows of many rooms along the way—

Noah spotted the floors above his workshop, the workshop still covered in debris from the wheel—and then the hallway outside his and Marie's rooms. In a matter of minutes, they reached the lower floors and climbed in through the hallway window.

"Curse him," Marie said. Her face looked chiseled from rock. "Planting a dark secret inside Elijah. He had no right."

They raced down the stairs and out the front door. Noah was tripping over his own feet with every step. "Who had no right?"

"Your father." Marie practically spat the words.

"But how? How did he do it?"

Marie pulled Noah across the yard, forcing him to run. "He knew Elijah's inner workings as well as I did. We built him together."

Noah stopped and yanked his hand away from hers as he tried to understand what was happening. He looked around. There were trees surrounding them, and something was wrong with the floor. No, not floor. Grass. Soft, cushiony grass. He was outside. He wasn't allowed outside.

"I can't be out here," Noah said. His voice sounded very small and far away and full of creaks. He wondered if he should just close his eyes and return to the house. *Am I safe?* he wondered. "There's a rule."

Marie covered her mouth and choked, then knelt in front him. "No more rules," she said. "I'm so sorry for them. The only rule now is for you to do as I say and we'll be fine."

Noah looked back behind him. There was something massive just beyond the trees—a weird giant house with oddly shaped rooms spiraling up above it, each level wider than the last so that it resembled a great swirling storm. "That's our house," he said.

"Yes."

"I've never seen it from the outside."

Marie sighed. "Those days are behind us. We need to hurry. Elijah will be moving quickly. We have to hurry before he gets much farther."

"Where are we going?"

"To the city," Marie said. "To Liberty."

Marie led Noah down a path winding through the woods toward the city. To Noah, the journey went by too fast. It was almost like traveling in a dream. One moment they were heading deeper and deeper into the forest, the next they crossed a bridge with a river passing beneath it, and then the towering trees were gone and looming above them were gray stone buildings dotted with dark windows. They stood at the top of a hill looking down a busy street that seemed to go all the way to the docks. Streetlights cast blurred halos of light that created more shadow than anything else. The buildings almost rejected the glow, and the people moving between them didn't appear to notice how dark their city had grown. The water of the ocean glimmered at the far end.

Noah took a deep breath. The babble of the people crowding the way and the whooshing and thunking of items being moved in displays in front of stores made him dizzy. "Where are we going?"

Marie knelt and pointed to the far end of the road where a black building loomed like a shadow from an invisible object. "There. My factory. There are people who need to know what's happened." She stood and brushed her hands together, as if wiping dirt away. Her eyes bored deeply into the ground. She looked scared. "They won't be pleased."

Noah didn't want to go any closer. He opened his mouth to say so, but before he could make a sound, Marie had grabbed his hand and they were moving through the street, through the crowds, through the city he had thought he'd never visit.

Noah, used to only Marie's and Elijah's faces, couldn't help but stare at all the strangers surrounding them. Here were more and more, popping in and out of windows,

passing through doorways, and walking along sidewalks. They looked odd. Every difference stood out. Noah wasn't used to difference. He had only two faces in his memory. Here were dozens—hundreds—and each was terrifying, even when smiling. Tall women and short men exchanged words too loudly. Children ran and screamed at one another. Was it a game? There was laughter, but it made Noah hold his breath, ready to escape at any moment. And the deeper into the city he and Marie passed, the taller the buildings grew and the more people swarmed around them. The buildings loomed above them. The people buzzed. Everything was in shadow. And still, the roar of the city pulled him forward.

Noah and Marie reached a line of shops. Across the front of each were signs: the names of the stores, the prices of goods. People haggled in doorways for bags and bundles of items Noah had never seen before. On the walls, posters had been plastered over brick and wood. Bold black ink and red splashes hammered at Noah's mind with their blunt, insistent messages.

The last had an illustration of a large man with a dark mustache holding a baby in one hand while fighting back monstrous gears with the other. Depicted with fearsome teeth and hungry eyes, the machinery appeared almost animalistic.

And then another:

THE HOMELAND EMPIRE
WATCHES AND WAITS

**DON'T TRUST
WHO YOU
DON'T KNOW**

GOVERNOR STONE: Liberator, Leader, Friend

It sent a chill down Noah's spine.

The Uprising, Noah thought. The great mistake his father had caused with his machines that had attacked the city. Apparently, this man, Stone, had stopped it.

Noah was suddenly dizzy. He couldn't breathe. The light was too bright, and he felt as if he were floating. People pushed past him too fast to see, even those standing still, and he found himself struggling to keep up with Marie as she drifted ahead.

He wanted to go home.

Reaching out, he caught her sleeve. She looked back, but didn't slow down. "We need to get through here quickly."

The crowds swirled, and Noah felt as if they were all lost in water, rushing, sinking, floating, and out of control. And then, through the bubbling noise of the street, a chorus of high-pitched voices rose up, chanting:

> *"Old lady Marie trapped a boy,*
> *Made from gears just like a toy."*

Marie stiffened and slowed, then took Noah's hand. "Don't look at them."

> *"Left behind by the machines,*
> *And the monster who set them free."*

Noah glanced back and spotted a group of children standing near a shop, crouching to gather gravel from the street and laughing.

Marie pulled him harder. "Don't stop."

The kids now held handfuls of large pebbles, adding a rattle to their chant:

> *"Old lady Marie hides in her house,*
> *While dying people scream and shout."*

A circle formed around Marie and Noah. The first stones clattered at their feet, but as people scurried away, the assault came faster. Rocks hit Marie, and she pulled Noah to her to shield him, turning her back to the children. Noah heard a murmur pass through the crowd. "Who is the boy?"

> *"Old lady Marie is caught like a rat. . . ."*

The chant faded to silence as the crowd stopped to gape at Noah. He took in the whispers, saw the horrified faces and pointing fingers. The silence passed up the street as a path before them opened.

"He looks just like the traitor," an old woman shouted, breaking the spell. Her voice shook with anger and fear.

"Let's go," said Marie, urging Noah forward. The adults around them slowly returned to their fish shops, fruit stands, and carts of bread, but they all kept a wary eye on the mother and son. The children gawked and trailed their steps. The last thing Noah saw as Marie drew him down a dark alley, which led toward the harbor, was the poster of Governor Stone . . . *friend*.

At the end of the narrow passage, they were welcomed by the sound of bells and the call of gulls. Noah tried to catch his breath, but the stink of salty water and fish hiding in it made him gag. The streets here were twisted, and the buildings crooked. No two sat at the same angle, the bricks and boards leaning slightly away from the dark waters ahead, as if blown by winds off the ocean. They'd been bleached white by salt air and sun, cracked and dry as if abandoned a thousand years ago. Nothing in Liberty was as he'd imagined it might be. *It's falling apart*, he thought. His hands clenched at his sides and he found he couldn't uncurl his fingers. *I shouldn't be here*.

Between the last of the small wooden buildings and the ocean stretched a long wharf covered by wooden planks as warped and bleached as the ones in the buildings. Nearby sat a heavy, granite platform with a bronze statue atop it—a man, ten feet tall, with his arms extended, his fingers spread, as if trying and failing to grasp something, perhaps trying to hold the sky itself. Beyond the statue and the wharf was the hard line of the horizon, ships floating nearby in the harbor and puffing smoke farther out. With his telescope, Noah had seen the docks and the water beyond. He knew the ocean was deep and wide and vast, but he knew it the way he knew that numbers could be large or that rain came from clouds or that the moon had a far side. He understood it, but he hadn't felt it in his gut. Now he felt it. In the soft, cold mist it left in the air. In the hush of the waves. It was deep and wide, and moved with a gentle power he couldn't experience through a lens.

And it stank. The air smelled of salt and rot. Noah stopped and looked out at the water and the row of boats and ships anchored at the docks. Some were sailing vessels with multiple masts and white sails tied into bundles like trapped clouds. Others had smokestacks as wide as the massive oaks in the woods, thin black wisps of smoke twisting out of them and reaching toward land. One giant gray ship sat closest to the city. From the house, it had been hidden by the buildings and forest, but here it was, the centerpiece of the harbor, covered in thick metal armor, and with large cannons mounted on the deck.

The ocean and the ships and the buildings of the city were all here, and they were *real*. He'd seen them from a distance, and now he could actually touch them. He could understand them in a new way. What Noah didn't understand—or feel like he wanted to—were the people. There were simply too many of them. He felt as if he had fallen into an ant nest, and was about to be picked apart by a thousand tiny mouths.

Dock workers and sailors hurried, hauled, and hollered from all parts of the wharf. They teased and taunted and sang bits of song to one another, and Noah wished they'd just be silent for a moment. A wagon rumbled past, just missing him, and the horse pulling it snorted gruffly as if offended. Across the street, emerging from another alley, was a small wagon pulled by a gray pony. The woman driving it smiled down at Noah, but the smile died when she looked from him to Marie. Noah hadn't smiled back at the woman, but now he wished he hadn't even seen her. Every stranger's gaze made him feel more and more out of place.

At the end of the wharf lurked a cluster of ancient and abused buildings, the largest of which was a black-windowed, smoke-hazed factory. Groups of blue leather-aproned workers huddled before its double-wide doorway, beneath metal brackets that might once have held a sign, but no sign was visible now. The brackets glowed with rust, an orange so vivid it appeared too hot to touch. Lines trailed down the brick beneath each one, showing how rain was slowly taking the metal, and maybe the entire building, one small piece at a time.

The building was enormous by design. It was black by accident. Where a scaffold had fallen, Noah could see red brick. The dark layer was from dirt and soot and time. Chimneys puffed coal smoke from the roof. Exhaust fans and open windows added to the grimy haze. The windows, high, oily, sometimes papered over, occasionally flashed with workers, women and men who leaned out to call to someone near the entrance or to simply get some air. Noises and smoke leaked from the windows more than anything else. Voices of people giving orders or asking for assistance. Belching smoke followed by foul curses and the clatter of metal. There was sometimes a heavy metallic thud, like something from another world putting its foot down, the sound of chains on wood, the high whine of metal scraping metal.

Noah didn't know what these people did or exactly what the building made, but it was the first place in the city that made sense to him. He could imagine what Marie did there, even if he'd never seen her in action.

The people in blue coveralls were filthy. The closer Noah got, the more he could smell them—a mix of smoke and sweat. They parted and glared. Marie passed them, entering the factory without a word, Noah trailing behind.

Noah took a deep breath, inhaling the smell of hot metal, and felt at home. *Marie could have brought me here any day. Instead, she left me in the house with Elijah. She kept the factory for herself.*

He hadn't been surprised that the workers—their whispered words still hanging in the clouds of steam rising from whatever their tin cups held—stopped and stared. *I would stare, too,* he thought.

He stared back. He stared at everything. He stared at the men and women in blue coveralls, headbands over their brows, goggles and face masks hanging around their necks. He stared at the entrance with its great sliding doors hanging from plate-sized wheels atop rusted metal tracks. He stared at the windows filled with cracked glass, and the woman shouting orders at workers moving too-fast-or-not-fast-enough. He stared at the cobblestones giving way to concrete, layered with oil stains, paint, and *is-that-blood?* He stared at walls, a mix of pine planks and broken boards, splinters as big as nails, nails that hid the wood they held.

Marie continued deeper into the factory.

Noah followed, but at a slower pace.

Around him were shelves and bins filled with shapes

he thought he recognized, though it was dark and hard to see. The lights overhead fizzled on and off and the windows were painted over with grime. He watched as some workers carried parts from the shelves as others unloaded carts to replace them. Noah found the workers, themselves, distracting—strange, bent, lumbering. Because sparks flew in all directions, the workers wore thick leather aprons, and fabric caps pulled tight over their heads, while bulbous black goggles covered their eyes—wide round circles that deflected and reflected sparks—and breathing masks with trunk-like tubes swinging below their chins. Noah couldn't help thinking they didn't look human.

But what they were building did. At each workstation, the engineers were constructing mechanical suits—suits that would make their wearers bigger, stronger, terrifying— like eerie armor. Noah recognized the gloves, the chest pieces, and the cast-metal helmets with expressions resembling stoic, focused faces. He knew them all because he had worked on them all. These were the parts he'd designed and built. The factory was turning his tinkering into terrifying suits of armor.

A firm hand fell on Noah's shoulder.

And then an engineer hauled Noah back as an arc of sparks skittered where he had stood moments earlier. The black glass saucers of a worker's goggles reflected the boy back to himself, and with a hiss and echoing metallic rasp, the worker leaned close and said, "Best not keep the missus waiting, lad." With one gloved hand, the man urged Noah deeper into the factory's depths.

Noah raced after Marie.

She stood in the doorway of a small office at the back. She clutched papers in one hand, her attention focused on a woman in orange coveralls with dark skin and curly black hair.

The woman was younger and taller than Marie, with a posture that revealed her strength. She stood silent, her goggles pulled up on her forehead, her mask settled just below her chin, but even so, Noah thought he could see the light of her thinking shine through her face. This was someone who understood everything in the factory as well as Marie did.

"I told you, Issa," Marie nearly shouted at the woman. She entered the room with pounding footsteps and looked as if she might push her desk to the far wall. "I told you he left the spideratus for a reason. The fact that he had changed the interior functions so I couldn't operate it or even understand it was likely a joke on his part. A little reminder that he's *smarter* than I am."

Issa smirked. "It's not a very funny joke."

"The man has no sense of humor!" Marie *was* shouting now, and shuffling papers around her desk. She looked for something in their details, and when she didn't find it, she tossed those pages aside and grabbed at the next ones. "He used Elijah as his messenger. Another *joke*."

Issa looked sidelong at Noah. He thought there was a hint of a smile, and a silently mouthed *hello*. To Marie she said, "How did you finally figure it out? The message, I mean?"

Marie wouldn't look up from her papers, though she'd stopped searching through them. "I didn't."

Issa narrowed her eyes. "Then how . . ."

Marie considered a spot immediately above Noah's head. Issa followed her eyes to the same spot, then lowered her gaze to Noah.

The boy felt his face flush with embarrassment, though why he was embarrassed he couldn't really say.

"They'll be coming," Marie finally said.

"Ma'am, we don't have enough."

"I know, but we'd never have enough, regardless."

"He asked for so many more."

"I know," Marie replied. "We have to do what we can. *Our savior, the governor* will be arriving soon." The words dripped from her lips. "I'm sure he's had someone watching the house. He'll know about the spideratus and Elijah."

"I'm sure he does," said Issa. "He's already been here."

Marie grabbed a stack of books from her desk, raised them into the air where they hovered for a moment before she slammed them back down with such force that pencils and papers were knocked to the floor. "Alton, how could you do this," she demanded through gritted teeth. She ignored Noah, or perhaps she'd forgotten he was even there.

Marie wiped sweat from her brow. Noah hadn't noticed until that moment how unbearably hot it was in the factory.

"What exactly is going to happen?" Issa asked.

"I wish I knew." Marie looked at Noah, staring right into his eyes. "His father laid a . . . no, not a trap. A *test*. And Noah passed it with flying colors."

"It wasn't much of a test," Noah said. "Just some secret buttons."

Now both women were looking at him, and Noah wished once again he was alone, back in the house that grew at night.

The forewoman smiled at him. "Just like his father, huh?"

"We don't have time for—" Marie began, when a

hammering of metal against metal interrupted their conversation. Three clangs, a pause, and three more.

Forewoman Issa glanced toward the entrance where a cluster of workers were gathered and gave a wave. One of the workers holding a wrench raised a hand in response. "He's back, ma'am."

Marie held her hands out as if trying to simultaneously catch her own thoughts and calm herself. "Noah, you'll wait with me." She turned back to Issa. "I'll never forgive his father for doing all this."

"No one is asking you to."

Marie nodded and revealed a hint of smile. "Let him know I'm ready for him."

The worker with the wrench was still looking intently at Noah. "Spitting image of his father."

Marie didn't respond to the man, except by clamping a hand on Noah's shoulder whispering under her breath. "Everything is going to be . . . fine."

❈ CHAPTER 4 ❈

The office had two lamps: one on the desk that cast a single yellow circle of light on a pile of papers, the other hanging from the ceiling, its bare bulb flickering depending on the amount of noise rumbling from the work crews' machines. Other than the cluttered desk and the chair beside it, a row of wooden crates had been stacked along one wall. Noah thought they looked familiar, and then realized they were identical to the ones Marie had spread throughout the house. Marie motioned wearily toward them and said, "Sit."

Noah didn't. He walked toward a crate, but instead of sinking down as he'd been commanded, he stood defiantly beside it.

Marie didn't even notice.

She moved toward the desk and frowned down at the

papers. Noah leaned forward, trying to catch a glimpse, but all he could make out were scribbles. Marie's handwriting was tight and jagged, so unlike the bold block letters on his father's plans. Noah couldn't help but wonder which of them his own writing resembled more.

"If there had been just a little more time, we might be ready," Marie murmured.

"Ready for what?"

"For whatever your father has planned. Or for *the governor*. Or . . . I just wish we had more time."

She turned to the wall behind the desk and grabbed the edge of a curtain. Noah was surprised when she pulled it back to reveal two large windows, each scrubbed clean, with a view of the ships and the harbor. The statue was nearby, and from here, Noah could see its face. The man appeared stern, somewhat sad, and angry. His expression made his grasping hands seem all the more desperate. The statue's face was covered in a thick mustache, and Noah realized he was looking at the same face as the masks he'd seen being built in the factory, the sorrowful face that had snapped into place over the worker's own, turning him into a mechanical giant. But Noah still couldn't recall whose face it was he'd seen on the machine men, though he couldn't help but feel it was a secret he knew.

Marie watched the horizon. "The governor will be here shortly. He's going to ask questions. Everything will be fine."

But when the door swung open and slammed into the wall, Noah knew her last claim had been a lie.

Standing in the doorway was the man from the statue and the mechanical suits, and Noah now realized, from the poster. The one holding back the Uprising while cradling a baby.

The hero of Liberty. Governor Stone.

He was tall and broad. His thick mustache hid his mouth like a shrub. His hands looked enormous as he pointed at Marie accusingly.

"Where is the boy?" Stone's voice rumbled out like a slow rolling boulder. "Where is my nephew?"

Noah was pinned in place by the question. What did he mean, *nephew*?

Marie held up her hands as if to keep the man from storming right over her. "Nicholas, please. We need to talk."

"It's already begun," he thundered on as if he hadn't heard her. "First the attacks on our ships, and now a contraption has been seen clattering through the city. Witnesses said it looked like a child. A child! Alton is up to something. We need to keep your son away from him."

Noah kept stumbling over the word *nephew*. If he was

the governor's nephew, then the governor was his . . . uncle. His *uncle* was worried about a contraption that resembled a child. "Elijah," he murmured.

Governor Stone eyed Noah as if the boy had just fallen from the sky. "What?"

"Elijah ran from the house. After I turned off the spideratus."

Stone put a hand out to silence Noah, even though he was done talking. Then the governor walked over, looking the boy up and down. It was unnerving. Noah felt as if he'd just been caught doing something terrible, and couldn't help but shiver under the man's gaze.

"What do you mean, after *you* turned off the spideratus?"

Noah opened his mouth, and the words came tumbling out: "There've always been noises . . . and I knew it was the house growing larger."

He explained how he'd always heard the banging and crashing, how Marie gave him tasks to complete, how the wheel had gotten away, rolled through the house, and smashed into the clock.

Stone stood before Noah, apparently speechless.

But Noah was *not* speechless. He explained how the spideratus's eyes had been switches, and that when his father's voice had erupted from the machine, Elijah had run off to prepare. When Noah reached the end of his story, he realized two things: he'd been talking very, very fast, worried he was in trouble, and throughout his story, Marie had been asking him to stop.

"Noah, be quiet!" Her face was red, and she rubbed at her temples as if every thought hurt. She closed her eyes. "Nicholas, let me explain."

The governor's face wasn't a matching red. In fact, it was as pale as ice, and his voice was equally as cold when he spoke. "You failed me, Marie."

"Nicholas, please."

"You failed me, and this city. By my count, you've also failed your son."

Noah had been sure that he was the one in trouble, and a flash of relief swept through him as he realized that wasn't the case. But there was also a twinge of something else: worry for his mother.

Governor Stone slammed a broad hand down on the desk. "You promised me that if I left you alone with those machines, it would be fine. 'Trust me, Nicholas.' You begged me! 'I can fix it,' you said. You told me you could figure out what Alton had done, and fix everything."

Marie grinned defiantly at the governor. "That's unfair, Nicholas. And you know it."

Unfair, Noah thought. *She thinks she's been treated unfairly.* He may not have been sure what promise she'd broken, but he knew something about *unfair*. *Unfair* was being locked away for things he didn't understand, all because of things his father had done. *Unfair* was believing his father was dead when he wasn't. This last realization settled, and it nearly took his breath away.

"What did she do?" Noah asked.

The room filled with a quiet Noah didn't know could exist. Even with the factory sounds on the other side of the door, the silence was like a fourth person in the room, threatening them all.

Governor Stone stood straighter so that he was taller than before. "She really never told you, boy? My sister never told you what it was you were doing, hidden away in the safety of that house?"

Noah wanted to fire back that he'd been held captive, not hidden. Instead, he simply said, "No."

"Then let me tell you. A long time ago, Liberty was a colony of the Homeland Empire. Our father's father founded it. Our parents worked hard to keep the city from crumbling, and eventually they found themselves pushing back against the Homeland Empire's iron hand. After years of unfair treatment, Liberty fought for and finally won its freedom.

But the Homeland never ceased its relentless attacks. They were determined to wear us down. I grew up in a city struggling to survive and protect itself. Eventually, I was elected governor, and I knew then the only way to persist was to find a way to hold the Homeland back permanently. Liberty was desperate. I was desperate. We needed a miracle."

"That's when your father built the robots," Marie explained. "The spideratus, and others even larger, all to fight the Homeland. To protect the city." She was sitting now, and her face looked as pale as Stone's. *Her brother,* Noah thought. He could see it. They looked alike, both tall, both dark-haired with intense, bright eyes. Marie seemed as if she was about to cry when she said, "Your father had plans to build machines that would fix everything. And they did, for a short time."

"You still defend him," Governor Stone said. Spittle came with the words and stuck in his mustache. "After all this time, you still believe that he did what was right. He built machines that turned against us!" The governor shifted to face Noah. "Your father built the machines, and then they turned against us. When the machines' attack ended, your father was somehow in control of them. And whether by design or by accident, he was to blame. This poor city was crushed. The dead lay in the streets, but your father was only concerned that his robots not be destroyed."

Noah's head was spinning. His imagination filled with images like the blueprint drawings he'd found, the sketches come to life, attacking a blueprint city. Blueprint people running and scared as a blueprint inventor stood defiantly with his creations. Noah felt dizzied by the vision, but also confused. It had all been so long ago, and yet the adults were still so very, very angry.

"None of that was my fault," he blurted out. The others peered at him as if just now remembering he was there. "Why did what my father did mean I had to be locked away?"

The lines in his uncle's stern face began to soften and fade. "Oh, my boy. You weren't locked away. You were hidden. We tried to arrest your father, but with any move we made toward him, the robots responded. In the end, I negotiated a peace: Alton would leave and take his contraptions with him. He was exiled to an island where he remains to this day. But I worry that he plots. He never accepted the blame for what happened. And the city needed someone to blame."

Noah looked across the room at his mother. "You? You were the one they blamed?"

Marie nodded. "And you along with me. I feared that the people of Liberty would think you . . . were like . . ."

"Like him," Noah whispered.

His uncle glanced at Marie, and in that flash of movement, Noah recognized something there, some kind of judgment. This man—his uncle—didn't trust him.

"But I *am* like him. When I turned off the spideratus, I proved it."

Marie shook her head. "Noah, you're not—"

"I am. I'm just like him! I saw the plans and I—" Noah suddenly couldn't breathe.

His uncle touched his shoulder and gave it a gentle squeeze. "As I said, Marie, you've failed. You said you could unlock Alton's secrets in the spideratus if I left it with you, and you could not. You said Elijah was nothing more than a caretaker. That because you had helped build him, you knew him better than anyone. But he had secrets. Secrets Alton planted that prove him a dangerous spy. And you said you could teach Noah to become a better man than his father. One whose obvious talents could help protect the city."

The governor stood, his gaze locked on his sister. "Yet, you've done nothing more than turn the boy into a prize for Alton to claim."

Marie shook her head. "Nicholas, think logically. The message was for anyone who turned off the robot, not for Noah specifically."

Stone kept his hand on Noah's shoulder. He squeezed it again, and Noah felt the tension in him start to lessen. He could breathe. He could breathe, and he could focus on what was happening.

"I've done everything I can to help this city," Governor Stone continued. "That includes trusting too often and too well. You are my sister, and my love for you runs as deep as my concern for all the people under my care. That's my weakness. That's my flaw. That's why I have ignored the sightings of Alton's machines in the waters near Liberty. It's why we haven't responded with force to the fact that ships have been disappearing recently. And it's why I let you keep a spy in your home, helping to raise an ally of our enemies."

Noah winced as the grip on his shoulder tightened.

Stone leaned down. "How did you know to turn off the spideratus?" he whispered into his nephew's ear.

Noah stared into the face of the stranger who was family. He knew there was a right answer and a wrong one, but Noah didn't know where to find either.

"I found the plans. It was . . . easy to tell, once I found the robot."

His uncle's whisper became softer, hissing, and even more secretive. "And how did you know how to read the plans?"

"Marie taught me."

Governor Stone looked up at his sister. "Are you insane? You're teaching him to be like his father?"

"I'm teaching him to be better!" Marie cried out. "He's not Alton!"

She rushed forward, but the governor put a large hand out, holding her off. "You deny the truth that sits right here before us. Guards!"

Noah's terrified gaze locked on his mother. "Marie, I want to go home!"

"The boy doesn't even call you *mother*," the governor spat. "He's as distant as Alton ever was. Maybe more so. Guards!" he shouted again, and six people in dark blue uniforms rushed into the room, carrying short clubs and guns on their hips. "Take the boy. Place him in custody for—"

"Nicholas!" Marie screamed. "You can't do this!"

"It's for his own safety, Marie. I'm not a monster. We know that the robot boy, Elijah, is on the loose. Until he's caught, he may try to get to Noah, and that we cannot allow." He nodded to the guards again. "Take him."

The governor's firm grip dug into Noah's shoulder for a moment more, and then vanished as two of the uniformed officers stepped forward. Noah was too stunned to speak.

"You can see him to his cell," the governor added off-handedly. "You'll see that he'll be well cared for. The guards will bring you back here immediately after. From that point on, you will stay in the factory at all times. You will make all preparations necessary to defend this city. Meanwhile, I've got to find the robot spy, Elijah, and prepare my city for the worst. Alton has made it clear he hasn't forgotten about us. He's returning, Marie. You must see that. That madman is coming, and at his back may very well be the machines he's spent years building to destroy us."

Marie reached out to take Noah's hand, but the guards pushed her away. And for a moment, as her fingers stretched for his, Noah flinched.

"I'll never forgive you, Nicholas," she spat.

Governor Stone walked to his sister, stopping before her. He looked down with pity in his eyes. "You were insane to think you could keep those machines from doing Alton's bidding." His gaze turned cold. "And I was a fool for believing in you."

Noah's mother gasped and began to cry. "Nicholas, how can you do this?" Noah couldn't recall ever seeing her cry. Especially not like this. Marie was focused, stern, sometimes detached, and distracted by the work she always seemed to be headed out of the house to pursue. She was not someone who looked ready to beg. "Please, Nicholas. You're my *brother*."

To Noah's surprise, Governor Stone began to cry as well. "I do love you, Marie, but I no longer trust you." He turned to the guards. "Take my nephew to his cell."

"But what did I do?" Noah asked, struggling for breath. No one answered. His stomach turned over again, the sadness and anger switching places, each struggling for control.

Six armed guards escorted Noah across the factory floor and out onto the docks. Marie trailed behind them. The governor had already gone on to other business, shouting orders to guards and factory workers alike. Noah no longer felt like he was floating. Now he felt made of lead. His feet were heavy, his eyes refused to stay open. Everything passed as if in a terrible dream.

They left the docks by way of the main street and headed toward a large brick building overlooking the wharf, which sat atop a short cliff that cut the docks off from the rest of the city. Uniformed guards lined the cobblestone street leading to the building, an uphill climb that left them all breathless. Brick walls and iron fences formed an outer barrier, broken by two massive gates framed by a rocky arch. Mounted above were the words LIBERTY HALL. On the other side, large mechanical statues moved about the courtyard. No, not statues—men in mechanical suits. Three officers patrolling, fitted in the lumbering armor Marie's factory had constructed. Noah heard the whirring of gears and twang of the springs inside the suits, and he watched the emotionless masks modeled after his uncle. For a moment, Noah forgot that there were humans inside.

They passed through the front doors into Liberty Hall, where more guards in mechanized suits stood at attention. Noah felt sick to his stomach. He'd had no idea that the projects he'd worked on—been forced to work on—would be used to imprison him in a worse place than he had already been. It was bad enough to have built the suits. Now they would keep him in a cell. The guards led him deep into the main hall, toward a set of stairs. On the far wall was a mural. Across the top was scrawled THE SALVA-TION OF LIBERTY. In it, his uncle held back a horde, this one a black cloud made of gears and a multitude of snaking black legs, with one hand, while the other was cupped over the city in miniature. On the far side of the mural lurked another figure—this one with thin limbs, and a puff of hair that stood straight up on his head. Thick glasses obscured his eyes, and his expression was one of wicked cunning.

Beneath him was scrawled THE TRAITOR ALTON PHYSICIAN. And beyond him, as if seen from far away, was a land covered with row after row of soldiers. THE HOMELAND EMPIRE.

Noah stopped before the painting and took it all in. Alton Physician was shown in detail. There were small lines around his eyes and mouth as he sneered contemptuously. Noah sighed. This was the first time he'd ever seen his father. He had no other image, no drawing, not even a description. And now, here was the man, a figure of doom, depicted as more dangerous than an entire enemy nation with its army of faceless soldiers. It made Noah's fists ball up at his sides. But why did he feel such rage? Was he angry at his uncle for depicting his father this way, or was he angry at his father for causing all this in the first place?

Noah was exhausted by the rush of thoughts.

The dark-uniformed guards were everywhere, and no one bothered to ask the escort of six soldiers and the small boy where they were going, though Marie's presence at the rear drew harsh looks and whispers.

The group reached the bottom of a spiral staircase, which rose to a small room with only one door. Another guard stood nearby.

Through the door they found their destination.

The room was long and wide. To either side were cells

with iron bars that ran from floor to ceiling. Noah had read enough stories at Marie's suggestion to know a jail when he saw one. Lamplight from the street entered through windows in the wall to their right, shining on a dirty stone floor wet with condensation. In fact, the air itself was thick with moisture, and somewhere close, water dripped, *plink-plink-plink*-ing in a way Noah knew would drive him mad.

Noah was led into a cell, where a metal cot had been bolted to the wall and a single window looked out over the docks. The guards seemed nervous to be leaving him there.

Marie tried to push past them into the cell, but was held back. "He's just a child," she pleaded. "And he's done nothing wrong."

Noah thought of the shock on his uncle's face when he'd learned the news of the message hidden in the spideratus. Governor Stone would surely disagree that he was blameless.

The highest-ranking guard was an older man with gray whiskers. He sounded as if he was trying his best to be kind. "We have our orders, ma'am," he said, studying the stone floor.

"Look at him!" Marie pointed to Noah. "Does he seem like a threat?"

The guard gave Marie a knowing look. "I'm old enough to know that some threats don't seem so bad at first."

In other words, Noah thought, *I remember what his father did.*

Marie gave up her protests. The soldiers withdrew, leaving Noah in his cell, a heavy *clank* echoing as they shut the metal door. As if the bars around him were as solid as panes of glass, he was suddenly trapped in a cloud of musty odors and found he couldn't breathe. The *plink-plink-plink*-ing of the *drip-drip-drip* was somehow louder than before. It echoed in his head. He thought the sound might drown him. He wanted to reach for help, but the only people nearby were Marie and the guard, and Noah wasn't sure he wanted help from either of them.

The old guard smiled weakly at Noah, then turned to face Marie. "You may visit for five minutes, but then I'm afraid we're to take you back to the factory."

She nodded, and the guard left.

Noah eyed his mother's face through the bars.

"I'll talk to your uncle. When he calms down, he'll see how illogical he's being. We'll make this right."

Noah felt a wave of heat rush through his stomach and chest. He was tired of Marie's assurances. She had promised she would protect him, yet she'd kept him prisoner in a house with a caretaker who turned out to have secrets. She'd kept him in the dark about his father, his home, and even what the contraptions she'd asked him to build were for. Her secrets and plans for stability had just fallen apart all around them, and she'd let it crumble. What did she know about making things right?

"Is it illogical?"

Marie's eyes popped. "What does that mean?"

"You've been telling me to trust you my whole life, but now I know you've been lying all along."

Her face went red. "Noah, you don't mean that. I—"

"You lied about my father being dead. You never told me I had an uncle." Now that Noah had started, he couldn't stop. "Elijah was my caretaker, and you didn't even know what my father had done to him. You kept me locked away because people are scared of me!"

"They're wrong!" Marie said. "They don't know you!"

"Neither do you! Because the first time I touched something my father made, it turned out to be dangerous. Maybe they're right. Maybe I am just like him, or even worse!"

"Noah, you don't mean that." She held out her hands to him through the bars. There was a time when he had wanted her to care about him like this, but now it was too late. The cell's bars were no longer the only things between them.

Earlier that day, Noah would have said that he and Marie shared a kind of trust wrapped in sadness. With that trust pulled away, only the sadness remained. Or so he had thought in the factory. Locked in a cell, he felt that hidden inside the sadness was something else. Something that had lurked beneath the trust. The idea *plink-plink-plink*-ed at the back of his mind. It was a *drip-drip-drip*-ing that had always been there, but he hadn't realized until that moment.

Alone in the cell, he realized he was angry. At his uncle, at the city, and at Marie.

"Maybe it would have been better if my father had taken me with him when he was exiled."

Marie's hands dropped to her sides. She breathed in the musty air and looked up at the ceiling. "You don't need to agree with me for me to get you out. But remember this: keep your head on the goal, and you'll find the path. Our goal is to get you out. Hate me or not, I'll still get you back."

She held out her hand again. Despite what she'd just said, Noah knew she desperately wanted things to return to what they'd been before. And she wanted him to want that as well. He could see in her eyes that part of her would always want him to be safe, alone, and locked away with her in a house that grew at night.

And a part of him did want to reach out to Marie, but he couldn't let go of the fact that she had left him every single day to keep her own freedom. "Your brother isn't the first to do this to me," he said. "You always kept me locked up, yourself. I don't see how this is any different."

He sat on the cot and faced the wall.

Marie stood at the door for another minute. Noah refused to look in her direction, but the longer they were silent, the more he wanted her to stay.

At last, he heard the shuffle of her leaving, and without saying another word, she shut the heavy door behind her with a solid thud.

Night had fully fallen, and the electric lantern outside the cell was so weak, Noah wasn't sure it was even on. He didn't think he would be able to sleep on the hard cot, but when he lay down, the buzz of the light bulb and the waves of the ocean lured him toward sleep. His last thought before drifting off was: *I can't hear the house growing larger.*

And this made him, for reasons he couldn't really understand, incredibly sad.

❆ CHAPTER 5 ❆

Noah woke to angry yelling. The window above him was still dark, and the bare bulb hanging outside the cells cast only a pale bluish light. A faucet dripped cold water into a pail, and the thin mattress below him creaked as he took in a hole in the floor covered by a metal grate that smelled suspiciously like it was to be used as a toilet.

There was a crash, and more raised voices, and when the door opened, two uniformed officers staggered in carrying between them a man who was at least two heads taller than—and twice as wide as—either of them. He looked strong and heavy, and the officers trying to guide him could barely manage. The man was sobbing, covering his face with one large hand, and this made their efforts even more awkward. Once they were through the door, two more officers joined them, and now all four tried to force the enormous man into a cell across from Noah's. He struggled a bit, but didn't appear to put up much of a fight.

"Sally!" he yelled. "Sally, how could you?" He stood to his full height and peered around the cell block. "Sally? Where are you?"

One of the officers pulled at his arm. "Sally's not here. Now, can you just come in here and rest and—"

"Sally!" He moaned.

Another officer pushed from behind with no effect. "The man's a lunatic."

"The man's a mountain," said a third officer.

"Shut it, you two." The oldest of the guards—a captain—had returned. He pulled a dark wooden baton from his belt and pointed it at the huge man. "Sir! Get in the cell! For your own good."

The giant of a man swayed a bit. The smell of him wafted toward Noah—ocean, tar, fish, and other curious scents.

"Sally's left me!" the man bellowed again.

"And I'm right sorry about that. But you can't go 'round knocking doors off hinges looking for her. Sir, get in the cell."

"But I love her!" The huge man raised his hands to the ceiling, and that's when Noah realized the man's right arm ended below the elbow. His hand was missing. Nonetheless, he gestured emphatically with the shortened arm. "She's like an angel."

The old captain nodded, then knocked his baton against the cell bars. "I know, I know. We've all been there. In love with them what don't love us. Hurts like daggers. Then we wake up, keep away from them for a time, and we feel better."

"Never!" The man's bald head nearly collided with the light hanging above him. "I'll never forget my Susie!"

The captain continued to strike the bars at a gentle rhythm. "I thought her name was Sally?"

The prisoner and the officers he struggled with went rigid. After a moment, the large man glanced from face to face, offering a small smile. "She's a complex woman?"

"Into the cell!" the captain of the guard roared.

The man stopped resisting, laughing as he fell forward onto the stone before him. The officers swore gently as they shut and locked the door, and then gathered the items they'd dropped or that had been thrown about in their effort to control the new prisoner: a hat, a pair of glasses, two batons, and a chair, which hadn't even been in the room before they entered.

The captain appraised the man through the cell's bars. "You'll wait here till morning."

The large man was sprawled out on the floor. He reached

up toward the door. "Take pity, sir. My arm? Sally took my heart. Don't you take my arm."

The captain shook his head and left the cell block. A moment later he returned carrying a wooden arm with a large steel hook at one end. "Here," he said, dropping the limb between the bars at the man's feet.

The man didn't move from where he lay, but Noah heard him mutter, "You're a gracious and handsome one."

The officer spat on the floor. When he turned to go, his eyes fell on Noah. He continued toward the door, then stopped. "Anyone feed you?"

Noah shook his head. "No."

The captain looked embarrassed. "I'll have something brought up."

"Eggs!" shouted the man in the other cell. "Over easy!"

The captain left without looking back.

Noah stood in the center of his cell and watched the exit door shut, listening for the click of the lock. The light was still low, but he sensed a new energy in the air. He saw that the large man was still lying on the floor, his wooden arm beside him. Not expecting him to move again, Noah turned and climbed back onto the bed platform.

When he glanced over once more, the man was sitting up and smiling at him.

"Mister Noah, sir?"

Noah was suddenly glad for the two sets of iron bars between them. *Mister?*

"A sign of respect for someone of such value." The large man stood and brushed himself off. "Sorry, not value. I meant importance." The man smiled again, and in that smile, Noah could see the man meant importance *and* value. Now that he was standing still, and not yelling about Sallys and Susies, Noah was able to get a good look at him. The strange man was taller than the cell doorway. His arms were as wide as tree trunks, even the one missing below the elbow, and both were painted thick with tattoos. His head was shaved clean, his skin dark, and he was imposing, though his fearsomeness was softened by the mischief in his smile.

"How do you know my name?" Noah asked.

"I was sent to rescue you by an interesting boy who ticks like a timepiece when he's worried."

Noah stood and walked to the cell door, wrapping his hands around the bars. "Elijah?"

"Aye, that's the one. Was going to say Susie. Anyway, he hired us to get you out. Here." The man knelt down and pinned his wooden arm beneath his knee. He reached inside with his one hand and Noah heard a pop as the man pulled a cork from inside, lifted the arm, and shook until a small metal tool fell out with a gentle *clank* onto the floor. The man replaced the cork, then set the wooden arm upon his stump and tightened a strap. A hook now glinted where his hand ought to have been.

"Take this," he said, and threw the metal tool between the bars into Noah's cell.

Noah picked up a thin, iron screwdriver. He looked at it and then at the man across the way. His eyes took in the heavy bars, the cell door, the massive lock, the bolted door of the exit. "I don't think this will be enough."

From beyond the exit came the clinking of keys hitting the floor and then a riot of swears as someone complained of dropping them. The captain of the guard's voice was clear. He was coming back.

The large man sat on his bed and pointed at the screw-driver. "Put that away, Mister Noah. No need to give it to them. They have keys. When they leave, use it to join young Winona there."

"Who?"

"Me."

Noah spun, expecting someone to be lurking right behind him. The voice had been so close, yet there was no one else in the cell.

"Down here," the voice called. Reverberating, it felt both close and far away. And still Noah saw no one. He scanned the room and almost missed that poking between the slats in the grate that smelled like a toilet was a finger. "Down here." The finger bent toward him and waved. "That's right. Here!"

Noah knelt beside the grate. Through the openings, he could see the shine of eyes. The finger retreated and the voice from below said, "Hide the screwdriver."

"What?" Noah didn't understand what was happening. Behind him, the exit door locks clanged and the door creaked open.

"Hide the screwdriver!" hissed the voice from the sewer grate.

The recently arrived prisoner let out a loud and obviously fake cough, which sounded clearly like he was saying *Hush!* Noah looked through the grate at the blinking eyes below and then curled his hand around the tool, stood, and slipped the screwdriver into his pocket. He glanced up just as the captain of the guard and two officers entered the block through the door. One of the officers was carrying a bowl and a piece of bread. Behind him came a man in uniform—though this one a different color from those of the other guards—along with a small black hat with a gold insignia.

"I understand your dilemma, Captain," the uniformed man said, but my orders are to get underway immediately. I assure you, you release my crewman to me, and you won't see him again."

The officer with the bowl and bread passed them through the bars of Noah's cell. The boy loosened his grip on the screwdriver, drawing his hand from his pocket to reach for the food, only in that moment realizing how hungry he actually was.

The captain of the guard continued his exchange with the newcomer as if the prisoners weren't there. "And what if he does come back? What then? He knocked a door clean off the hinges at the bakery screaming for a woman no one knows."

"Trust me. My captain won't be granting him shore leave again soon. You have my word as the first mate of the *Colossus*."

"I should hope not," said the captain. "I'd think your commander would want all his men out there hunting down the smugglers who've been lurking about the city."

"Oh, yes," said the first mate. "He does, he does. Terrible smuggling smugglers. We're—you know—going to stop them."

"Good! That trash belongs in the sewers."

The first mate smiled and darted his eyes at the grate beneath Noah's feet. "You don't say."

The captain of the guard looked wary and tired. "You're lucky I haven't filed the papers yet. Otherwise, it's my neck on the line."

The sailor swept his hat from his head and saluted the commander. His skin was tanned and weathered, and Noah noticed lines on his face that showed years at sea. "I'm forever in your debt, sir. And if we do come back this way, I promise to bring you a crate of the finest drink you've ever tasted."

"No debts here, especially if this is what that drink does to a man."

With that, the captain opened the large man's cell and stepped back. His officers looked like tightened springs, ready to uncoil the moment the giant of a man moved.

But he didn't. He just lay there.

Noah wondered if he'd imagined the man had spoken to him at all. He'd seemed so alert, but now there he was sleeping peacefully on the floor. Noah's fingers twitched with longing to check for the silver screwdriver in his pocket, but his hands were full with bowl and bread. He glanced back at the grate. He no longer saw fingers or the flash of eyes. No sign of a Winona.

"Wake up!" hollered the captain.

The large man snorted, but didn't move.

"Come on, Steem. Captain's waiting."

The large man, Steem, scraped his hooked arm across the floor. The prison guards shifted warily, and their captain muttered oaths, cursing himself for giving the dangerous-looking false hand back to the prisoner. They were all focused on Steem. All except the first mate, whose eyes were locked on Noah. Still holding his hat, he saluted the boy.

"Come on, Steem. Tide's turning and our friends need to get aboard ship."

Steem sat up, looking around as if seeing the cell and all the people gathered there for the first time, and grinned broadly as if recalling a secret. "Yessir. Sorry, sir."

He climbed to his feet and ducked his head as he exited the cell. The officers and commander shuffled back.

"For the last time," the first mate chided. "Don't go into town after you've gotten sad news from Josie."

"Susie," Steem murmured.

The captain of the guard shoved the cell door, and it crashed shut, leaving the bars ringing. "I thought it was Sally."

The first mate and Steem both eyed the jailor for a long moment.

"Well," the first mate finally said, "she's a complicated woman."

"Get out of my jail."

Steem and the first mate backed toward the door, promising a delivery of riches. The captain wanted none of it.

"Just get out of my jail, my harbor, my city. If I see either of you again, I'll arrest you for every crime committed in the last ten years!"

The sounds of the sailors' footsteps faded as they fled down the stairs.

"See to it that they reach the *Colossus*," ordered the captain. His officers saluted and ran out the door.

The captain and Noah regarded each other through the bars. Though the red-faced commander's eyes were locked on the boy, he muttered away, and it was clear his thoughts were occupied by the two men who had just fled. At last, he cleared his throat and he started for the exit. At the door, he paused and glanced looked back at Noah. "Best eat that stew while it's hot. It doesn't get better as it cools."

"Yes, sir."

Silent, the captain took in the empty cells. "It's not a cold night, but will you need a blanket?"

Noah's gaze flicked to the bed and its thin mattress, then at the drain in the floor. "No, thank you."

"All right then. I suppose your uncle will stop by tomorrow. He didn't say so, but . . . well, I suppose he will."

My uncle? For a moment, Noah didn't know who the commander meant. It was all so new: Uncle Governor Nicholas Stone. Noah doubted his uncle would remember to visit him in the morning. The man had seemed all too happy just to have Noah locked away.

"I suppose," Noah replied cautiously.

The captain slowly pulled the door shut behind him, and Noah was once again alone. He set the bowl and bread on the mattress, then pulled the screwdriver from his pocket. Rolling it between his fingers, he wondered if he'd taken too long—if his chance at escape had passed. Would the girl in the drain still be waiting?

As if hearing his thoughts, Winona called out from below. "Hello? Please say you're there."

Noah crossed to the drain and knelt down beside it again. It was impossible to tell Winona's age from a pair of eyes and a hand pressing against the wrong side of the slats. He leaned over the grate as close as he could without gagging. "What are you doing down there?"

"Breaking you out, obviously. Use the screwdriver. Take out the screws. We'll slide down this way."

"I'll never fit," said Noah.

"Trust me, you will. I'm bigger than you, and I made it all the way to the grate. We had doubts about that. That's why Steem got himself arrested. We weren't certain I'd reach the grate to be able to pass the screwdriver to you. But this sewer's as roomy as it is disgusting. All that trouble for nothing."

Noah looked at the screwdriver, then examined the screws in the tarnished metal. There were five of them. They looked old and were caked with dirt and other, nastier muck, which reminded him why the grate smelled so terrible.

"Your ship. It's nearby?" Noah asked.

"Move the grate, and we'll be there in minutes. Trust me. No one wants out of this sewer more than me."

Noah's hands shook as he started working on the first screw. By the third, his hands had calmed, but he was sweating. The tool was small, and the screws rusted and crumbling. It took him twice as long on the third as it had the first two.

"You're doing fine, Mister Noah, but the tide's coming in. When it's high, this tunnel won't be a way out anymore. Hurry."

Noah nodded and focused on the work. He finished the third screw and started on the fourth. It slid out on its own, so rusted that it no longer had threads to keep it fixed.

Winona's smile caught the thin light and glinted happily at Noah. "That's the way!"

Noah's hands shook with excitement as he fit the screwdriver into the final screw. He'd never felt so nervous using a tool before, but he'd also never felt what he worked on mattered so much. One tiny, rusted screw was all that kept him from finding his way out of the cell. He was about to say *That wasn't so bad*, but when he gave the first twist, he felt a snap. The screwdriver's tip had split in two, and the sharp point still attached to the handle was far too small to turn the screw.

"Oh no." He thought he might cry.

Winona muttered a word Noah hadn't heard before, but he was certain it wasn't kind. "We're sunk."

The sinking Noah felt was in his chest.

Winona pushed up on the grate. It shifted a little, but the remaining screw was enough to keep it in place. Winona grunted and then abruptly stopped, her fingers poking up feebly through the metal slits. "I'll be back. Not for a few hours. Try to sleep."

Noah didn't want to spend another moment locked up. He'd been locked up in the house his whole life, and locked away from the truth—about his family and what he might be capable of—for just as long. He wanted out, and away. And he knew how to get both: find his father. Elijah would see to it.

Noah grabbed the spoon from the bowl and wiped it clean on the mattress. It was wide, but pounded thin, and the edge of the handle was almost sharp. When he placed it into the slot of the screw, it crumbled a bit.

"Push down," commanded Winona. "Make it bite."

The spoon dug in, and he turned counterclockwise, feeling rust and dirt grinding as the screw loosened. On the third turn, the head of the screw crumbled; the spoon scooped through the metal and turned it to dust. Winona sputtered as the remains rained down on her.

"Ah, right in my eyes."

"Sorry," Noah said as he put down the spoon with a sigh.

Winona pushed up on the grate again, and this time Noah helped, taking hold of the metal, standing, and pulling up with as much strength as he could muster.

"If only Mister Steem was here," hissed Winona. "He could do this even with his missing arm."

There was scraping and the sound of dirt and grit tumbling down. Winona coughed, and then called, "It's moving!"

Before Noah could tell if it truly was, the remaining

screw snapped, and the grate lifted and slid away from the opening. Noah fell back, landing with a yelp on the stones.

Winona pulled herself halfway into the cell. Now that he could see her, Noah realized she was his age or barely older, though taller by a head. Her skin was copper, her eyes a deep brown, and her hair umber with honey streaks at the tips. Slimy water soaked her from her chest down, and she stank like the tunnel.

She grinned at Noah and tipped an imaginary hat to him. "Look at what we've done. Broken out of jail. Shame, shame. Now let's get going. And I hope you're partial to the smell of rot, Mister Noah, because this tunnel is made from stink."

❈ CHAPTER 6 ❈

Winona wasn't wrong. The tunnel was filled with a stench that burned Noah's throat and eyes, and felt like a slap every time he inhaled. What he hadn't expected was that everything below the streets would be coated in filth and rot. He'd only ever seen the forest from above, and the city from a distance. He'd never imagined what might slosh beneath the surface. What had the people of Liberty done to create such a disgusting underbelly for their city? Slime coated the curved rock walls, iridescent, with an eerie glow that colored everything a sickly green. The light made Winona's face look like the skulls Noah had seen in drawings in some of Marie's books. He wondered if his face looked as ghastly.

Things better not named floated in the water around them, bumping and brushing past their legs. As Winona was a head taller than Noah, the water, though rising, came to the middle of her chest. Noah, however, was neck deep. He hopped as they walked, trying to breathe only when he was sure he was fully above the sludge.

Winona had instructed Noah to remove his shoes. He carried one in each hand, raised high above his head. Below the surface, his feet felt a different current, faster, and slick. "The water is so cold at the bottom."

"Aye, that's the tide coming in. It slides in underneath, and then pulls this junk out when it leaves." Winona pushed forward a few more steps. "We're cutting it close. This tunnel will be full soon. The mouth's likely under-water already. We may have to swim the last few yards."

Noah realized they were slowly making their way down a gentle slope. The water was deeper here, and he was hav-ing trouble getting breaths. Winona pushed on, the water now to her armpits.

"Miss?"

"No 'miss' here. Just Winona."

"Winona." Noah spit out the word along with a mouth-ful of green water. "I can't swim."

As if triggered by this, the tunnel floor crumbled beneath him. He tried to hop forward, but felt his feet slip into a gap in the rock and he sank beneath the surface.

His vision filled with the green glow of the water. He swallowed another mouthful, sputtering for air. Just then, a hand landed on his head, grabbing his hair, and he was yanked straight up. He yelped as he emerged, or tried to. A gush of water spewed from his mouth instead, followed by coughing and choking.

Winona held him up by an arm. "Never would've thought a boy living by the ocean couldn't swim."

"Never . . . been . . . to the . . . ocean."

Winona grinned. The greenish light and the gleam of her teeth made her look disturbingly even more like a skull. "Just hold on to me, kid. We'll be out soon."

Noah scowled. He was no more a kid than she was.

Winona guided Noah's hands to her shoulders, then continued forward, pushing against the tide. Noah could feel it was getting stronger. Soon, he felt that they were both floating, and ahead was a different glow. Bluish-white, it churned, growing and shrinking, as if the tunnel, itself, were breathing. From far away he heard a rising and falling roar.

"Our way out," said Winona. "It's covered by the tide, and there's more on the way. I need you to hold your breath now. It's not far." Noah gripped Winona's shoulders tighter. "No worries, kid, we'll see stars soon enough. We go under on three. Ready?"

Noah wasn't ready, but he knew he had to be. His heart beat hard, and the slimy green walls seemed too close. He couldn't look away from the whitish glow. Winona was saying something, something about numbers, and then it was clear she was counting. Noah sucked in as much air as he could.

They went under just as the glow was at its brightest. Noah was already wet, but the shock of the cold water was so intense, he nearly gasped. At first the glow hung before them. Noah could see Winona's head before him, could see her arms working and feel her legs kicking, but there was no progress. Then the glimmer started to shrink, and it felt as if all around them the water took hold, and they rushed forward. The current forced them into the light, which grew quickly, but they'd lost all control. They were spun around, and Noah's grip slipped. The glow was somewhere behind them, and then a jolt as Noah crashed into something—the rock wall. He saw a burst of sparks in darkness. Pain sliced through his head.

The trailing arcs disappeared as the darkness faded. Noah choked on seawater, trying to again get his bearings. The light was to his right, and he tried to grab it, but he couldn't reach. Winona was gone, and as Noah kicked and sputtered, he saw the darkness returning, and saw the first and brightest stars start to shoot across his vision. Once again, the current took hold, and the light began to shrink, but this time, Noah rushed with it. A dark form drifted in the water beside him, and when Noah touched it, he felt a hand. He gripped it, but it didn't squeeze back. The stars were shooting faster, the darkness growing, and what he could see at the center was white and loud and angry. He reached out with his other hand and felt the bricks of the tunnel wall rushing past. His fingers scraped against the rough walls, and he struggled not to swallow down more of the salty water. Everything went dark, and then his eyes were full of stars and the moon.

He couldn't hear from the crashing of the waves, and spat out more foul water than he remembered taking in. Instinctively, he kicked at the water, trying to keep his head above the surface. The air was cold, and his breath puffed above him. Beside him floated Winona, facedown. Noah reached over and took her hand again and struggled to turn her onto her back. Relief washed over him as a moment later he saw the same tiny puffs of steam come from her mouth.

Searching around, he realized they must be in deep water beside the stone pier. The tunnel mouth was behind them, and ahead stretched only the ocean. Overhead, the moon looked enormous, its light dancing across the waves.

Another broke in front of them, threatening to push them back into the tunnel. Noah caught hold of an iron bar, which jutted from the rock, and held on, though it was short and sharp and cut his hand. The rushing water was so loud, he could barely hear his own cries for help.

A swell dragged Winona farther into the mouth of the tunnel, and Noah called out again as he tried to keep his grip on both her and the rusty bar.

Exhausted, throat raw, he could barely hear his own shouts when a deeper voice roared with the crashing waves. "Hold on, lad!"

Noah looked over his shoulder just as the next wave rushed in. Riding the surge and blocking the moon's glow, he spotted a rowboat with three figures inside. The one in the middle was the tall man with the shaved head and the hook for a hand: Mister Steem.

"At your service, Mister Noah," he called as the boat moved in beside the tunnel's mouth. The two rowers kept their oars churning the water, and even though they didn't exchange so much as a word, they worked together, perfectly in sync, to keep the boat in place.

Still, the ocean rocked so violently, he had no hope for getting a hold on the boat. It moved up as he swooped down, and flew past at a terrifying speed.

He need not have worried.

"Hold on. I'll take young Winona first!" yelled Mister Steem. He plunged his hooked arm into the water beside the unconscious girl and lifted her easily, the hook tangled in her clothing.

For Noah, the few seconds it took to lift Winona into the rowboat were the most terrifying of this ordeal. Rescue was there, but what if it wasn't for him?

"Got you!" shouted Mister Steem as he hooked the back of Noah's shirt and hoisted him clear of the water. The boy swung limply in the air above the boat for a second, before landing against the bottom with a thud.

He gasped for breath, all the while marveling at how calm and quiet the sea was now that he was out of it.

"Get us along, now," Mister Steem instructed the rowers. "These waves and rocks will smash us to bits.

"Aye," said one.

The other broke into song:

> "Wooden Ivy *was her name.*
> *I loved her strong and true.*
> *But when the storm winds blew her in,*
> *'Twas nothing I could do.*

> *I saw her sink beneath the waves.*
> *No rescue was at hand.*
> *So poor* Wooden Ivy *sank,*
> *Despite all her demands.*

> *'Save me,' she cried. 'Jump in*
> *And pull me straight to shore.'*
> *I smiled and waved and danced a jig,*
> *But then did nothing more.*

> *I heard her call some more to me*
> *Through waves of ocean foam.*

She wished she danced high in the air
'Stead o' sinking like a stone.

My guilty heart loves her still,
But yet I will admit,
That her shrill commands to do her will,
I miss them not one bit.

The sun was bright when she was gone.
The wind made not a sigh.
As for that storm that blew her in,
My guilt did know was I."

Exhaustion and the lull of the song pulled Noah to the brink of sleep. He lay at the bottom of the boat, wedged between the feet of the rowers, across from Winona, who coughed and spit up seawater that blended with the brine already sloshing at their feet.

Mister Steem knelt over Winona and turned the girl's head to better face the moonlight. A gash ran from her eyebrow up to her hairline, the blood running down her face, thin and inky as it mixed with the salty water. Mister Steem held a rag over the edge of the boat and brought it back sopping. He rubbed it across the wound.

Winona gasped. "What happened?"

Mister Steem continued to clean the wound. "Smashed yourself against the sewer wall, I imagine."

"Why did I do that?"

"Impatience. You should've waited on the tide."

"What tide?"

Mister Steem patted the girl's shoulder. "You did well. You saved the lad."

"I did? Good." Winona's attention shifted to Noah. Her eyes were wide and black, and she couldn't hold herself up. "Who's this?" she demanded, a wobbly finger pointing in the boy's direction.

"Don't you worry," Mister Steem said. "You only saved his life." His gaze then locked on Noah. "And you went and saved her right back. I won't soon forget that. Neither will those aboard ship when they hear it. Am I right, Gentleman Nest? Lady Byrne?"

The rowers both nodded. The man who'd been singing, tipped his chin at Noah and said, "I'm working on a ditty about it right now."

The other looked at the moon, her tattoo-covered neck illuminated in the glow. "Aye. And it will be a good one."

Gentleman Nest laughed. "She only talks when she's right."

Just a few minutes earlier, Noah couldn't hear for the ocean's roar. Now, all seemed quiet enough to hear the fish breathing.

The moon followed them as they rowed away from the breaking waves toward calmer water, under cover of the docked ships. The first was the largest, a great gray monster with three smokestacks and five rows of windows above the waterline, making it taller than the buildings lining the port. Noah couldn't help thinking it was like a wall in the ocean. Gentleman Nest silenced his singing as the rowboat crept beside it. There were letters painted near the bow, but they were at the far end, and Noah couldn't read them.

Mister Steem leaned forward and whispered, "The *Colossus*."

Noah wondered why they were being so stealthy. "This is your ship."

Mister Steem shook his head. "Not exactly."

"But the first mate said you were from the *Colossus*."

"Don't worry what that other first mate said," Nest advised. "Worry at what this one does." He nodded his head toward Mister Steem, who smiled in return.

Nest and Byrne pulled their oars so quietly, not even a drip could be heard as they cut through the water close beside the *Colossus*. So close, Nest's oar almost tapped its side. Once they cleared the stern, the rest of the port drifted into view. Beside the *Colossus* was another large ship—a freighter—low in the water, but long and wide. Peeking out from between its massive smokestacks were the masts of sailing ships. Older than the steam-powered vessels, the sailers were wood and white cotton lit with blue moonlight. They looked ghostly, silent, and the dark figures on their decks and in the ropes and rigging were worrisome.

Noah sank lower as their rowboat made its way past each ship in turn. Nest was whistling another tune, and Winona was either asleep or lost in a long blink. No one seemed concerned now that they'd passed the *Colossus*. Mister Steem was gazing at the stars.

The last of the tall sailing ships was ahead, and beyond them, a few small craft, and then rocks and cliffs that ripped straight up from the water. Noah looked back toward the *Colossus*, illuminated by electric lanterns lining the decks, while the windows beamed out bright watchful circles. Beyond it was the city. Strings of lights hung along the edge of the wharf and outlined the streets beyond. Above, lights sparkled in the windows of buildings and homes. Noah even found the factory, and though most of it was dark, smoke and a reddish glow were visible above the chimneys. His eye followed the sparkling trail until he spotted one glimmer far away.

It was the house atop the hill where Marie and he lived. The sky behind it was starting to turn purple; the sun was just about to rise.

Home, he thought. But not home. He had never called it that. Knowing only the house, he'd never needed to give it a name. And now *home* didn't fit. It had been more of a prison, and he wouldn't be allowed back by his uncle, he knew. How could it be home if it wasn't safe?

"Where are we going?" he said to no one in particular.

"Home," said Mister Steem.

Noah looked at the big man and saw he was pointing to the horizon. Ahead was ocean and stars, but in the middle of the vast emptiness was another, darker hollow. A splotch in the field of stars. "The *Abbreviated*."

As if hearing the name was the key to seeing it, the ship began to emerge from the dark. It was three decks high, but strangely short from bow to stern, capped with one massive smokestack. The deck was unlit, but as they drew closer, Noah could hear sailors calling to one another, a few lines of song, and harsh, happy laughter. They were almost to the ship when Noah spotted figures on deck moving about.

"Ahoy," called Mister Steem.

"Ahoy," came the reply from somewhere above them. How had they gotten so close? The stars disappeared as they coasted beside her. It was like sailing out of the world.

A splash sounded nearby and Mister Steem dipped his hook into the water. When he lifted it again, he was spooling a length of rope around it as if that were his hook's very purpose. Sailors on deck snagged the rowboat with long wooden poles and quickly tied it to the *Abbreviated*'s side, before a flurry of hands pulled each crew person aboard, and then, finally, Noah. Winona reached the deck with Mister Steem's assistance, and a swirl of sailors gathered around her. Whispers were followed by dark eyes darting in Noah's direction.

It was hard to see details on the dim deck, but from what Noah could glimpse, the ship was less than half as long as the *Colossus* but almost as wide. It was a strange vessel, and when Noah turned around to get his bearings, he nearly fell overboard. Someone gruffly grabbed his shirt and yanked him back hard from a drop to the black ocean peppered with a tantalizing swirl of stars that weren't in the sky.

Still clutching a fistful of fabric, the figure pulled Noah back farther from the edge. The boy looked up. His eyes were adjusting, and the glow from the city and its reflection off the water was enough to show him Elijah's calm face. Just below the calls of the sailors and the rise and fall of waves lapping the ship's sides, Noah heard a gentle *tick-tick-tick*.

A tightness Noah didn't know he'd been carrying released at the sight of his caretaker. Seeing Elijah again was like remembering to breathe.

"Elijah," he said, starting forward to hug the robot.

"I'm afraid I must encourage you to the pilothouse, Sir Noah. The captain wants a word, and by now your escape isn't a secret to your jailers."

Noah thought Elijah's smile was ghastly in the low light, and his ticking like that of a clock just before the alarm that jars you into panic.

Elijah led Noah to a metal staircase, stopping at the bottom step. "Better to let me lead the conversation, Sir Noah. The captain is a bit"—*tick-tick-tick*—"cautious."

Noah patted his caretaker's arm. "It's good to see you, Elijah. I missed you."

Elijah looked at Noah a moment, but said nothing before turning to climb the ladder.

They ascended to a small room atop the ship, the highest structure, and there found two figures waiting in the dark. It was too dim to see the man in the back. The closer man was old, with several days of gray beard on his face, and he leaned heavily on a large steering wheel. Nearby, a table held some cups, a broken mug, a kettle, and pots. It looked as if the pilothouse was also home.

A panel before the pilot was dotted with gauges and knobs and levers, but the engine wasn't running. The man rubbed at his eyes as if he'd been sleeping. The small room smelled of his breath. "Not even big enough for ballast!" he roared loud enough to hurt Noah's ears. His accent had curls and ripples that made the words into adventures. Elijah didn't respond.

"Maybe," said the man at the back of the room. "But their money will let us buy some ballast." He stepped close enough for Noah to see that this was the man who'd claimed to be the first mate of the *Colossus*. The sharp, clean-cut uniform was gone. In its place was a worn black wool coat and filthy gray pants. The dark-haired man pointed out to sea. "Pilot, those jailers are going to sound the alarm at any moment. Take us out of the harbor."

Elijah stepped forward to put himself between the younger man and Noah. "Captain Moor, may I introduce you to Noah. And I wish to thank you for your excellent plan to release him from the jail."

Captain Moor laughed heartily, then said, "Watch this clockwork boy, Pilot. He'll sink us with sugar."

"Aye, Captain," shouted Pilot.

Captain Moor stepped past the others and thrust his head out the doorway. He whistled once, and pointed to someone on deck. "Tell Mister Steem I need him. Now." There was a quick response, and then Moor returned. "I'll have the second half of that payment," he said to Elijah, ignoring Noah's presence.

"Of course." Elijah reached into his pocket and pulled out a leather pouch, then counted out a handful of gold coins, and held them out for Captain Moor to take.

"Where did you get those?" Noah asked.

"Your father left some items hidden around the city, including some money. He anticipated that leaving might be difficult. His commands to me were clear: 'When the one who understands my work is discovered, you will have to flee.' That day is apparently today, as we are now fleeing."

"Fleeing," said Moor. Without counting, the captain tossed the coins into the broken coffee mug. "So, you've fled. Now tell me why I shouldn't put you in a life raft and be done with you."

Elijah ticked away a few moments before saying, "I have paid for passage to Singe." His ticking was calm, his face expressionless.

The captain nodded, as if considering this for the first

time. He looked surprised and a bit grave. "Singe isn't a place anyone wishes to go. There are strange things lurking in its waters that can pull a ship straight down. No struggle, no sinking—just straight down into the depths. There's also said to be a mad scientist who lives on the island—one who loves his work enough to destroy his home and the people in it. I wasn't sure how I'd like working for a mechanical, and now I know. Your type might walk the streets freely in the Homeland Empire, but you're insane."

Noah took a deep breath and held it. The captain's words made him feel sick to his stomach.

That and the gentle sway of the *Abbreviated* with the ocean. Elijah leaned as the ship moved, keeping himself vertical at all times, but Pilot and Captain Moor both stood still as timbers, moving with the ship as if built into it, and while Pilot rested his weight on the wheel, the captain had nothing but his will for support.

Noah feared he would be sick. He couldn't remember when he'd last eaten, and now he felt lightheaded and dizzy. "I have to go to Singe."

Captain Moor shook his head. "It's covered in monsters. What could possibly be on Singe for a boy like you other than death?"

Noah didn't want to say. After the captain's warning, he

worried the answer might give even more reason for Elijah and him to be put off the ship. "My father."

A series of bells sounded. First just a few, then more and more added to the chorus. The ringing was drowned out by a whooping siren.

Mister Steem entered the pilothouse and stood behind Noah. With him he brought the salt air of the ocean and a shadow that darkened the entire room. His head nearly touched the ceiling, and while the captain was not a small man, he was a full head shorter than his first mate. "That's the *Colossus*, Captain. She's preparing to launch."

Captain Moor nodded. "To chase us and recapture our little escapee." He studied Noah for a moment. The words Noah had said—his reason for going to Singe—had finally sunk in. "Your father can't be on Singe. The only man on Singe is—"

"Alton Physician," Pilot said, then gasped. "Oh, mermaids, take me now. That's the boy's father?"

"Yes, sir," Noah replied.

The captain narrowed his eyes and frowned. "My mother was right. She has a fool for a son."

"Please," Noah said. "They'll lock me up again! I just want to find my father. He's waiting for me." This last part wasn't entirely true, but it wasn't untrue, either. Alton

Physician was, in fact, waiting for the one who found the secret to the spideratus. He just didn't know it would be his son.

The room was starting to twist around Noah. He reached out and tapped Elijah's arm, then took hold of his sleeve. "Elijah," he said as something in his stomach rolled over. "I don't feel well."

Mister Steem patted Noah's shoulder and stepped beside the captain, whispering something into the man's ear, a string of words Noah couldn't keep up with as his nausea refused to settle. But he did hear Winona mentioned. As the men spoke there was a boom, and far off ahead of the ship, a plume of water rose into the air.

Pilot smiled. "The *Colossus* is giving us warning shots! As if they could ever sink a ship this pretty."

The captain pushed Mister Steem away and stepped forward, looming over the terrified boy. He looked exasperated. "Just had to complicate things, didn't you, Mister Noah? Saving our young Winona. Heroes like you are always trouble."

Noah felt his stomach shift one way as the ship moved another. "Hero, sir?"

"Saving one of my crew." Captain Moor snorted. "Probably even did it because it was the right thing to do, didn't you? No thought of getting one over on me, no expectation of a reward."

The room swayed around Noah, and he wanted to shut his eyes. There was another booming warning shot, though this time he was the only one to flinch. He held on to Elijah's sleeve as he looked at the captain, though he couldn't make out Moor's expression.

"I'll regret this, no doubt," Moor finally said. "Mister Steem, our guest is exhausted. Prepare him a cabin. Pilot, make best possible speed to Singe."

"Aye, Captain," said Mister Steem. He smiled at Noah, then walked to the door. As Pilot held the wheel and muttered to himself in a language full of ripples and rolls, Noah wondered if the room would ever stop spinning.

"We'll get you and your caretaker onto Singe," Captain Moor said. "Or as close as the monsters that protect it will allow."

"Thank you."

"Don't thank me until I'm done complaining about the headaches ferrying you about will give me."

Elijah's ticking sped up as another warning shot exploded ahead of them. "Captain, what do we do about the ships chasing us?"

"You said it yourself: we flee. We're faster than their

sluggish gunships. And we'll have to pray their gunners are poor shots."

Noah nodded and felt his knees buckle beneath him. He took hold of Elijah's hand, but his caretaker didn't offer any support, and so Noah hung there awkwardly for a moment before falling to his hands and knees. When he landed, his stomach lurched, and he threw up, his mouth still filled with the taste of salt.

"Half drowned, by the looks of him!" Pilot shouted. "Filled with naught but the ocean."

Captain Moor knelt beside Noah and gently lifted him from the mess. "When did you eat last, lad?"

"I don't know."

The captain looked up at Elijah. "Day's just starting, but I think he needs to sleep."

Noah never heard the reply, because his ears rushed with the sound of waves crashing. He looked up and saw Elijah peering down at him as if he were something beneath notice, like a curious bug that had crawled across his shoe. Noah wanted to ask for help, but the room had finally stopped spinning. All went black.

❂ CHAPTER 7 ❂

Noah spent the next day trying to recover. Everything had become a blur in the wheelhouse after he fell to the floor. He knew Elijah and Mister Steem had helped him to his feet, and he'd been taken to a cabin below deck. The ship seemed to roll beneath him. Elijah kept watch. Noah was given water and food—mostly stale bread—but it was enough, and he was able to keep it down for the most part. Sleep came and went, but Elijah was always there.

Throughout the entire ordeal there were reminders the *Abbreviated* was under pursuit. Sirens called across the water, their whine crescendoing and fading on the rise and fall of the ocean and the direction of the wind. Cannons boomed occasionally, though the warning shots were farther away each time, and by noon it was almost possible to ignore them.

At midday, Captain Moor visited Noah to reassure him. "You're their prize. They won't sink us."

"But will they catch us?" Noah asked. "Is Singe far?" He lay on a bunk bed with a single pillow and a wool blanket too scratchy to use. A wooden chest sat beneath the bed, and a single porthole on one wall looked out on the rolling waves. Other than that, the room was plain, empty and gray. And Noah felt as gray as the walls.

"They won't catch this ship," Moor said. "We slip in and out with prizes more secret than you. We've already made it past their patrol ships. The *Colossus* is giving us a good chase, but even they're falling farther back."

Elijah stood at the foot of the bed, ticking away. "When will we arrive at Singe, Captain?"

"By early evening. The approach will be . . . interesting. I've heard rumors about the island. And what with our pursuers, we won't make a direct approach."

Noah tried to sit up. "What rumors?"

Moor laughed. "Monsters, of course. Protecting the island, some say. Likely just stories spread by Liberty to keep away the curious. We'll see soon enough. In the meantime, you rest. If you're feeling up to it, there's a visitor who'd like to stop by."

Noah couldn't imagine who the captain might mean.

He'd never had a visitor before. "Okay," he finally said.

Once Captain Moor left, Noah asked Elijah, "Do you know what monsters he's talking about?"

Elijah's ticking sped up slightly, then skipped a beat—a small, silent gap that sounded like an error. "I don't know of any monsters, or anything else that will stop us from trying to reach your father."

Noah nodded. He couldn't help but wonder why Elijah said *trying* to reach Alton Physician. It made him feel like the trip might suddenly be doomed. He hoped it was just an odd choice of words by his caretaker. Since he'd learned of his father's whereabouts, reaching the island and finding him had been all Noah could think of.

"What . . . is my father like?" Noah asked Elijah.

Despite his face being cast of immobile iron, Elijah looked back at Noah with something like embarrassment. "Your father is gone, I'm afraid."

This was the same answer Elijah had always given to Noah whenever he had asked about him. Years earlier, he'd finally stopped asking. But not anymore.

"I know he's gone. He's on Singe. But I thought he was dead thanks to Marie's lies. I asked you *to describe* him."

"He's gone."

Always the same, Noah thought. Even when everything

else was different, Elijah was still an unchanging machine. Except, Noah realized, he wasn't. Not really. He did have secrets: he'd known about the spideratus, and he'd kept silent about Alton Physician's mysterious mission. Perhaps this was just another secret.

"Why won't you tell me about my father?"

"I'm afraid your father is gone."

Noah sighed. "I know. I asked *why* you won't talk about him. Don't tell me about him. Tell me why you won't."

Elijah's gears sped up for half a minute as he thought very hard about what Noah had asked. At last he said, "Your mother forbade it."

Of course, Noah thought, his heart feeling tight in his chest. Marie had more secrets than his father ever could. Noah wondered if he would ever know why she had treated him the way she had.

Outside, cannons boomed as the chase continued across the ocean.

Hours later, Noah was finally feeling like himself again, and his appetite had fully returned. A dinner of stew had been delivered by the visitor Captain Moor had promised.

Winona entered the cabin without knocking and nearly

dropped the bowl into Noah's lap. "Here, and thanks."

Noah caught the bowl and managed to keep most of the stew in it. "Thanks? What for?"

Winona wouldn't meet his eyes. She stood at the door with her arms crossed and a look on her face that alternated between embarrassment and anger. "You know. That thing. Back at the jail."

Noah felt as if she was speaking in code. Understanding Elijah's ticking was simpler. "The jail?"

"It's where you were locked in the cell," said Elijah, trying to help.

"I know what the jail is, Elijah."

Winona kicked the doorway. "You saved me from drowning. That's what. *Thank you for saving me from drowning*," she said in a singsong tone, as if it was a joke. She still seemed embarrassed, but the anger was gone. "Blimey, you're supposed to be bright, kid."

"You're . . . welcome?" Noah said. He still didn't like how she called him *kid*.

"I said thanks."

Noah nodded. "Okay."

Another cannon shot called out. No one responded. The booms were ever farther away.

Winona looked around the room, her discomfort

obvious, but Noah didn't know what was causing it. "The *Colossus* isn't giving up easily," she said suddenly. "You must be very important."

Noah shook his head. "I'm not. But my . . . family . . . doesn't want me to reach my father."

"Why?"

Noah shrugged. Now it was his turn to be embarrassed.

"His father is blamed for the Robot Uprising," Elijah said. He looked from Winona to Noah and back. "But now I'm afraid he is gone."

Winona looked at the caretaker with apprehension. She almost seemed afraid of him.

"Are you okay?" Noah asked.

Before she could say anything else another cannon shot called out. This one was closer, and it was followed by the rush of a watery explosion beside the ship.

Elijah looked at the porthole. "That sounded quite close." He put a hand on Noah's shoulder. "Perhaps you should get under the bed."

Instead, Noah and Winona both rushed to the small window, each trying to shoulder the other away to better see outside. The sky overhead was darkening as the sun set, but because they were headed west, the way forward was a blur of light on the water. Behind the *Abbreviated* were the ships from Liberty. They had sounded farther than they actually were. The massive *Colossus* was close enough to see sailors running on deck.

"We've stopped," said Winona. "Can you feel it?"

Noah could not. The ship swayed as it always had. "Why would we stop?"

In answer, he received a deafening mechanical scream that sounded like dozens of heavy chains quickly snapping over a metal blade. The din lasted several seconds and then stopped abruptly. Noah and Winona exchanged looks of terror.

"Oh good," said Elijah. "We must be near Singe."

Once again, the pair looked out the porthole. In the light from the setting sun, it was hard to see what was happening. The mechanical scream blasted again, and Noah watched the glass in the window vibrate, and then crack. The tilt of the ship grew steeper. This wasn't the *Abbreviated* being chased. This was something far worse.

The screeching faded, and the sounds of gunfire and sailors shouting took its place. Screams filled the air from above deck as the ship suddenly began listing in the opposite direction.

Then the roar rose again. Light sliced through the porthole at a new angle and the ship lurched backward. There was a squeal like metal being bent, and then a shudder ran through the deck.

Noah gripped the frame of the porthole to keep from falling. He held on tight enough that the sharp edges and bolts dug painfully into his fingers.

There was more screaming, and the *Abbreviated*'s crew shouted to one another. Noah recognized certain voices, the captain's most easily calling for lanterns and guns. The ship shuddered to a new angle and something huge loomed into the dim light. Whatever it was, it moved too fast to be a ship. It rose and fell as it swam past the porthole and left a swirling current in its wake.

Something crashed on deck, and there was a scream followed by a splash.

"Man overboard!"

Noah craned his neck, trying to see what had caused the latest panic, but the porthole was at times brilliantly lit and then painted with darkness, like a shadow was passing over the *Abbreviated*.

Winona gasped. "Something's *holding* the ship."

"Holding?"

The mechanical roar blasted out again. It now felt as if it was coming from inside the cabin. Winona and Noah covered their ears, wincing. Noah hoped that Winona would know what to do, but when he turned toward her, tears were gathered at the corners of her eyes. Her mouth moved, yet he heard nothing but the roar. The floor vibrated beneath them. Noah couldn't stand to be on it. He tried to scramble to the bed, but slid away as the ship tilted even further.

The roar ended as suddenly as it had started and the ship righted itself partway. There was a knocking in the floor as something that had been twisted near to breaking returned to its proper shape.

Winona looked up at Noah and wiped the water from her eyes with the back of her hand. "Something's trying to crush us," she said, her voice shaking.

Off to the side, Elijah calmly watched the window. "It's the octochines, I believe."

Winona grimaced at the robotic caretaker with obvious dislike. "The what?"

"Octochines. The giant machines that nearly destroyed Liberty. They were always a bit . . . nervous."

The horn's blast sounded again, this time so constant Noah almost couldn't hear it anymore. Then the volume rose to wall-shaking levels, and Noah could hear nothing else. He watched a sailor swim desperately for a rope, but the cries of the man, the splashing of the water, and the creaking of the ship were all drowned out by the terrible roar.

The ship shuddered again, the light shifting as they changed direction. And then, at last, he saw the source of the sound.

The monster resembled a great, mechanical octopus, one that could turn a ship in the ocean as easily as Noah could turn a stick in a puddle. Sailors aimed a spotlight on the face of the machine's enormous, egg-shaped head, which rose out of the water atop eight tentacle-like legs. Noah couldn't help but be thankful that they had such a light. He wanted to study the machine. He wanted to understand it. He couldn't help himself. He even—for just a minute—forgot that the robot was threatening the lives of everyone aboard the ship.

He quickly spotted that the whole thing—legs and body—looked like it had been formed of cast iron, with rusty patches marring the dull sheen. The creature's head was actually two parts. A seam ran around the circumference, allowing the top half to swivel and turn the creature's spotlight eye, though the maneuver was accompanied by a high-pitched grinding. Beneath the seam, several large holes ran in a ring, like a series of mouths. When they were partially submerged, the horn-blast roar quieted. But when they rose above the water, fully exposed, the alarm reached such levels, it sent the ship shaking. The holes looked large enough for Noah to crawl through, and part of him wished he could do so—just to see how the mechanisms inside were put together. Even with the creature thrashing around, and the ship's lights chasing it, Noah was able to spot spinning wheels and churning pistons, fast-moving machinery steaming against the ocean swells. Beneath the head, a cluster of legs disappeared into the water. Could they be long enough to support it against the bottom? Two legs curved back up out of the water, large metal coils wrapped around the deck playing with its prey, shifting it first this way then the other, as the great eye searched back and forth across the deck. All the while, the angry horn bellowed down on the scrambling crew.

Noah couldn't help but be awed by the magnificence of its construction. "It's beautiful," he whispered to himself.

"What?" Winona cried. "It's a monster!"

Elijah shook his head. "It's an *octochine*. As I said, a nervous one."

Noah didn't know whether to laugh or scream. Inside he was a mix of terror and excitement. The octochine might destroy the ship, but Noah couldn't help but feel like he was one step closer to his father. A thrill ran through him at the thought that he might find the person who made such things.

Another cannon shot echoed overhead. It sounded now

like the *Colossus* was no longer firing warning shots. They were engaged in battle. Noah tried to spot the ship approaching from behind, and could just make out black iron legs rising from the water to grapple with this new threat.

"I hope they don't hurt it," he said.

Elijah patted his shoulder. "Oh, they won't."

"You're both out of your minds," Winona replied with a shake of her head.

"Get those lights over here!" Captain Moor shouted, his tone one of command, not panic. "Where are those guns? Don't just stand there. Get moving!"

Feet pounded the deck boards. Hatches clanged. A rattling and a flurry of competing voices. These faded beneath the sound of strong sticks breaking, harsh snaps one after another. Sparks flew off the mechanical octopus's head, a layering of small explosions. Noah realized it hadn't been sticks breaking, but the crack of gunshots.

Winona ducked. "Away from the window!"

"I want to see!" Noah said, pressing closer.

"You stupid kid!"

"You stupid . . ." He paused. "Sailor!" It felt silly the moment he said it, and her laughter proved it so. She took hold of his belt and tried to pull him away from the window, but he held tight to the latch.

"Get down, kid!"

"Leave me alone, Miss Bossy!" That was even worse.

The bullets had no effect on the octochine. The giant robot didn't bother to hide, didn't turn, didn't shy away at all. Its eye-light stayed fixed on the ship, swinging a bit, continuing to examine the top deck and some of the portholes, including the one Noah and Winona hid beyond. With a sudden rise in volume, the octochine rose taller and lunged toward the ship, its roar turning to a rumble through what Noah realized must be bubbles erupting from and around the machinery of its mouths. Every time it lowered into the water, a cloud of steam and spray rose up, and the sailors' spotlights showed the height of the waves battering the ship. A swell more like a wall than a wave—at least as tall as the ship's smokestack, perhaps taller—surged toward the port side. It seemed they were caught by both high seas and a sea monster.

Noah shifted his focus from the ocean back to the octochine's searching light. "It's like a giant eye," he murmured.

As if he'd heard the boy, Moor shouted, "Aim for the eye! The eye!"

Winona grabbed Noah and pulled him away from the tiny window. "Why do you want to see such a terrible thing?" she demanded, her frightened face lit by the roaming light. "Who could have built it?"

It *was* a terrible thing. It was a marvel. But Noah didn't need to wonder who could have made such a terribly marvelous thing. *My father.* Winona didn't seem to actually expect an answer, though, so he pressed closer to the glass.

The ship groaned again, tilting toward the octochine. The monstrous machine pulled the *Abbreviated* ever closer in a painful hug, and the ship sank lower into water so black and thick it appeared ready to swallow the *Abbreviated* whole.

A lantern came arcing through the sky, starting at a point just above Noah's porthole, flipping in the air once as it streaked toward the eye of the roaring thing, the octochine, before striking there with a double smash, as both spotlight and lantern cracked. In a blinding white flash, the lantern exploded, the lamp oil spraying, fire spreading over the beast's eye.

The reaction was immediate. The octochine stood even higher, its body leaving the water entirely, as its legs released their hold on the *Abbreviated.* The knocking and grinding of metal scraping across the deck reverberated through the hull as the creature's arms pulled across the ship, tearing away loose plating, breaking railings, and snapping cables. The horn roar of the machine made Noah's teeth ache, and though he was certain the thing was about to strike the ship a terrible blow, he couldn't help but press himself even closer to the porthole.

Now free, the ship rocked back to level and drifted away from the burning face of the octochine. The arms pulled back, two giant metal whips preparing to snap down across the middle of the ship, when there was a pop and a spark, and the spotlight eye went out. The fire had caused the bulb to explode. Captain Moor had blinded the octochine.

In the sudden darkness, there was only the nonstop roar of the thing in the water. It sounded like a wounded animal, the pitch keening higher as the machinery inside spun faster and faster. The captain called for another lantern. The sailor's spotlight turned again and the octochine's blindness was confirmed as it lowered back into the water. Two legs swung wildly at the sides of the ship. The roar gurgled down to a tortured moan, quiet enough that the crew's voices could once again be heard.

"What am I doing?" Winona grabbed Noah's arm. "We need to get away from the window."

Noah pulled back. The panicked voices from above deck were too interesting.

"Turn us about, full speed!"

"Did you see it?"

"It's from the island, I tell you! The island!"

"What if it's not alone?"

"Get away from that thing!"

"Is it chasing us?"

All the voices blended in a mess of panic and commands.

"You stupid kid, get away from there." Winona pulled hard on his arm, but still Noah clung to the porthole.

The ship turned. As it did, Noah's porthole gave a clearer view of the machine.

"Look at it," he murmured. "It's beautiful."

The pair watched the octochine stop, shudder, then lurch forward. Its face was blackened with soot, the shattered eye nothing but a white web of cracked glass. Three of its legs reached to attack the ship it couldn't see.

Maybe it surprised itself when it did find the ship. Found it with one sweeping leg, the pointed whip of which tore into and through and up the *Abbreviated*'s side, ripped into it like a hatchet into a tin can. Ripping it open, emptying some of its contents into the sea.

Ripping it right where Noah's cabin was located.

Winona pulled Noah clear of the porthole just in time, as rusted jagged metal swept past his face. He, Winona, and Elijah stood against the far wall of the cabin, water splashing just below them, the cold wind swirling.

Winona pulled at Noah's arm. "Follow me. We'll head above deck."

But Noah couldn't move. He gazed down at the swirling black water below, and tried to breathe. He thought nothing could pry him from the spot, until his caretaker leaned forward.

"There," said Elijah, pointing to a speck nearly lost in the last sliver of sunlight on the water. "There is Singe."

Noah could barely make out the island ahead of them. Winona yanked his arm again. "Who cares."

"I do." Noah leaned forward for a better view, as if he might see his father standing on the horizon. As if his father *was* Singe.

But he couldn't see. Moor had ordered a retreat, and the ship was turning. The island was dropping away. "We can't go!" Noah shouted. "I have to find him!"

There was a splash in the water just below the damaged cabin. Noah and Winona looked down, spotting a wooden trunk bobbing in the water like a cork in the waves.

Elijah came beside them. "That landed nicely."

Winona gave him a puzzled look. "Why did you just throw that in?"

"To make it easier for both of you."

Noah was about to ask what Elijah meant when his robot caretaker put a hand each on his and Winona's backs and gave a single, shocking shove, sending them sailing down to the sea below.

❂ CHAPTER 8 ❂

Noah plunged into the icy water. As he flailed about wildly, his hand found and then clutched a leather strap. He sank beneath a wave and felt the water vibrating with the octochine's scream. He pulled himself up by the thing he held on to—the handle of the trunk. It bobbed, and Noah felt like he was the rope in a tug of war. The cold, black ocean water drew him one way, and the trunk tugged him the other. With a burst of effort, he managed to pull himself on top of the trunk, ending the battle.

Another pair of hands grasped at his makeshift raft. Noah reached out, helping Winona to safety. The trunk was big enough for them both.

Noah lay against the trunk and felt his heart beating hard in his chest. He wanted it to calm, he wanted to catch his breath, but there wasn't time. An ocean surge pushed over them. He took a deep lungful of air and held it just before another cold wave slammed down. The currents were already pulling them away from the *Abbreviated*. The people on deck looked so small.

Winona gripped his arm and hissed into his ear. "We need to paddle back to the ship!"

Noah looked back toward the ship, but it already appeared too far away. He wanted to scream at Elijah, to ask him why he'd done such a reckless thing.

But before he could, the robot boy stepped off the deck and plunged into the water, disappearing into the inky cold with barely a splash.

"I hope he sinks like a stone!" Winona cried. "Why did your stupid rusted friend push us into the water?"

"I don't know."

Noah scanned the water, but Elijah was nowhere in sight. What if he never saw his robot caretaker again? He was angry with Elijah. Confused. And still, he could not imagine a day without Elijah beside him.

The ship slowly motored away, water churning behind it. The lamps and lanterns the crew held high were by then brighter than the natural light. The gaping hole in the *Abbreviated*'s side looked dark and empty. Noah found it difficult to make out details. The ship was becoming a fading silhouette hidden among the waves. "They can't see us."

"That's not the worst of it." Winona pointed at the churning water between them and the ship. "That thing is still trying to kill us!"

"No." Noah shook his head. He knew the octochine was dangerous, but from its thrashing, he could see it wasn't intentionally attacking anything. His fear shifted to curiosity. What might the machine do next? Would it give up? Find a way home? "It can't even see us."

"Look at it! It knows we're here!" Winona clutched at the strap and screamed for the ship.

Several of the octochine's legs thrashed against the water as the *Abbreviated* barreled toward the horizon. The ship was already just a cluster of lights reflected on the water. Winona shouted again, but even the sounds of the sea lapping around them seemed louder than her screams.

The octochine's egg-shaped head was almost submerged, its roar now drowned out to a pitiful whine. The eye, cracked, black, and useless was already halfway under the water. The machine's legs had stopped their flailing, and now that it had stilled, the ocean around it calmed, too. The waves rose and fell over its legs and body, but its head sat like a strange rock in the water.

The *Abbreviated* floated, but the rows of lights along its aft and atop the smokestack showed it listed heavily to one side. Ripped open, she must have been taking on water, so it was lucky she was moving at all. "She might be sinking," Noah remarked.

"She won't sink." Winona's grip on the trunk tightened. "She can't. She just can't."

Noah realized he was trembling, from fear or cold or perhaps both.

"Don't be scared," said Winona, holding tighter on the trunk to stop her own hands from shaking. "The captain will come back. When he sees we're gone he'll make way to find us and—"

Her eyes widened.

In the water, the octochine's head had swiveled, stopping when its eye faced them. Noah thought it looked like a shattered dinner plate that had been poorly reassembled. He wondered how the creature had ever seen, or how it could see now, and for a moment, his curiosity outweighed his fear.

Then the monster began to move toward them.

Noah and Winona clutched at the trunk, their only protection against the machine. Noah's insides trembled and Winona gasped as the octochine sank just below the water's surface and knocked lightly against the bottom of the box. As it passed beneath them, Noah couldn't be sure, but he thought he heard a *tick-tick-tick*. And then it was gone.

"If that thing comes back and kills us, I'm going to rip your robot apart gear by gear."

Noah gritted his teeth. He didn't like how she talked about Elijah, but she was right about one thing: he *had* pushed them into the water. Ever since Elijah had spoken in Alton Physician's voice, his behavior had been focused on getting Noah to Singe. Noah hadn't thought to question whether this meant he'd be safe. He didn't want to question it now, either. *Elijah will always be Elijah*, he told himself. *He has to be*.

"I've known Elijah my whole life. He wouldn't do anything to hurt me." Noah wondered if he sounded convincing.

"He should be sunk like an anchor."

"He had to have a reason!" Noah looked at the disappearing ship. It was barely a glimmer on the horizon now. Once it was gone, there would be nothing for miles.

"He should *be* an anchor."

Noah was about to ask Winona to stop dreaming up ways to destroy his caretaker when he saw something behind her, far in the distance.

"I know why he pushed us in," Noah whispered.

"Sure, you do." Winona's fear seemed to have disappeared along with the octochine. Now she was just angry.

"I do." He pointed to the horizon behind her. She turned to see the island of Singe sitting there, only a few miles away. Behind it was a dark sky full of stars. "The ship had turned around," Noah said. "Elijah wanted to make sure I reached the island."

"That's a really horrible excuse to push you in the water," Winona fumed as she splashed angrily in the direction of the shore. "And why did he have to drop me in, too?"

Noah didn't know for sure, but he was sure Elijah would have a reason. "Right now, we need to get to Singe."

Winona gave a tired nod. "I know. This trunk won't float forever. We'll have to paddle there."

They shifted so they could both kick and push in the right direction.

After a few silent minutes of work, Winona said, "I wish you were wrong about needing to get to the island."

"Why?"

"Because the island is where that monster robot was headed."

The ocean sounded like a thousand whispering mouths. The sky grew darker until the island was a jagged band of missing stars. Winona guided them by looking at the constellations, and neither of them spoke much.

As the island drew nearer, the ocean's whispers became louder and more constant. There was no telling how long they'd been kicking, but judging by how exhausted he felt, Noah figured it had been hours. The ocean's whispers grew to a loud shushing; they'd found the surf. Waves rushed against a sandy beach. Soon enough, they took hold of the trunk and pushed it and its passengers, until it hit a sandbar and rolled, and the survivors tumbled off. Noah swallowed more than a mouthful of water, choking as he dragged himself to the beach. His body burned from the salt. His clothes were already full of grit. Reaching dry sand, he kept crawling, stopping only when he came to a cluster of trees.

Despite his exhaustion, Noah felt electric with excitement. Somewhere beyond the forest was his father waiting for the one who could help him with his work. The machine that had attacked the ship was only an example of what Alton Physician was capable of building. Noah knew he should be terrified of the machine that had nearly sunk the *Abbreviated*, but it was just too marvelous. Maybe his father had found a way to control his creations. Maybe the machine was just protecting the island.

Noah's wonder evaporated as he suddenly realized he

was alone. "Winona?" he called. No answer but the surf's murmuring. "Winona!"

The gentle shushing of the ocean was interrupted by a horn blast. It lasted just a moment, stopped, then repeated. Noah scanned the water and saw the octochine emerging from the ocean. As the waters rose and fell around it, the noise of its horn was cut off and returned. Its blast followed the rhythm of the waves until at last, it surfaced completely. Then the noise reached full pitch, and wailed on. The giant mechanical octopus staggered forward, water rushing from every opening, dragging lengths of seaweed behind it. Lit from behind by the moon, it looked like a black void outlined in white.

Noah ran up the beach to the nearest clump of trees. They were scrawny and felt fragile beneath his touch, but he had nowhere else to go. From his new hiding place, he watched as the machine continued to pull itself from the water.

It stood taller than the trees, on stretched legs, but staggered and tripped over the sand and some fallen trunks, moving up the beach in a zigzag pattern. Noah grew braver as he saw the thing struggle. He almost pitied it.

He stepped from behind the trees and followed the machine as it stumbled on.

Its head swiveled as the machine staggered back and forth at the edge of the beach. Stepping forward, it thrashed into a tree, then stumbled. It tried again, this time disappearing onto a path Noah could hardly see. *It's blind,* he thought. Despite this, it had still been able to find its way back—able to make it home. Noah felt a swell of pride at the thought that his father had made this remarkable contraption. His pride soured to shame. This machine had nearly sunk the *Abbreviated*.

The horn-blast cry faded, and Noah rushed to catch up. He was surprised to find the path wider than he'd expected, but in the dark it was still hard to navigate. Snapped and toppled trees lay everywhere. Noah couldn't find an easy way around them, so he wove between the trunks on one side. Soon enough, he saw how the path had been made. Up ahead, the giant mechanism lurched, moaning. When it veered too far from the path, it knocked into trees, tearing their roots from the ground, or snapping them in half before stumbling back. Still, the path appeared to be well-used. The octochine evidently came this way often.

The ground grew slightly steeper. *It's headed up the mountain,* Noah thought. *To the city. To my father.*

"Hsst! Noah!" a voice called from the trees nearby.

Beyond the first few trunks it was impossible to see

into the dark palms. Noah kept one eye on the staggering machine as he approached the edge of the woods. "Winona? Where are you?"

There was a rustling to his left. "Here! And keep quiet. That thing will hear you."

"You don't need to hide. I think it's trying to find its way home. It's not looking for—"

His explanation was interrupted by a sudden harmonizing as another horn joined the first. Ignoring Winona's calls for him to hide, he rushed ahead, darting between trees to get a better look. He'd just reached the wide entrance to the path when a beam from above swept over him. Another machine had found them. It towered above Noah, its light just missing him as it focused on the damaged unit. The giant metal octopuses swayed, their horn blasts rising and falling in synch.

"Don't you ever learn?" Winona asked as she rushed from the tree line and grabbed Noah's arm. "Listen to me just once and we might survive." She pulled him back into the forest, but Noah struggled against her grip. He wanted to understand what was happening between the two robots.

"You don't need to take care of me," he said.

She snorted. "Of course I do. Captain would have me locked away if anything happened to you."

"Well, who saved who back at the jail?"

Winona bit her lip. She apparently didn't like being reminded of owing someone a debt.

Noah returned his attention to the octochines, which were still bleating back and forth to each other. "I think they're talking!"

"That's lovely," said Winona. "Probably discussing how easy we'll be to crush."

The undamaged machine stood tall. Its head swiveled to face the path ahead while its horn blast shook the nearby trees. Noah covered his ears. The machine started to move, the light from its beam scattering through the tree branches sending birds fleeing. The machine took a few massive paces, then turned and gave a series of blasts, as though urging the damaged unit to hurry up. The grinding of gears and the rattle of what could have been broken machinery filled the air as the struggling octochine tried to climb the hill. Now guided by the sounds from its companion, it managed to mostly stay to the path.

Even slowed by the damage, the machine was faster than Noah could run. He rushed ahead, trying to keep the octochine in view. Winona called his name again, but he didn't turn back. The light of the lead machine helped him see a bit, making for a faster pace. Noah's breathing was heavy and his chest hurt, but if he stopped, he might lose the way. His father's city stood at the top of this mountain. He could reach it before dawn. He felt as if the machines, even though they didn't know it, were leading him home.

"What are you doing?" Winona demanded. She'd had no trouble keeping up. "We need to stay away from those things!"

"They'll lead us to my father."

"One almost destroyed the ship, and two will have no trouble with us! Why would you want to find whoever built them, even if he is your father?"

"You don't get it. I just have to."

Winona looked at him thoughtfully. "Yeah, I get it," she said, sounding a little sad. "But I still think a bad idea is a bad idea, kid."

She steered him back toward the beach and he struggled, pulling himself free before pushing her away. It was too dark to see clearly, even with the light from the mechanical eyes sweeping over them, broken into bands by the trees.

"If you keep going this way, you'll end up dead," she said. "Your father is one thing, but those machines will kill you."

"I need—"

"We *need* to stay on the beach. We *need* to find water.

We *need* to light a fire so we can be spotted and rescued. If Captain's even able to reach the island while it's protected by those things."

Noah looked back at the machines striding away. He could still find them by the crashing of their footfalls. He had to hurry.

"You don't know they mean to attack us."

"Don't I? That thing put a hole in the side of the ship."

Noah looked back at Winona. "You don't have to come."

"Captain Moor would want us on the beach."

"He's not *my* captain."

"No, but he's mine. And I'm in charge." She took hold of his hand again. He could feel an urgency in her grip. She wanted to get away as badly as he wanted to find his father.

"You may have been in charge of me on the boat, but we're not on the boat!"

He could hear the robots thrashing through the woods. And though they were loud, he feared he would lose track of them soon.

He decided to try a different tack. "Listen to me, Winona. I spent my whole life locked in a house like a prisoner, forced to do as I was told, and never told why. Now I have a chance to find out what's happening. To find my father.

There have been so many lies, so many secrets, and I'm done with them."

"That all sounds terrible, but just because you were unhappy doesn't make you right." She shook her head, then let go of his hand.

Noah backed away. When he turned to climb over a pile of fallen trunks, he realized all was silent behind him. Winona was neither following nor trying to talk him out of chasing the terrible machines.

Fine, he thought. He was used to being on his own, even though he really never had been, not with Elijah, and not with Marie.

He headed deeper into the woods listening to Winona not following.

After ten minutes of rushing through the dark, Noah caught up with the wounded machine. The other octochine must have gone on ahead. He thought he could hear a siren sounding deeper in the woods.

He stayed out of sight, running from tree to tree, but soon there weren't any more trees to hide behind. Looking around, he saw he was no longer on a path, but in an expansive flat area covered with wooden planks, similar to the dock in Liberty. Ahead of him, a large black building loomed, nearly identical to Marie's factory, and was backed by cliffs that rose up to the mountaintop.

The wounded octochine blasted its horn. A single, short blast came from the building. The robot gave another burst of sound and the building answered again. Windows lit up. The area around the building filled with light, and the damaged machine hobbled forward, its noise deeper, more violent. The ground and surrounding trees shook.

Noah continued forward on shaking legs. He was no longer sure he wanted to follow the machines, let alone go inside.

The damaged robot made its way into the wide entrance, and the horns stopped. The only sound now was distant machinery.

There was a great ticking, rhythmic as time, coming from inside the building, and the glare from the windows and doorway blurred Noah's vision.

When his eyes adjusted, he saw that while the building resembled the factory Marie ran back in the city, this one was even larger. The front door was three times as tall and wide, and hung from massive wheels that looked rusted. The door stood open, and must have been for years. Instead of three rows of windows, there were seven. The ones closest to the ground remained dark. Many of the panes were broken, and Noah watched as birds flew in and out of them, screeching about the light interrupting their sleep.

Noah crept closer. There might be someone inside—maybe, even his father.

A row of workstations sat near the door, but only one was in use. The damaged octochine had made its way to the nearest stable and now stood in the center of the whirring machinery as automatic arms pulled it apart. The body of the mechanical octopus shook. Its legs twisted and spasmed. If Noah hadn't known the device was made up of unfeeling gears and springs, he might have thought the repair work was painful. The workstation's arms clattered, and steam-driven motors hissed, the sounds blending with the muted mechanical whimpering of the damaged machine.

Its gears slipped, and the blind eye lantern swiveled back and forth with a grinding sound, like sand was trapped in the grooves.

Noah walked past the repair station and deeper into the factory. A fine black dust covered the floor. Aside from his footprints, the grit was undisturbed. It didn't look as if anyone or anything had walked through the cavernous room in a long, long time.

Noah walked to the end of the row of workstations.

They looked like versions of the ones in Marie's factory, but much taller. There were ladders and platforms where workers could climb to the top. The tools hanging at each station were large, connected to gears and cables that ran to machines at the ceiling, attached to steam pipes and wires that led to massive boilers at one end of the room.

As Noah pushed farther inside, the room grew warmer. From what he'd seen, the building was nestled against the mountain. No, not a mountain. A volcano, he realized. One that supplied all the power the factory could ever need.

Noah poked his head around the edge of the last station and saw another row just like the first. He quickly counted them, two rows of ten, and wondered where all the other octochines might be. He had seen two, but there ought to be twenty or more. The factory had clearly been built for dozens of octochines to be worked on at once. And in the floor's dust, Noah spotted no signs of human life. Just the prints of the octochines—circular imprints with long lines where the ends of mechanical tentacles had left winding trails.

No one—not even his father—had been to this factory for ages. And upon closer scrutiny, Noah now could see why: the machines took care of themselves. Just the thought gave him a sense of pride. His father's inventions *took care of themselves*.

Noah returned to the first row of workstations and found the octochine was nearly done being reassembled. The automatic arms swung around, adding rivets and tightening bolts so swiftly, it was hard to follow the movements. Even though he knew how dangerous the machine was, he couldn't wait to see it walk again. His father had built an amazing factory—one that ran itself—and the octochine was the most amazing contraption he could imagine.

Until something went wrong. There was an explosion from somewhere deep in the building. The lights flickered and a rattling of metal parts ricocheted inside the workstation. The rebuilt robot slouched to one side, half its legs hanging uselessly, and its other arms reached out to push against the stall. Its dark eye swiveled in a panic. As the legs jerked, debris flew in every direction, and Noah suddenly realized that the robot's flailing tenacles were sending enormous metal containers of bolts and gears high into the air with no effort. Metal rained down around him, and Noah scrambled back against the factory wall, though there was nothing there to protect him. Steam shot from some broken pipe, and the workstation arms all slowed until they all finally hung limp. The robot released a stuttering siren that sounded almost like a cry of fear or pain. The scream stirred something in Noah. He knew that the octochine had been a threat, but in that moment, it sounded terrified, as though it simply wanted a chance to be safe.

Without thinking, Noah rushed forward and began scaling the ladder. The octochine thrashed against the workstation walls with its functional legs as Noah climbed higher and higher until he was near the head. The eye was still dark. The repairs weren't complete. Through one of the mouthlike openings, he could see gears lined up improperly. Hanging nearby was a mechanical arm with an assortment of tools at one the end. He managed to work a wrench loose and leaned out to tinker with the octochine's inner workings.

He'd never seen plans for this contraption, but it had been built by the same man who'd built the spideratus: his father. He even recognized some of his mother's touches. His father's focus was a direct line from the desired purpose to the tool to accomplish it. His mother's designs often included subtle additions that might aid the goal indirectly. It was the difference between the spideratus's straightforward building tools and Elijah's sense of helpfulness.

For the first time, it occurred to Noah that they must have worked together on so much.

His thoughts returned to the work before him. Bolts were loosened and gears moved into better position. The pieces were all there, but the whirling mechanical arms, on the verge of breaking down, hadn't gotten components in the proper places. The octochine bucked a couple of times, making his work more difficult. Noah heard himself whispering quietly to calm the machine, reassuring it that everything would be okay.

Noah was exhausted, but the work didn't feel like work, and so he kept at it for hours. Only once did he stop and think about the fact that he had paddled ashore on a trunk. Only for a moment did he let himself feel how he missed Winona. He hoped she was safe. He hoped that when morning came, she would be found by the crew. As for him, he let those thoughts go and focused again on the task at hand. He was here for this. For the machine. For his father. For the secrets they contained. The octochine was a marvel, and as he lost himself inside it, time ticked away and the moments drifted into hours.

And then he was done. The gears fit together and began to spin. The springs started to sing and the sirens stopped. The body shifted and the legs tensed beneath the robot as it prepared to stand. Despite Noah's successful repairs, age and lack of upkeep had left one of the machine's legs nearly useless. He wished that he could see the original blueprints. It was likely he could figure out what was wrong with the one leg if only he could locate them. Peering down, he wondered if there was an office in the factory where he might find the plans. Only then did he notice how high he'd climbed.

His knees shook on the way down, but once back on the factory floor, he congratulated himself on the work he had done during the night.

Then another thought occurred to him: What had he done?

He'd just repaired one of the robots that had nearly destroyed Liberty, attacked the *Abbreviated*, and tried to hurt him and Winona.

The steam thinned. In the weak light of the ceiling lamps, Noah could see the black shape looming. It was thirty feet tall, and it suddenly seemed much larger. There was a short honk, the sound of gears shifting, and the eye popped on and shone down on Noah.

He froze.

Chains rattled, followed by the clicking of gears into place, and the machine stepped forward, limping on its one bad leg. The beam of its light closed tighter on Noah. And then the octochine released a horn blast so loud, it rose to a scream, and took another shaking, sudden step forward.

Noah fell and scrambled back, but the octochine lowered its eye, its massive body hanging over him like a fist ready to crush him. As the eye beam focused on Noah's face, the boy was too stunned to move. Beneath him, the boards shook from mechanical vibrations as the great machine examined him.

And then it honked. It was a small sound, almost friendly. Like a goose.

"*Honk?*" Noah repeated.

The octochine honked again. It continued to watch him. The beam widened, and it stood to its full height, but it didn't scream again, nor did it attack. For a moment, Noah wasn't sure what to do, so he carefully rose while keeping one eye on the octochine. When he finally risked taking a step toward the door, the machine only watched, but when he exited the building, the octochine followed, walking with its odd limp.

"Are you going to follow me from now on?" Noah asked, spinning around.

Two honks was his answer.

The way the octochine studied him made him think of Elijah, and Noah smiled to himself. "Maybe there's hope for you after all."

The sky was starting to turn bright on the horizon. Instinctively, he ran toward the light, across the wooden decking that reminded him of the city docks, stopping only when he reached the edge. Leaves waved in the wind just a few yards from his face, but they were a hundred feet above their roots. The ground was lost in the dark below.

The octochine followed on its seven good legs. Its bleating started and stopped at strange intervals. It seemed to be talking to itself.

As the machine crossed the wooden dock, its feet struck hard enough to splinter the wood planks. Noah hadn't noticed how warped and worn the platform was. Neither did the machine, and it was halfway to the boy when one of its legs snapped a rotting board in two. When it struggled to push itself free, two more legs smashed through the mushy wood. The mechanical octopus fell. Its horn squeaked and its eye rolled forward, trying to examine the holes trapping it. It yanked at the boards, but its nearly useless leg remained stuck. And then, with a metallic snap, the leg broke free, and the octochine collapsed to the platform, shuddering. When it quieted, Noah and the now seven-legged octochine eyed the detached leg. The octochine honked, then looked away as if embarrassed.

"You're just Seven now, aren't you."

After a moment, the machine continued forward, joining Noah at the platform edge. The giant robot walked carefully now, checking the spots where it could safely put its weight, until at last it stood beside the boy and gazed out over the forest. Noah couldn't help but laugh at the way it imitated him. The boy and the machine studied the trees, the way the canopy of leaves swayed in the breeze, and beyond, the lush green of city spires that reached to the sky.

Noah sighed. After the hours of work and exhaustion, he was left, now, with a giant pet robot and his worry for Winona. He felt bad about their argument. He should take the path back to see if he could find her, even if it meant having to explain his new pet. It would be the right thing to do for his new friend.

Instead, he looked toward the city he knew must be his father's home. The towers were just beginning to catch the rising daylight. And in their midst, he spied a new marvel— a giant contraption sitting at the edge of a platform atop the highest tower. It looked like a great insect, a beetle with its hard outer shell opened and gleaming wings that stretched hundreds of feet wide.

Only my father could have built that.

The limping octochine, Seven, staggered beside Noah, still examining its detached leg.

"Hey, I have to get to that city." Noah pointed. "Over there. I need to get over there. To those towers. Take me there."

Seven looked at the boy, then the boy's hand, and then the horizon. Whether it understood him wasn't clear.

"Come on," Noah urged. "Take me there. To my father. Take me to Alton Physician."

Seven released a series of bleats and one long gasping sound, then walked to the far end of the platform and stopped. It looked back at Noah, and for a moment the boy was unsure what was happening. With another series of quick honks, Seven made its intentions clear.

"You want me to follow?" The machine gave one more blast of its horn, a burst that sounded like a reprimand. "I'm sorry. I'm not used to giving orders."

Then Noah followed Seven down a path that would lead them to the city with the glittering towers and, Noah was certain, to his father.

❈ CHAPTER 9 ❈

Seven zigzagged through the forest. Its torso kept spinning, and Noah realized the machine was trying to find a way to remedy the missing limb, but there was no remedy. The machine would take a dozen awkward steps, the torso would spin again, and off it would go in a slightly different direction. It bumped into trees and honked in annoyance. Yet it was always headed toward the glittering towers.

Noah followed behind at what he hoped was a safe distance.

Soon, he thought. *I'll find my father soon.* But he couldn't help wondering what had become of Winona. He hoped she'd made it back to the beach, that she'd signaled Captain Moor and been rescued. As for himself, he needed no rescuing. He just needed to find his father.

The city would be different, he told himself. "All I have

to do is find that glittering building, and I'll be there." His voice sounded small in the sprawling woods, but he reminded himself of what he'd find when he arrived, including protection from the machines. *They were just malfunctioning,* he thought. He'd fixed one already. Seven just needed some adjustments. The others could be fixed as well. They could be corrected to leave him alone. To leave Winona alone. And the city.

Noah's thoughts drifted to the little machines he'd made. To the small adjustments that changed their behavior. He'd managed all that alone. With the help of his father, who'd made all these wonders to begin with, who knew what he could accomplish.

If his uncle and his mother had wanted him to be free in Liberty, they wouldn't have kept him prisoner in his own home. To be hidden away again would be miserable. But here on the island, with his father and the machines, repaired and working and amazing—this was all he wanted.

He stumbled as the realization of what he'd finally found took hold: *home.*

Noah couldn't help imagining the city, itself. It would be like paradise when he reached it. A marvel. After all, it had been built by a genius. Built large, and it ought to be filled. He wondered how his father had managed alone all this time. Wouldn't others have wanted to join him in his pursuit of his marvelous inventions? Wouldn't he have wanted others to help him achieve his dreams? Even if the island had started as a prison, could he have changed it into so much more?

Noah pushed through branches, eager for another glimpse of the contraption perching atop the tower. The massive beetle, its wings shimmering with refracted light, sat like a monstrous guardian over the island. He could see it more clearly now. The body appeared to be one solid piece, but a seam along the edges ended near the "head," with what could be hinges. Hinges meant movement, and movement could mean wings or some other mechanism beneath the outer shell designed to take the enormous contraption into the air. *Can it fly?* Noah wondered.

He imagined himself aboard such a craft. He'd built small contraptions that could hop, even a couple that had managed to stay airborne for short periods. Something the size of the craft he saw above them would have to be tremendously powerful, perhaps able to keep itself aloft for hours. In his imagination, he was already up there, beside his father, looking down at the island from high above.

A shriek from the other side of a nearby copse shook him from his daydreams, and Seven marched on, its eye occasionally swiveling back around to check on Noah.

The horn sounded again and Noah froze. He'd only repaired Seven. What if the other machines attacked? The horn blasts were behind him, and farther away. Still, he wouldn't feel safe until he crossed into the boundaries of the city.

And then, all at once, he did.

Without warning, the trees gave way to the towers, as if the buildings had grown out of the forest. Spaces between the structures were a mix of rough paths and finished streets breaking apart, returning to wild. The enormous towers stretched upward like grasping fingers into the sky, and like fingers, they weren't quite straight. They bent oddly. Some appeared to have fallen into others. Through a gap, Noah thought he spied the rubble of one that had collapsed completely.

And then he realized the entire city was glittering towers of wreckage. Only as he took it in did it occur to him how much he'd hoped to find. Where he'd expected streets of brick laid flat and even across wide avenues, he saw instead uneven terrain spotted with piles of rotting wood, overgrown vines, and bursts of wildflowers. Where he'd anticipated heavy foundations of stone and metal would stand, he instead found simple wooden constructions pinholed by insects and worms. He'd envisioned grand entrances to magnificent buildings. In their place were dark, empty maws yawning like gaping mouths. And where he'd imagined floor after floor rising toward the sky, he saw only haphazardly placed rooms stacked in the same fashion as the house he'd lived in his entire life. There were no cheery glass windows. Instead, empty shafts allowed him to see straight through to sky on the other side. Noah had hoped for pinnacle towers — markers of his father's genius. Instead, he saw abandonment.

And the worst part: in taking in the decay of buildings built as mindlessly as the house he knew at home, he realized how much he'd hung his hopes on finding a city full of people who would welcome him. This was perhaps his greatest delusion. *I didn't even need it to be people. A city full of robots living as people live might have been enough.*

Noah stood beneath the crumbling towers, alone.

He swallowed his disappointment and tried to focus on what *was* there. This tangle was clearly the work of a spideratus, and more than one — a massive number working unstopped and unchecked for years. As he considered this, he searched the ruins for signs of movement and quickly spotted it. Climbing high among the wooden towers, and in and out of windows reflecting the sunlight off glittering metal bodies that he'd mistaken for glass and steel, were countless numbers of spideratuses. They scaled the sides of the buildings, carrying wood beams and planks. Noah spotted a line of them in the distance coming from the woods dragging fallen trees stripped of their branches. It took two or three of them working together to move the massive trunks. Once in a clearing, they lifted their forearms to reveal the spinning saws beneath, then set themselves upon the logs, cutting them into beams, planks, and shingles. Other builders dropped from the constructions to gather the fresh supplies, only to immediately return to their work atop the growing towers.

Noah could hear it now in the distance—the banging and crashing and sawing. The work of buildings growing. He thought if he listened closely enough, he might hear a ticking of a clock . . . or a caretaker.

Noah walked to the nearest structure. The base was covered in vines, and he had to tear them away to find what he knew would be there.

It was the house. The same one he'd grown up in.

Noah's heart sank. No matter how much he tried to escape the home that had held him captive, he was already finding his way back inside. He pulled at the door, and it opened with a dusty snap, debris falling from the frame.

The house was made of raw wood. Unpainted and unprotected from the weather, it had warped. Between cracks sprouted roots and vines and small flowers. He peered into the dark entryway, but it was, of course, empty. There were no pictures bolted to the wall. There was no stuck clock.

He looked up again at the massive beetle, and saw now that it, too, was covered in vines. The underside had gone green with growth and tarnish. It might not work. It might not even be meant to move. It might just be a statue.

From somewhere at the other end of the empty city came the sirens of the octochine. Noah didn't know where to go, but he knew he couldn't be trapped in the city. If the machines surrounded the buildings, he might never escape. Seven stood in front of the house. Its eye never left Noah, and its honks were almost like impatient complaints.

"Is my father even here?" Noah asked, not expecting Seven to answer.

Another siren blasted from just behind a nearby cluster of trees, and then a trio of octochines stepped into the clearing. There was no doubt they saw Noah, and his mind went blank as all three focused their eyes on him. Their sirens wailed and they moved forward, but before he could respond, Seven stepped to stand immediately above him. Now Noah's thoughts were racing with worries about being crushed by his savior. The three attacking octochines circled Noah and Seven looking for an opening to strike at the boy. Seven deflected their swipes and butted against them with its own head, all the while sending out deep bell-like clangs that echoed into the distance. Noah barely had time to think as he dodged between the legs. He pointlessly yelped for help, and shouted excitedly at Seven to somehow magically get him away from the attack. *If only I'd been able to fix more than one*, Noah thought, but he knew it wouldn't have been enough. How could repairing only one at a time hold off an army?

Noah ran in one direction and then another. He wanted to return to the building, or to the forest. "Please, let me go!" he screamed as he dodged a robotic leg sweeping over the ground. "I didn't do anything! Let me go!"

"You haven't done anything?" a voice shouted from behind him.

Noah turned to see a man in dark coveralls emerge from the tallest of the buildings. He looked odd, his face partially obscured by what seemed like a helmet of spare robot parts. He appeared to be holding dozens of gears, springs, levers, bolts, and wrenches. Noah didn't know it was possible to carry so much. It was as if the parts were clinging to the man.

"What have you done to my robot?" the stranger demanded. As he approached, the robots formed a respectful ring around him, lowering their gazes to the ground, hopping as he passed them like an electric current traveling between the octochines. Even Seven had joined in. It was clear they were excited by the man's presence.

The man, however, was not excited to see Noah. "You've brutalized the poor thing!" he yelled.

"It wasn't me," Noah insisted. "It was in a repair station. The machinery broke and—"

The man raised a wrench into the air like a sword. "My machinery doesn't break!" He held out a hand and Seven approached. It turned and lowered its body so the gap with the missing limb could be examined. "Hmm . . . However, it does wear out."

Noah watched the man as he worked. The gears and machine parts weren't just hanging off his clothes. They *were* his clothes. Machinery wound along each arm, ending in a mechanical contraption on each hand that added additional fingers and tools at the ready. It was as if the man had twenty fingers instead of ten, some with cutters or clippers or wrenches or screwdrivers. They moved quickly and seamlessly, extensions of his body.

The man's work inside Seven was as fast and precise as

if a team of three people were working together. Above the stranger's right eye was a gear with different lenses mounted into it that spun, snapping back and forth from one magnification to the next, so he could examine Seven's injuries. The man kept up a steady stream of muttering throughout the process. Noah noticed that the right leg of the man's coveralls was cut away, revealing an iron leg of springs and gears, with a knee that bent the wrong way. The leg looked like that of a giant bird, and the sounds it made were like those of the octochine.

This man, Noah realized, had to be Alton Physician.

Noah was transfixed by his father as he worked on Seven, all the while speaking quietly to the machine. Meanwhile, the other three octochines continued their investigation of Noah, and though he no longer thought they'd attack, he was still too scared to move.

At last Alton Physician spun around and pointed a mechanically enhanced hand at Noah. "All right, so you didn't break him, but you did, ahem, alter him. How? How did you do it? How? What did you do, and how?"

"It was in the factory," Noah explained. "It was being repaired. Its eye was replaced, and the machinery broke, so I finished the repairs, and after, it just . . . *liked* me."

His father's lenses spun so that a massive, magnified

eye fixed on Noah. "It doesn't like you." Alton Physician slapped Seven's side, and the octochine responded as if it were a loving pat, honking gently, swinging its eye to look into its maker's face.

"It imprinted on you," Alton Physician continued. "Every one of my metal friends knows exactly who takes care of it: *me*. I made sure to be there for every one of them when their gears first spun. They see me as a father. And you . . . you tricked it somehow."

Noah was confused. The city had turned out not to be a city at all, and now his father was blaming him for tricking a robot into being friendly. Nothing was going as he'd hoped.

"I only wanted to help it. It was broken."

"Was broken? Is! It *is* broken." Alton Physician pushed at the massive egg-shaped body, raising a scraping sound as his metal fingers met the hull. "It's almost cruel what you did. Still, it doesn't seem too unhappy, and it can walk."

Physician walked toward Noah staring down at him again. He shooed the octochines away with a wave of each hand. They stepped back, but stayed nearby, continuing to eye Noah suspiciously. All except for Seven, who honked happily to itself as if glad to have everyone together.

"How, though?" the man demanded again, his lenses

spinning. "How did you know what to do? I can count on one finger the number of people who understand my work, and that woman is a day's journey from here. How did you know what to do? And more significantly, who are you? And wait! Better still, what are you doing on my island?"

Noah took a deep breath. So much had happened, and he didn't know where to start.

"This is Noah," said a familiar voice. "And he's here because you invited him."

Elijah emerged from a nearby tower. His clothes were torn and filthy, and there was green seaweed dried to his torso and legs. A sea snail sat on his shoulder, slowly making its way toward his ear. His face, which had begun to look a little rusty years before, now also had green-blue corrosion at the edges, and in the creases around the eyes and nose, from the saltwater he'd been bathed in. His ticking, though, was as steady as ever.

"Elijah!" Noah shouted. It hadn't really settled in that he might not ever see Elijah again. He'd watched his caretaker fall into the ocean, and then he'd been glad to be on his own on the island. To see him here so suddenly made Noah's heart lift in his chest. He was thrilled to see Elijah return, and ashamed that in wanting independence so badly, he'd ignored the long absence from his best friend.

He couldn't recall thinking of Elijah's safety even once. *It won't happen again*, Noah promised himself. *He won't leave my side.*

Noah rushed forward and took the robot's hand. Elijah seemed smaller than Noah remembered. Though his hand was cold, Elijah squeezed back.

"You made it safely to Singe," he said, stating the obvious as always.

And with that, Noah's anger at Elijah returned. "What were you thinking?" he demanded. "Why did you push me and Winona from the ship?"

"What ship?" Alton Physician asked, impatiently. "What is a 'Winona'? And who is this 'Noah'? Elijah, explain."

Elijah's ticking sped up as he looked from Noah to Physician and back. After a moment, he replied, "Noah is your son, Doctor Physician. He found your message in the spideratus."

"Oh my," said Noah's father. He now appraised Noah with a glimmer in his eyes.

Noah thought the man might cry. His own eyes began to burn, and he realized he might, too. *He's proud of me.*

Then Alton Physician said, "What took you so long to get here?"

Noah felt as if he'd been struck. "What do you mean?"

Alton bent and studied his son's face. "I've waited so many years. My work has suffered. I thought of leaving a thousand times. I've only kept myself sane by working on my children."

His children. What did he mean? But before Noah could ask, Alton shouted, "You should have been here years ago! The message wasn't hard to find."

"I'm . . . sorry?" Noah felt a wave of hot shame. "Marie wouldn't let me near the spideratus. She had Elijah keep me from it."

"Marie!" Alton Physician's eyes darted around wildly. "Always meddling!"

All this time, Noah had been so desperate to finally meet his father, and now that he'd found the man, he was raving in a forest. Elijah stood nearby, calmly watching Noah watch his father shout at the trees.

Noah wanted to be angry with something himself. He wanted to rant at the trees, or even the man who had just blamed him for something he couldn't control. Instead, he decided he was very angry with his caretaker. "Elijah! You pushed me and Winona off the ship!"

"Yes," replied the robot matter-of-factly. "The ship was turning around, and we would not have made it to Singe. You swam here, Sir! It is nice to see you again."

"But . . ." Noah knew from the years of growing up with Elijah there would be no apology. "But how did you get here?"

Elijah tilted his head as if that should be obvious. "I walked."

In spite of his frustration, Noah couldn't help but laugh.

Alton, meanwhile, had stopped his tirade and was now walking in a slow circle around Noah. The lenses spun away from his face and his mechanical fingers tapped and snapped nervously against one another.

"I had thought the spideratus lost long ago. I assumed your uncle destroyed it."

"Marie wanted to figure it out," Noah explained. "She knew there was a secret inside."

Alton smiled. With the lenses pulled away from his eyes, Noah could clearly see his father's face. It was thin and lined. His hair was graying at the temples. He was filthy. He smelled. And there were scars on his face and hands. He looked tired in a way Noah didn't know a person could be.

"Yes, that sounds like Marie. Smart, dedicated, and always getting in the way."

"Noah is your son," Elijah offered.

"Yes, I know."

"Marie is his mother."

"Yes, Elijah."

"Noah does not call her 'mother,' but nevertheless—"

"Stop, Elijah." Alton held up a hand, The clicking and snapping mechanical fingers waved at Elijah as if to unmake him.

"Yes, Doctor Physician," Elijah said. His ticking slowed, and he quietly watched the two humans.

It seemed odd to Noah that Elijah referred to his mother by her first name, but to his father by his last. The formality was surprising, given that Elijah had been programmed by both.

Alton took a deep breath. "You figured out the spideratus?"

Noah nodded. "Yes."

"Without instructions?"

Noah shrugged. "I saw your designs. And Marie, she teaches me things. I tinker. Make my own contraptions and . . . I was helping build defenses for the city."

"Defenses? From what? The Homeland Empire? They have come close to these shores and retreat in fear. My children sink their ships." Alton smiled at the octochines. "What could Liberty fear?"

"The Empire is part of it. So are—" Noah glanced at

Seven. The octochine honked happily and staggered toward him.

"Ignorant, fearful Nicholas. All of them, ignorant and fearful. Even Marie." Alton Physician's smile faded. "They never did understand. They wouldn't listen. Worse, they worked against their own interests. They sometimes even worked against me."

He turned away to look at the tower Elijah had come from. Like the others around it, it had started as a house, spiraling to a high pinnacle, but this one had a large platform near the top with the massive beetle contraption sitting on the haphazard boards as though it were surveying the island.

Alton started toward the tower. His robot foot clinked on the stones with every step. "Walk with me, boy," he said without looking back.

Noah rushed to catch up, and Elijah slowly followed behind them. The octochines remained where they were, chirping noises that sounded to Noah like they were worried their maker might never come back.

CHAPTER 10

Alton Physician didn't wait for Noah to keep up, and the faster the inventor walked, the faster he talked. They had entered the tower and were climbing a series of ladders and shortcuts through holes in ceilings and out windows and through haphazard doorways, higher and higher.

"The city didn't deserve my help," Alton said. "Nicholas, especially. Have you met your uncle?" He spun around, lenses whirling.

"Uh, yes. Just once."

"Moron!" Alton climbed through a hole barely wide enough for either of them. "He refused to understand that my little metal family was special. Delicate personalities require patience and sensitivity. 'Make them build! Make them protect us! The Homeland Empire is coming! Blah, blah, blah!' "

He scaled a ladder that looked climbable only if you had

a robotic bird leg, and Noah stood at the bottom, wondering what to do. Without warning, Alton's robot-enhanced hands reached down and scooped him up. Noah saw Elijah still slowly following.

"You've seen my family, boy. The marvels that they are."

"Yes," Noah said, his eyes shining. "In fact, I tinker on contraptions that are very similar. I've made—"

"These are not contraptions. My children are so, so much more."

Alton led Noah to a window that looked out at the forest and the ocean beyond. "This island has grown beyond nature. Singe is more than a laboratory. It's the modern equivalent of primitive ooze. New life is here. Truer life. Better life. It's why the Homeland Empire keeps testing these waters, looking for a way in. It's why your uncle and mother and the other shortsighted in Liberty . . ."

Noah waited for his father to finish his sentence. No end came. Instead, Alton turned, and his lenses spun to examine Noah. The man had already carefully studied him in the forest. Noah wondered what he might see now.

"Did they send you?"

Noah squinted. "Who?"

Alton stepped back, as if struck. "Nicholas. Or Marie. Or even the Homeland Empire."

At the far side of the room, Elijah ticked happily away. "Sir Noah found your message in the spideratus. He—"

"Did he?"

Elijah's ticking paused and then restarted. "Yes. He did."

Alton Physician peered intently through several of his spinning lenses. "I don't know," he said at last. He leaned forward, a single finger pointed at Noah's chest. "Could you have unlocked the message by finding the key in the spideratus? Possible. Could someone have simply corrupted Elijah and unlocked my message by deceit? Tricked him into being their ally? Also possible." He turned away to look at the tree line and tapped his chin with a long, mechanical finger.

Noah couldn't believe what he was hearing. His father seemed content to wander into mazes he made for himself. "I didn't deceive anyone."

"But you might have. There is a chance you unlocked the key as designed. There is a chance you lucked into it. There is a slim possibility you, or someone else, have tricked Elijah."

"I recall no tricks," Elijah said. "I recall Noah."

"Still, there is only one I know of who could have unlocked the key at such a young age."

"Who is that?" Elijah asked.

"Me!"

Elijah nodded. "That makes sense."

"I've got to sit down," Noah murmured. "I swam to this island, wandered through the forest, and I've been up all night fixing your machines. I don't know how else to prove to you—"

"My machines need no fixing!" The flash of anger appeared to surprise even Alton. He stood up straighter and again considered the treetops. "However, your . . . poorly chosen words . . . do give us insight into a plan."

Elijah nodded toward Noah. The snail was now fixed to the side of his face. "Plans are helpful."

He's like the octochine, Noah thought. *He's eager to please my father.*

Alton narrowed his gaze at Noah. The boy expected another burst of buzzing and swirling of the many lenses. Instead, his father leveled an appraising glare that made Noah long for shade. "I shall give you a test."

"Please, can it wait?" Noah said. "I just want to rest." The thrill of meeting his father had given way to exhaustion so quickly.

"Rest is the luxury of the unmotivated. The fact that you are even here demonstrates you are not so. In a sense, it was the first test. Come! We shall see if you truly are who you claim to be!"

Noah wiped grit from his eyes. He was so tired. "You mean a test to prove I'm your son?"

"No, a test to prove you're the one who unlocked my message!" And with that, Alton Physician walked into the tower's next room. "Follow me, in here, your test awaits!"

Elijah stepped before Noah and tilted his head quizzically. "Family reunions are so interesting." The snail climbed across Elijah's eye.

Noah couldn't help but sigh. Reluctantly, he followed his father farther into the tower.

He found Alton in a room several floors up with his ear pressed to an outside wall. It was made of drab, unpainted wooden planks that were slowly giving way to the forest. The nearest window was nearly choked with vegetation, leaving only splinters of light to illuminate the mostly empty room. Vines had snaked from the window and across the wall in wavy patterns, and the smallest of leaves at the ends looked like hands reaching farther still. Noah's father studied the wall as if it were whispering to him.

"I have a question for you," Alton said.

Elijah stepped into the room behind Noah. "Do you mean me?"

"Of course not."

Elijah tapped Noah on the shoulder. "He means you."

Noah nodded. He felt confused by his father's ability to help create Elijah. The man didn't seem interested in others at all. How was Elijah so skilled at keeping the needs of everyone around him in mind at all times? Was this solely his mother's doing?

Despite his announcement, Alton Physician was now silent as stone. He moved his head a little, listened, then moved again.

Noah said, "You have a question?"

Alton switched ears, turning his head the other direction so that he was able to see Noah. Lenses spun into place magnifying the eye. He leaned back and studied the wall through the glasses. The wall remained unchanged. His gaze didn't land on any detail, but roamed over the uneven, mottled surface. He reached out a hand, his robotic digits tapping against the thin panels—the hollowest of sounds—until, finally, came the thinnest of scraping.

"My question," said Alton at last, and then was silent once more. He balled up his fist. The robotic fingers wrapped around his hand to create a large, hooklike shape, and without warning Noah's father drove his hand directly through the panel. He gripped at the edges of the broken wood, then pulled them into the room. Large pieces tore free from the wall and exposed the moldy frame beneath.

While the room was just beginning to be overtaken by wandering vines and the window was full of branches and leaves that had found their way in from the outside, the interior of the wall was an enclave of growth, a habitat all its own. The smell of rot escaped into the room, and Noah staggered back and put a hand over his mouth to stifle a gag. His father didn't react.

Inside the wall, black mold grew on the wood, and rooty white tendrils hung between and from the wooden beams. Pockets of dark soil and sunlight sparkled through pinholes bored into the outer wall by worms and insects probably long gone. Along the beams, the light hit tiny bits of reflective metal, casting rainbow refractions into the dark spaces.

The smell was soon forgotten, and Noah stepped forward to better see what his father had revealed.

"Here is my question," Alton Physician said. "What is happening here?"

The robotic hand, which was clearly strong, released the pieces of wooden panel it had ripped from the wall, and a long and delicate finger pointed into the dark space, catching the smallest of glimmers from the metals inside.

And then Noah looked closer. They were moving.

Some followed others. Some scurried for the darkest corners, as if trying to hide. If there was a pattern to the movement, Noah couldn't see it. Not yet. Especially not from where he stood, far from the wall and behind his father.

"There appears to be something in the wall," Elijah said.

Noah stepped forward for a better view.

"Yes, take a look and let me know what you think is happening. Not what they are. *That* is obvious. Let me know what is less obvious." Alton stepped back to make room. Noah leaned in.

Marvelous tiny machines crawled inside the dark space. Tiny robots appeared to be taking the wall apart. Or perhaps they were putting it back together? A handful looked like centipedes, others were ants. A worm wriggled through a hole, but its body was a single thin strip of metal wrapped around delicate inner workings. Each creature seemed to have its own task. The worm simply chewed its way through the wood and vegetation. The ants carried bits of material from one spot to another. The centipede had some kind of goo coming from its mouth that hardened into the white tendrils—a kind of manufactured substance, slowly replacing the natural wood.

"What are they doing?" Noah asked.

Alton huffed. "That's what I've asked you."

Elijah came forward, standing behind Noah, with his

head nearly resting on the boy's shoulder. "Oh, it appears that they—"

The robot was pulled away abruptly. "Silence, Elijah! This is not a question for you. It's for *the one who found my message.*"

Noah could tell he was being mocked. He remembered feeling similarly small and foolish in front of his uncle. Small and foolish and then thrown in a cell.

"They're robots, and they're . . . converting the building into something else?"

Alton stepped back farther. He sounded far away despite the room not being overly large. "That's the obvious part. I did not ask what they are doing. I asked, *what is happening?* Something more important than gears and springs is occurring in that wall."

For a moment, Noah wished his father would just tell him what it was he was meant to see. It would be simpler in the long run. But as he watched the small machines crawl past and over one another, he put that idea aside. It wasn't how he really felt, he realized. *I have been told what is going on for too long. I wanted to find out things for myself, and that's what's brought me this far.*

The tiniest of the robots carried bits of wood toward a hole in the outer wall. Noah wondered if there might be a nest—

if the creatures that looked so much like ants were designed to mimic the insect—or if they'd learned the behavior from being in the wild. Could such small robots learn? Elijah learned all the time, but his design was so much more complicated. And these were simple machines created for a lone task. At least, that's what Noah thought at first.

As he watched the robotic ants scurry in their line, the mechanical worm approached, moving with a hypnotic twist. The single thin membrane of its body constricted, making it thinner and longer, and then as it loosened, the entire contraption pulled itself forward with such apparent ease its speed was almost simple to ignore. Noah reached out with a single finger to touch the shiny, metal creature, but stopped when it twisted itself into a circle around two of the methodically marching ant machines. Without warning, the end of the worm uncoiled and created a looping ramp that led into its interior. The body shifted itself, tightening its circle around the ant machines, forcing them along the spiral into the almost mouth-like opening. As soon as the ants pushed inside, the coil reformed, and the body of the worm shut around them.

Noah could hear the tiniest of clicks. There was a series of gearish snaps, as quiet as a watch being wound, and the worm, with a bulge where its meal sat, twisted and tightened. Noah took a deep breath. He hoped that the machines did more than just destroy one another. Consumption would be boring. And then it happened.

The worm shifted, and from its side emerged a series of small legs. Only six were visible, but the moment they appeared, they gripped the soft rotten wood. The worm now moved with such speed that Noah almost missed it dart into the dark.

Noah's breath started burning in his chest, and he let it out in a tiny whistle. "They're evolving."

The silence that followed was surprising. After all, he was watching these machines in the wall chase after one another because his father had directed him to. He turned to see if the man would confirm his suspicion. Instead, he found that he was alone.

From behind him came tiny metallic clicks and whirrs as impossibly small machines consumed one another and altered themselves. Noah forced himself to ignore the sounds and walked toward the far door.

"Hello?" he called out.

"Yes, yes. In here." His father sounded impatient and distant.

In the next room, Noah found the man. Alton Physician's back was to the door, and his mechanical fingers clicked away on something on the table before him.

"They're evolving," Noah said.

"What?"

Noah cleared his throat. Talking to his father was exhausting. "The machines—you've built machines that change themselves. They're evolving."

Alton stopped and turned to glance over his shoulder. There was no clear expression on his face. "They are, indeed."

Noah let himself smile, feeling both wonder and pride. "It's amazing."

"It's inevitable!" Physician said with a dismissive wave. "It's my legacy. *This* is the future. These creations are my legacy. I have introduced new life to this odd world. So much chaos, so much out of our control, so much that doesn't make sense inside us. But these . . ."

Alton reached out an arm and brushed the vine-covered doorway. A couple small contraptions resembling ants crawled onto his hand and up his arm. They were so small, and Noah couldn't help himself. He wanted to understand how they worked, so he reached out a hand.

Alton hissed at him to hold still.

They both watched as the robotic ants crawled onto his arm. And then from the vines emerged another robot, this one circular and ringed with legs. It almost hovered as it whirred into sight, before coasting onto Alton's hand and arm, and then in an instant, sucked the ants into its body. There was a moment of high-pitched ticking, and then the spinning circular robot changed direction and sent out feelers toward Alton's face.

The inventor smiled. "And now this one is different. It has moved forward the tiniest step, thanks to what it took from the other two."

Noah was stunned. "Why did you design such a contraption?"

"I didn't." Alton's smile fell, and he looked closely at the robot spinning up his arm. "These children of mine will interact, mix, find what fits. Find what's new. Find what works. They will not have any of the obstacles that hold us back—the worries and fears, the clashes, the wars. They won't need them. My creations will have everything because what they become will fit, will work, will belong. They will make sense. None of the chaos that we drag around with us. Conflicts of different desires. Desires that others can't understand, that we don't understand ourselves. All that . . . gone. Instead, order."

"They build themselves?"

"They do. They see what is needed. They know what

they are. They mix and match and experiment until what is needed exists. They are evolution itself. They are *perfection*."

"I was right. They are evolving." Noah smiled. "So I passed the test?"

Alton Physician studied his son's face. The corner of his mouth curled in a way that said that smiling wasn't typical, or comfortable, or even desired. "That wasn't the test. That was a distraction. I needed a moment alone."

The man stepped away from the worktable mounted against the wall. Elijah was lying on it. He was suspiciously silent. By now, the robotic boy should have been describing to Noah not only that he was lying on the workbench, but how he had gotten there, and what his view from the bench was like. Instead Elijah's face remained calmly aimed in Noah's direction, the eyes locked in place. Not a word was uttered.

And then Noah noticed how complete the silence truly was. The constant ticking of his friend's thoughts was gone. His gears didn't turn, his springs didn't whine.

Elijah had been turned off.

Alton Physician walked to the far corner of the room and pointed many of his fingers at Elijah. "This is your test. Fix him."

❀ CHAPTER II ❀

Noah was certain all the air had left the room. It must have. He couldn't breathe. When Elijah had pushed Winona and him from the *Abbreviated*, it hadn't occurred to him that he might not see his companion again. It wasn't until he was alone for long enough that the worry crept in. Now, the idea of being lost forever without his friend lay on the table along with the robot boy.

"What did you do?"

His father's lenses clicked slowly as they spun from high to low, his eye getting smaller with every switch. "I created a test," he said. At last, his eye was unmagnified, though still behind a lens. It was, Noah thought, how this man saw the world: through a distorting glass he kept on his own face. It was the way this man *chose* to view the world.

"He doesn't deserve this."

Alton didn't respond at first. He bit his lip and his eyes shifted. He suddenly darted away from the table, as if distancing himself from a mess he didn't want to be blamed for.

"Deserve." The word slid from Alton's mouth. "Does anyone *deserve* anything?"

Noah walked toward his friend. He put a hand on a cold, metal arm and looked into Elijah's face. The snail was on the other eye now. *He's had this done to him because I wanted to come here.* The arm felt as if it were getting colder. "No one deserves to be treated like a plaything. Or to be punished for others' mistakes."

Alton muttered under his breath, pacing the far side of the room. One flesh finger was in his mouth while the mechanical fingers tapped at the side of his face and temple.

"Deserve . . . deserve . . . no . . . no one . . . . It . . . it's done now. You'll do it. I know . . . I hope you can do it." There was only Noah there, and still Alton didn't look his way.

Is he talking to me, or himself? Noah had spent so much time alone with Elijah. He wondered how he might sound talking to himself if he hadn't had the robot with him. After all, Alton Physician had been that alone for as long as Noah had been with Elijah.

The pacing stopped. "It's done. This is the test. I . . .

hope to see you pass." Alton seemed to shrink a bit. His loneliness was like a weight, and it made him smaller as it settled into place.

Alton left the room, and for just a moment, Noah listened to the uneven steps upward into the tower. His father's single robotic leg made each footfall with solid confidence. It was the human leg that seemed to drag.

On the table waited Elijah. The snail waved its antennae and slowly moved on from Elijah's face.

Noah wished his robot friend could say something. Elijah's support would be helpful now. Especially now. "Ironic," he said to his motionless friend. "I need you now, more than ever." He leaned forward and intently scrutinized the recently corroded face. The greens and blues gave Elijah an ancient look.

Noah pulled at a dried piece of seaweed that had adhered to Elijah's cheek. "I've taken you for granted for far too long. I'm sorry."

He searched the seams that ran down Elijah's sides. He found the clasps he knew would be there, and pulled at them. The chest plate designed to look like a well-tailored suit swung up and out of the way, revealing the robot's inner workings. Noah took a deep breath and marveled at the complexity. He'd never built anything nearly so intricate.

The only contraption he'd seen with so many parts had been the octochine, and when he'd worked on Seven, he'd been happy to discover that the machinery was enormous. He'd nearly climbed entirely within the octochine's body to complete his task. This time, the work would rely on the tiny assortment of tools arrayed on the table. Noah took a deep breath and leaned in.

"What would Marie say about you right now?"

In his head Noah heard Elijah's response: *She would say you need to pick your goal, and work in the most direct way toward it. She would say to believe in yourself. She would also say that she is your mother, and you should call her that.*

Noah whispered, "I'll fix you, my friend."

Noah worked for a long, long while. He was already tired from his time spent fixing Seven the night before. By late afternoon, his eyes were heavy and he was struggling. The tools on the table were no longer well-ordered, and gears and springs he'd removed were laid carefully on the table, but very little else had changed.

He became aware of a presence behind him, and when he turned his head to the door he saw Alton Physician watching him.

"As I suspected. Very little progress."

"I need to rest," Noah said. "I can barely think straight, and I'm having to teach myself how he works before I can discover what you did."

"Methodical. Logical." Alton made a deep humming sound as he considered the scene before him. "It is possible there has been no deceit. We shall see." He pointed at a tray he'd quietly set on the far end of the table. "Here is some food. You may rest. I shall not time you, nor will I pull the work away from you before it is complete. I am far too busy to look after you every moment."

"You've barely spent a moment with me!" Noah said. He was surprised by two things: First, that he'd said it at all. And second, that Alton Physician's reaction was to raise an eyebrow, spin his lenses, and say, "It's that which makes you so intriguing. Someone your age is usually . . . lonely . . . when left alone."

At some point Noah couldn't recall, Alton had brought a lantern with a single bulb and placed it on the table's edge. It cast a beam of light that sent their shadows up the wall—shocking, harsh angles that moved as they moved.

"I don't want to be intriguing. I want to help my friend."

The lenses whirred again. "See! There! Again! Intriguing. You may or may not be the one to have found the message, but I can see how you've laid the tools out on the table. I can see the parts you've removed from our Elijah, and I can see you're on the right path. Whether you found the message or not is, at this point, irrelevant. You are on your way to passing my test. Set your sights on what you want to do. Help your *friend* . . . if that term fits for you. Help your friend by moving beyond what you knew. Challenge yourself. Too many people see a challenge and a failure as obstacles to shrink from. Even if you don't awaken Elijah, pushing yourself to do so will change you for the better!"

"But what if he won't wake up?" Noah was so frustrated he thought he might cry.

Alton Physician shrugged. "There are unfortunate byproducts of failure. Your growth is not one of them. I was able to disable Elijah because I have been in his workings countless times. I knew what I was doing. You're having to find your way on your own. From where I stand"—the man leaned forward again to eye the pile of gears Noah had removed from Elijah—"you're something of an inventor yourself."

Noah took a deep, shuddering breath. He wasn't sure, but he thought that maybe his father was actually trying to be . . . *helpful.* "I'm not sure I believe that anymore."

The gears on the eyepiece swirled again. "Believe it or don't. There are sometimes solutions that are correct, even when they appear incorrect. It is the true scientist who can accept that." Alton spun on his robotic leg, and without another word left the room.

Noah set down the tools he held and took hold of the tray. *He actually seems to think he's helping.*

He was starved, and only realized it as he grabbed the first piece of food. He ate it, though he tasted nothing for the first few bites. The bright orange fruit was cut into large chunks that he bit into with pleasure. They were sweet and juicy and filled his stomach quickly.

From where he sat, he could see the side of Elijah's face. If it were a person on the table, he might have looked asleep. "When I get you working, I have so many questions for you."

His questions were not pleasant ones. *Where can we go? What will we do? How can we be safe?*

One thing was abundantly clear: Alton Physician had no need or desire to have Noah around.

He swallowed the last of the fruit, almost too quickly. With the tray clear, he rested his back against the wall, closed his eyes, and fell asleep.

Noah worked throughout the night. He took short breaks and napped, but his worry for Elijah always woke him and he set back to work. At last, either very late in the night or very early in the morning, he was finished. Light leaked through the overgrown window as he made the last adjustment. He finally understood what his father had done to Elijah. It had taken a different approach than any other work he'd ever completed. Tinkering for Marie had always been done with her guidance. He knew what each part did. He knew what parts he was to improve upon. For his own contraptions, it had been even simpler. He started with an idea and fiddled with it until he found some parts that achieved his goal. Neither of these methods would work with Elijah. Noah had no guidance, and he couldn't risk simply seeing what would happen were he to pull out a specific gear or modify a certain spring. This was his best and oldest friend. This was someone who needed to be as they were and as they should be.

For that reason, he had carefully studied each part and how it joined the next. He had examined how each gear interlocked, where the springs were located, and why each piece might shift depending on what Elijah was doing and what he was thinking. After a long while he'd finally begun to see the patterns. There were links that were active all the time. There were others that would only be engaged in certain situations. Yet all of them followed a logic. If one thing was true, then *these* gears. If another, then *those* others. And so on, and so on, until at last Noah stood beside his oldest friend, having replaced each and every gear. He had put each and every spring and lever and switch into its proper position. He had reconstructed Elijah in the only way that made sense.

There was a tiny switch at the back of Elijah's head that needed to be in the on position, but it was hidden beyond reach, between and beside tiny gears so that it was almost invisible. He'd need some sort of tool. Noah searched the worktable for something the right size and length.

What if I've done something wrong? What if I activate him, and something breaks?

He had no choice. This was the test, his father had said. That didn't matter. But it was also his only chance to save his friend.

He no longer cared that the fantasy city he'd dreamed of with his father at its center wasn't real. He no longer wondered if he and his father could be happy building contraptions and inventions together. It stung that Alton Physician didn't care about his arrival. Noah hadn't realized it before, but he'd wanted excitement and celebration.

Instead, he'd received this test. This chance to save Elijah.

He looked into Elijah's face and whispered, "I've done everything I know to do. I hope it's been enough."

A long, thin screwdriver shook in his hand as he maneuvered the tip to flip the switch.

Nothing happened.

There are many gears, Noah reminded himself. And then with a sudden rush, the air was full of the sound of gears clicking into motion. They overlapped in a scary way at first—a scurry of sound as if making up for lost time—but then they settled into a recognizable rhythm. Noah had never considered that his friend's ticking was as familiar as his voice. Now that the room was filled with it again, he realized how much he'd missed it.

"I am lying down," Elijah said. He looked one way and then the other before focusing on Noah. "May I sit up?"

"Of course." Noah was laughing without fully knowing why. *It's fine*, he thought. *I'll laugh now and figure out why later.* He stepped back, making room for Elijah to climb down from the table.

"I followed Doctor Physician into this room. I do not know what happened after that."

"After that," came a voice from the doorway, "my son passed his test."

Noah wasn't sure where his father had gone but it would be no surprise to find out the man had also worked through the night. He did not appear to be someone who willingly slept. Or rested. Or simply took a moment. Alton Physician was in the same clothes as the day before. Fresh streaks of grease lined his hands and face. He was a little dirtier and possibly a little more exhausted, but now the man had a strange smile on his face.

"Which gear was it that I halted?"

Elijah looked from Alton Physician to Noah and back. "A gear was halted?"

Noah gestured to the table. "There was a tiny bolt loose that didn't belong anywhere." He'd placed the bolt on the table with the intention of giving it to Alton as proof of finding the problem. During the process, the bolt had fallen and was now missing.

But as Noah scanned the table, he saw something else. A single gear. Gold and slightly smaller than his palm, it glimmered in the growing light. He remembered finding it and removing it, but now he realized he'd neglected to put it back. He had followed his father's advice: one step at a time, so each thing made sense. Elijah was awake and aware. Yet there, plain as day, sat a piece that hadn't been replaced. Noah quickly covered it with his hand and waited for a moment to slip it into his pocket. He darted his eyes to Elijah, worried to see any sign of malfunction.

Alton stepped into the room with a hop that showed excitement hidden until that moment. "Yes! The bolt, easily placed but hard to spot! Big enough to stop our Elijah's clockworks, but not damage them! Oh, the test is passed! Now the real work begins." Alton's celebration ended as quickly as it began. His eye lenses whirred, and he turned and marched to the door again. "Follow me! We eat because unfortunately we must, and then we work. At last."

Elijah watched Alton leave the room. "I was broken?"

Noah wanted to take Elijah's hand and leave. But beyond the doors was a forest. A forest filled with unfriendly octochines. And beyond that an ocean. Winona should have been gone by now. Gone to the *Abbreviated*, and back on the ocean, headed toward the city or some other port. Noah wanted to leave with Elijah, but with nowhere to go, he knew he would have to stay.

"Yes," he said. "You were broken."

"I was broken? I was off? I was . . . . a test?" His caretaker's ticking sped and stopped and sped again. Elijah's face could not change. It would never change. Its expression would only shift with shadow and rust and corrosion, but Noah knew his friend's moods. The ticking told of them.

Elijah was confused.

Elijah was hurt.

Elijah might even be angry.

"Doctor Physician turned me off?"

Noah slipped the tiny golden gear into his pocket. "Yes," he said quietly. "Now, let's see what else the building has. We'll need to stay safe from the octochines. And let's figure out if there's a way for us to get off this island."

"We will look for a way to escape!" Elijah said.

Noah covered his friend's mouth and hushed him. When he removed his hand, Elijah looked quickly to the door to see if it remained empty and said, "We will also make sure to keep our escape a secret!"

✸ CHAPTER 12 ✸

Noah and Elijah found Alton talking to himself in a room with a wall unlike anything they had ever seen before. Across its surface teemed a seething, clicking, snapping, and whirring tangle of tiny machines that climbed over, under, and around one another. Their movements made the wall seem to undulate, as if it had waves. There were so many small machines moving about, it was hard to see any of them individually. The wall looked like a great mechanical mass. The sound coming from it was a constant rising and falling song of clicks, pings, and metallic whines. Without having to look closely, Noah could tell by the sounds that the evolution he'd seen in the other room was happening here. Only faster, and harsher, and scarier.

Alton Physician ignored the swarming wall. Instead he gave his attention to a plate of sliced fruit that sat on the table. He ate a piece and stared at a point far off in the distance. The room around him held little interest. A simple wooden chair and table sat at the center. Worktables lined the other walls, and on those lay dozens of tools of sizes and uses unimagined. Everything gleamed with a whiteness hard to look at, despite the still soft, early morning light.

"You should eat." Juice ran off the man's chin. "The fruit refreshes, but I find it needs to be eaten constantly to keep the mind sharp."

Elijah continued into the room, but Noah thought the robot kept his distance from Alton. There was a new wariness there. He was a little relieved that his oldest friend might no longer trust his father without question. Noah tapped at the small circular gear in his pocket. Was it responsible for the devotion? *Was it an unnecessary addition, and that's why I couldn't find its place?*

Noah watched the wall organize and reorganize itself. Patterns seemed to rise to the surface, only to break apart and reform elsewhere. It was as though a conversation was being had from one side to the next, like ripples in a pond receiving ripples in response. "What's this?" he asked. He hated this surge of curiosity. He hated that the question came without his being able to stop it from crossing his lips. *I should be looking for a way out of this tower, not wondering at his work.*

Alton continued to chomp at the fruit, juice slicking his chin. "That? Early stages." He pointed his constantly clicking and mechanically articulating digits at the wall while his flesh-and-blood fingers fed his mouth. "That wall, mechanically confined and limiting to those tiny machines, is the earlier version of what you saw in the other room."

Noah peered back through the door. He could no longer see the place in the wall where the roots had grown and the tiny machines consumed one another, but in his mind, it was very, very clear.

Elijah ticked up beside him, and looked back the way Noah did. "What did we see in the other room?"

"Evolution," Noah said, and smiled, despite his worry. These contraptions didn't seem easily understandable, and his father had already made machines that became dangerous. He didn't like that part of him was still a bit thrilled at the idea of what was happening.

Alton finally wiped at his chin.

Noah pointed back the way they'd come. "That's them in the wild."

Alton nodded. His eyes flashed.

He wants me to understand, Noah thought. "There are so many more right here. It's so much more complex. This is the next step?"

Alton slowly shook his head. His lenses pulled away from his face and he beamed at his son. "No. The complexity here is due to these little ones being physically limited to this wall, and the long . . . long period of time they've been . . . playing."

Something in the way Alton said *playing* made Noah feel as if small machines had just crawled up his spine.

He walked away from the teeming wall and turned his attention to the worktables on the far side of the room. Each was covered with tools and equipment. Spanners, wrenches, pliers, screwdrivers. Multiple sizes and types of each, each arranged in rows by size, each equally spaced. The organization here was carefully maintained. Noah was a bit stunned at the idea that his father—a man who looked like he was put together out of spare parts—was this careful and particular about his workspace. It was clean. Scrubbed. Organized. And perfectly focused on one thing: the wall.

"This is a lab," Noah finally said.

His father smiled again. Noah decided he didn't care for his father's smile.

"How are they held here?"

"Electromagnetism." Alton motioned to the wall as if there were a window in it. "I generate power at the volcano.

As long as its lava runs hot, my little ones here will remain in place on this wall. Despite their ambitions."

Noah struggled against a shudder. "And you're studying this . . . the evolution of these machines? And you've released them into the wild to . . . do the same to the island?"

Elijah walked between Noah and the wall. "What did we see in the other room? What are they doing to the island?"

"They're changing it," Noah said.

Alton consumed the last bite by tossing it into the air and catching it in his mouth. It was swallowed without chewing. "They're perfecting it. You see, don't you? The organic chokes itself out. But the mechanical . . . it only exists."

"The patterns," Noah said. "It's talking to itself. There's harmony."

"Yes," Alton said. "They reorganize and perfect. They work together. They remove conflict. They avoid any sense of personal whim and replace it with collective good. They are one. They stretch out and make the one larger, more inclusive, and more perfect. Eventually, those out there will be as advanced as this." His gaze stretched out past the wall and his eyes glazed over.

Elijah's ticking sped up. "May I ask who is it that is doing all this perfecting?"

Noah looked at Elijah and whispered, "His machines."

Alton's gaze snapped back into focus on the room, on the wall, and on Noah. "My children," he said sternly.

Elijah's ticking sped to a buzz, and he looked from Noah to Alton.

Noah stepped away from the tables. Something about how all this work was done and why was confusing. It made him uncomfortable. His home with Marie was largely like this very tower. Room after room haphazardly laid one upon the other, and inside a confusing mess of work and storage. Yet in that mess there were jobs to be done to improve the lives of the people of Liberty. Even the building of the soldiers' armor had a clear goal Noah understood. But here, his father was organized and directed, but toward something so distant, disconnected, and abstract. What was the point? He understood the desire to create, but not the way his father described. "But how do your contraptions help people?"

Alton Physician's face screwed up in confusion. "Why should they help anyone?"

Noah watched the wall pulse. For a moment it turned into a swirling black vortex. An illusion, he knew, as the wall underneath was still flat, but the concentration of the small machines at the center and the pattern of movement they created at the edges made it seem as if a black void had opened and would suck the room, the building, the forest into its maw. Just as the illusion became overwhelming and Noah could almost feel the room tilt beneath his feet, it shifted again, and the vortex turned into a single black circle like the pupil of an eye that shifted its focus from Noah to Alton to Elijah and back to Noah.

It's watching us, Noah thought. *They. They're watching.*

Elijah said, "These look like your contraptions, Sir." His ticking rose and fell, and he leaned forward so that his nose almost touched the wall. "Do you also think of them as children?"

Noah wanted to tell Elijah to back away, but bit his lip instead.

Alton looked shocked. "What do you mean, Elijah?" His lenses spun and he examined Noah intently. "What does he mean?"

"Sir Noah builds contraptions like this. He releases them outside, and we would see them sometimes. They hid in the woods."

"You do this?" Alton asked, his eyes fixed on the boy.

Noah nodded. He'd tried to tell Alton all this before, but now that his father actually understood, he suddenly felt reluctant to share. Something about Alton's interest was upsetting. *He finds me useful, not interesting.*

"Yes," Noah said. "But when I tinker, I don't make anything like this. I—"

"Why do you say 'tinker'?"

"It's what I call making contraptions."

Alton leaned in. "That doesn't explain *why* you call it that. *Tinker*. A small word. A silly word."

Noah didn't like the smell coming off his father. The man had been alone on Singe for a long, long time. "It's what Marie calls it. When I made something, she called it tinkering. If it's not a useful project. . . ." He leaned away, a little confused and a little scared.

Alton pulled back and stood to his full height. "You don't tinker, boy. You *design*. You *create*. Never think of yourself as a mere tinkerer! You do not play at it. Not if you make children like these." He gestured at the robots turning the wall into a great black eye. "It is not tinkering to make such wonders, to make an octochine or an Elijah. It is *creation*. It is *evolution*. You wonder what might be, and then you make it. And then, when it is done, it will be the solution that the world needed. Even if the world doesn't want that solution!"

He took hold of Elijah, and before the robot could react, Alton spun him in a circle and lifted the caretaker's chin to reveal the gears and springs that ran along his neck. The interlocking parts ticked at a speed faster than usual, but Elijah did not struggle.

"This is not tinkering. Put that word away. I won't hear it again. Not if you are to join me."

Noah watched the glittering gears spin inside Elijah. He silently promised himself that he would never utter the word *tinker* again, if only because he was now terrified of the reaction it brought. "Join you?"

"Boy . . . Noah. Do you believe in fate?"

"I—" Noah pulled his eyes from the hypnotic, sparkling clockwork that made up his caretaker. "I don't know."

"I do not," said his father. "I believe each of us finds our fit, filling in the missing pieces with the parts that belong. Like the gears in Elijah here, or in any of these other little family members."

Alton took hold of a lever on the wall and drew it down. A trapdoor on the ceiling opened, and a ladder that seemed to be a robot itself descended, leaned into place, and waited to be climbed. Alton didn't explain. He scaled the ladder up into the hole in the ceiling and disappeared from view. Some stalks on the ladder that may have been eyes watched Alton ascend, then bent to examine Elijah and Noah closely, almost expectantly, until Noah reluctantly took hold of the lowest rungs.

"Follow me, Elijah."

"I will," Elijah said. "Are we still working on our secret mission?"

Noah nodded, and put a finger to his lips.

Elijah mimicked the gesture, but still spoke at a normal volume. "We should hurry after your father. The ladder appears to be anxious."

The eye stalks focused again on them, and the entire contraption shook. The ladder wanted to retract, and they were keeping it from doing so. They climbed without apology.

At the top of the ladder, they found themselves outside the structure, looking up at the remaining floors of the tower. Alton, Noah, and Elijah clustered together on the overhang. Above them, only a few floors remained before they would reach the final platform. Below, the forest stretched out. Occasionally a burst of octochine calls sounded in the distance. Noah noticed an enormous box that had dozens of legs clinging to the side of the building. Alton stepped inside it, and the box shifted to adjust to his weight.

"My work has carried me to great heights."

Noah looked out over the narrow ledge and then took in the uncertain footing of the climbing box. It was the long, tragic drop to the forest below. "I can see that." He gripped the building's outer wall. Something shifted beneath his fingers, and when he moved his hand, a row of his father's evolving machines scurried away. It was disturbing how the machines ignored him. They demonstrated the same disinterest in people that his father had proudly bragged of minutes earlier. Noah worried about what that would mean if more people came to the island. *Does anyone affect them?*

Alton paid the machines on the outer wall no mind. "As high as I've reached, there are yet greater achievements. Logic dictates that you join me. Every gear has teeth that need other gears. What one gear has, another does not. Yet, put them together and you have perfection. You should join me. You must. Now. Now!" He motioned impatiently. "What are you waiting for? Come aboard."

Noah hesitated. The box shifted legs, grabbing hold of the exterior of the building with a different set every few seconds. With a sigh, Alton reached out and yanked Noah aboard. The box shuddered, seeming to struggle.

Noah clutched his father's arm, but the man offered no support in return. Just a mixture of confusion and annoyance, as though he couldn't fathom why a child might be terrified of falling countless feet to the forest floor. Noah had just caught his breath when Elijah calmly stepped aboard and some of the legs lost their grip completely.

Noah gasped, but Alton continued, oblivious to his surroundings. "My whole life, I have been looking for someone who fits me in that way. I once thought that person
was your mother." The box had thankfully found its footing
and was now slowly climbing the outside of the building,
carrying them to the uppermost levels. "But Marie, she was
missing something else. I believe she thought you were that
missing part for her. Maybe. Maybe she didn't. I thought
she was my missing part, and she thought you were hers.
But now, now that I see you . . ."

Noah suddenly couldn't get enough air into his lungs,
and his eyes began to water. In the house, he'd only known
true fear once, as he searched for the spideratus. This felt
similar, but with a giddiness mixed in. There was so much
here to be worried about. His father's attitude toward the
people in the city was upsetting, and the goals he'd set for
the machines he had already unleashed upon Singe was
unclear. But the man was also inviting him to be a part
of his life, and no one—not even his mother—had ever
invited him to be a part of anything. Everyone had simply
forced him. To build contraptions. To stay in the house. To
remain ignorant of the truth. Alton's goals were confusing
and unclear, but he was at least *asking* for Noah's help. And
he was suggesting that Noah *fit*.

Is that all I want? Noah asked himself. *To feel welcome?* How could he trust the man after what he had done to Elijah?

The box shuddered to an uneasy stop at an upper floor, teetering as Alton stepped off without looking back. Elijah helped Noah onto more solid ground, and almost immediately, the robot box made a grinding noise, then began to descend, as if complaining about the work it had done.

Alton walked ahead. They passed through another door that led back inside to the final rooms of the tower. "We have such wonderful work to do, you and I."

Noah's excitement grew. This was beginning to feel like everything he had ever hoped for. And yet, with the excitement lurked guilt. Downstairs he'd thought that fleeing was their only option, and part of him worried—no, knew—that Alton's willingness to use Elijah as a test was a dangerous sign. And what did the robot pursuit of *perfection* mean? Noah couldn't catch his breath. The wind whipped around them, and it felt as if the air had vanished. He was exhausted. When had he last slept? He tried to recall. The tower seemed so tall now. He could see all the way to the ocean, and yet nothing was coming into focus. Was any of this right? Was staying with his father a good idea?

Alton stopped abruptly. His lenses shifted and he seemed

impossibly distracted by the act of trying to see. "If my work is to advance, I will need your help. Will you help me?"

The answer escaped Noah before he even knew what he wanted to say. "Yes," he whispered, the word barely audible.

"Noah." Alton knelt before his son, taking hold of the boy's chin and lifting it as if searching for gears. A magnifying lens snapped into place. "Why are you crying?"

Noah shrugged. "It's hard to explain. I guess I'm just . . . excited." The word he wished he'd said was *happy*.

"Hmm, I see." Alton stepped back. "So we are agreed. You will be my assistant."

Something deep within Noah shrank. There had been a great swirl of energy in his chest, but now it imploded, turning into a tiny pebble in his heart. "Your . . . assistant?"

"Yes, finding the message in the spideratus was only the first part of your test, but then you proved your worth down below when you recognized what my Evolved have accomplished," said Alton, turning away. "Proving that you could build, that you have vision, that you're worthy of my offer . . . that was even more important. As I said, I had previously thought that Marie might be the one—she is a brilliant engineer—but you found my hidden message, and you have built similar contraptions." He looked back at Noah. "Yes, you shall do quite nicely. For now, at least."

His whole life, Noah had ached to find the place where he fit. He had long known that it wasn't trapped in a cavernous house alone with a robot. He'd hoped his father might want him in a way his mother never had. Instead Alton Physician saw him exactly as his mother did: as an assistant. Not a son. Not even a friend. *Assistant.* It sounded like another word for *prisoner.*

"Does being your assistant mean I'll tinker—I mean, work on contraptions that you need help with? Will I build more of these?" Noah gestured to the room full of crawling contraptions. "Will you assign me projects?"

"Oh my, no." Alton crossed to the door leading to the next level of the spiraling tower. "I have grander plans than simple evolution. Something larger. And smaller." He began to laugh. It sounded like a laugh meant to hurt— sharp, loud, and mocking. If there was a joke, Noah didn't understand it. "We will look beyond what is right in front of us. There are gears of reality invisible to the naked eye, and we will dig to find them."

Noah closed his eyes and tried to make sense of what his father could possibly mean. When he opened them again, he was alone, staring at a platform covered in tiny, wandering mechanicals. He had already been disturbed by how the small machines ignored him. Now he saw, his father didn't care for him any more than the Evolved did. *How could I have been so tricked?* Noah wondered. *I saw who he was down below when he hurt Elijah. How could I have been convinced he saw me as his son?*

Alton Physician had stepped through the door, and the light that filled it seemed to swallow him. "Are you coming? Now that you are here, we can finally get to work. Mysteries await." The man smiled broadly. That's when Noah saw it. The cause of his confusion.

Despite the dangerous forest his father had allowed him to wander in, despite the damage he'd done to Elijah for his *test*, and despite being called *assistant* instead of *son*, or *family*, or even just *Noah*, Alton Physician's smile and grand words were enough to make Noah question his choice to leave. *Because he knows the gears that turn in our heads as well as he knows the gears of his machines, and he makes them fit for his own purposes.*

"I think we are going on another trip," Elijah said.

Noah suddenly wondered if his father thought Elijah fit in the same way he did. A wave of guilt rose up to swallow him. His oldest friend had already been used once for a cruel test. What else would Alton do to him?

And Noah had been ready to stay.

I'll never forgive myself for that, Noah thought. *Never again. I won't put myself ahead of him ever again.*

Noah and Elijah followed Alton Physician through the

last few rooms, and then outside to a wide platform that sat atop the tower. At one end, a group of spideratuses continued to build the platform. Alton ignored them, focusing his attention on the massive beetle contraption ahead of them.

"Have you ever seen anything like it?" Alton asked.

"Yes," said Elijah. "Sir Noah has built flying insects before."

Alton flashed a grin at Noah. "I'm happy to hear that."

The boy blushed. "They didn't fly well," he said. "Or far." Why was it, he wondered, that even when he didn't know if he could trust his father, he wanted desperately to please the man? Even Elijah—though he had been talking loudly about their *secret plan*—didn't seem interested in escape. Noah looked out over the forest. In every direction he could see beyond the trees to the ocean, which spread to every horizon. Could this machine make it far enough to reach another shore?

"Don't worry," Alton said. "She flies well and easily. And as far as we want. Other than getting supplies for us, she won't need to land at all."

Noah breathed in the cool air. It was exciting to imagine flying high and far to any place they'd please. He'd watched pelicans that flew in great, free circles above the harbor and Liberty, and the flocks of sparrows that chased one another in a chaotic cloud. He'd been fascinated by the hunting hawks that flew lazy loops, motionless on updrafts, and the seagulls that screamed and swooped looking for food. Now he could join them. He and his father. They would rise up and soar above the world. It could happen, but only if Noah could forgive the man for harming Elijah.

Such forgiveness seemed to escape him.

As he considered his dilemma, he searched the sky for birds above Singe. In his memory, the birds had been calming. He could use that comfort. He looked for wheeling clouds of small scavengers or the slow circling hunters. He saw neither. He thought he spied some seagulls out on the horizon, black specks far, far away, above the water. There was no birdsong, either. The forest all around them should have been noisy with screeching and whistling, but instead there was only silence.

Noah walked to the platform edge, where a railing had been constructed, and peered down to the clearing around the towers. He could see the neighboring building covered in spideratuses and hear the hammers and drills, the slams and saws of their busy building. But he heard no birdsong, no insect buzz, not forest animals of any kind. He tried to recall hearing any during his time on Singe. He tried to recall seeing any animals. He couldn't. If he really concentrated, all he heard was the singing pings and whirring springs of his father's evolving contraptions. The mechanical creations were everywhere. The gears and metallic clicks of ever-changing machinery had replaced the gentle songs of nature.

"What happened to the animals?" he asked.

His father, distracted with gears beneath the beetle's wing, was fiddling with a wrench, his eye lenses spinning back and forth. "What animals?"

Noah pointed out at the forest. "The animals that should be here. There are no birds or animals. I don't even hear an insect."

Alton finished his adjustments. "As far as I know, there have never been any animals here. I don't bother with such details."

This seemed odd to Noah. He turned and watched Elijah, who was walking up the gangplank into the belly of the tremendous beetle. A moment later he appeared in the glass eye of the machine. *The controls for flying the contraption must be there*, Noah thought. The robot boy waved through the window.

"I'd like to go somewhere with lots of animals," said Noah. "And people."

Alton was now under the other wing making more adjustments. "What do you mean, *go*?" he asked.

Noah rubbed at the side of his head. Talking to his

father was giving him a headache. The man was confusing, almost intentionally so, it seemed. "This flying machine. Won't we be going somewhere to do your . . ." He wasn't sure what to call his father's efforts. Work? Experiments? What did he mean by *invisible gears of reality*?

Alton turned and blankly considered Noah's question. "We won't be going anywhere. This lovely creature brings things back to me. Things that I need."

Noah felt suddenly cold. "What kinds of things?"

"Metal. Fuel. Assorted items of value. I send it out and it scavenges. It brings back all sorts of . . . interesting items."

Noah looked up at the massive robot. The beetle's head was small compared to its body, and it was covered with massive black eyes that were made from dozens of smaller glass orbs. Beneath the contraption were impressive legs, especially the pair in front, which were long and arced and ended in jagged points that hooked backward. Noah could imagine this thing descending from the sky and taking what it wanted. It might even be able to take away the *Abbreviated*. His father had called it scavenging, but what the beetle did sounded more and more like something far more sinister: attacking and stealing.

"So we'll stay here?"

Alton continued to gape at the boy. "Of course."

Noah's headache was growing worse. This scenario was sounding awfully familiar. "Won't we be seeing any other people?"

"People get in the way."

Noah considered the structure beneath him, just like the house he'd grown up in. He thought of all the time he'd been locked away, dreaming of escape. And he'd ended up in exactly the same situation in the same house.

"But won't it be lonely without people?"

Alton's lenses shifted, his eyes flickering and changing size as the gears whirled. "Who needs people? Us? No! They don't understand us. You and I, we're not like them. We seek perfection. They seek minor convenience. We seek truth. They don't understand what we do. They don't understand my children. And my children don't like them."

Noah felt a chill run down his spin. His father had referred to the contraptions as his children several times, but this was the first time he'd said anything about them liking—or not liking—something.

"*What* don't they like?"

Alton poked his head inside an access panel on the side of the mechanical beetle. When he spoke his voice echoed, its volume increased by the hollow spaces inside his creation. "They don't like being bothered. Especially by people. Nicholas couldn't understand that. 'Build me great defenders,' he begged me. And when I did, he kept pestering them. Kept putting his soldiers in the way. And his workers bothered the spideratuses. I couldn't be everywhere at once. An accident was bound to happen."

An accident.

"What accident?" Noah asked slowly. His mouth was dry.

Alton's wrench clanged from inside the panel. All Noah could think of were the monsters his father had brought with him to the island, the truths he'd forgotten, and the history of Liberty. The very things that had caused his father to be exiled to Singe, and had trapped him in a house that grew at night.

"What do your contraptions do when they're bothered?" he asked, though he knew the answer. All of Liberty knew the answer.

"They defend themselves, of course. I told Nicholas. 'Don't bother them,' I said. 'Let them alone. They will grow. They will multiply. They will be strong and powerful and everything they should be.' But he wanted . . . pets. He wanted mechanisms that would take *commands*. *Never*." Alton reached up into the panel and opened a hatch, then crawled inside, talking to himself, his tools clanging against the metal interior.

Noah looked out over the island again, listening to the silence. What his father had called an *accident* had another name in Liberty: the Uprising.

He had more questions, but he wasn't sure he wanted to ask them. "What do you mean, the machines defend themselves?"

Alton's hammering stopped. "They will do what they must to continue their work."

Noah pictured the posters plastered around Liberty—the images of his uncle fighting back clouds of gears and mechanical arms. "Would they hurt people?"

There was a long silence.

"You should help me with the repairs to my beetle," Alton said at last. But it was in a whisper, as if he were hiding. "The beetle takes such a long time to take off. Won't you help me speed that up? It takes such a long time. Too long. The wings beat, but it can't lift off. It struggles."

Noah shook his head. "Not until you answer me. *Would they hurt people?*"

Another long silence. Noah thought he could hear his father sliding farther into the hatch.

"I don't have time for such questions," Alton said. His voice was very close, but Noah still couldn't see him.

"Were you alone here? All these years?"

There was no answer. Noah heard the sliding sound again. He was sure his father was just on the other side of the dark opening.

"Did the people of Liberty get in the way?"

A wrench dropped from the hatch. It clanged onto the walkway and landed between Noah's feet.

"They had work to do. To build a city. To protect it. If only everyone had let them do that . . ." Alton lowered himself through the hatch. Despite the robotic foot and extra fingers, he landed silently on the platform. "People are chaotic. They don't fit. The machines need things to fit. And when they don't—"

A siren rose up from far below. Another joined in, and then a third. They warbled around one another, harmonizing. Alton Physician didn't react. He watched Noah, his face lined and filthy. His machines were attacking something or someone and he would do nothing about it.

"Aha!" called Elijah. "There is Winona from the *Abbreviated*! She seems to be looking for you, Sir Noah. And she seems to be running for her life!"

⚙ CHAPTER 13 ⚙

Noah rushed to the end of the platform. "Where is she?"

Elijah pointed and Noah gasped. Winona was running along the edge of the clearing. A group of three octochines were following right behind her. She tried to lose them by dodging between trees, but the machines swept their legs through the trunks, knocking them to the ground. She was headed straight toward the building Noah and his father stood atop. He hoped she made it.

"I thought she was gone!" he yelled. "I hoped she got back to the beach and was found!"

"She did not," Elijah said. He stood next to Alton, who chewed angrily on one robotic finger.

"She's bothering them again," Alton growled. "I thought they had successfully chased her off."

Noah clenched a fist. His father was infuriating. "How do I stop them?"

Elijah looked up. "I'm not sure I know what you—"

"Not you, Elijah." He turned to face his father. The man still stood silent on the platform. *How do I stop them?*

"You stay out of their way. You let them do their work, and they will . . . take care of things. . . ."

An accident. The Uprising.

"They don't like people because *you* don't," Noah snapped. "And they attack immediately. The spideratus, the one with your message, it went after me before I unlocked your secret."

Alton twitched as if an insect had crawled across his face. His lenses withdrew so that he was looking at Noah with unassisted eyes. "Well, what did you do to upset it? You must have done something. Hurt it or scared it in some way. What did you do? You didn't break it, did you? *Did you?*" The inventor took a step forward, panicked, his voice shrill.

Noah darted out of the way, pushing past his father. "You weren't exiled. You ran! You ran and hid! And the machines followed you, but you don't control them."

Alton grabbed hold of Noah's arm and spun him around, squeezing the boy's shoulders. With his mechanical fingers Noah worried his father might crush the bones.

"Yes, I fled! My children were in danger!" Alton gave Noah a shake. "What would you have me do? I told the city to stop. I warned Nicholas. But no one would listen. 'Control them,' they said. Control them? My creations are life! Who can control life? My children followed me because I am their father. *They attack because no one understands them!*" The mechanical appendages squeezed even tighter until Noah cried out in pain.

"You're just like the others," Alton continued, his eyes wild. "You pretend to understand, but you do not. Not at all. Try to help that girl, if you must. You've proven you don't fit. Try to help her and fail. Fail like the others."

Fail like the others, Noah thought. *Fail and die.* Noah shook his head. "Just let me help her."

"If you truly understood my work, you'd do anything you had to. No sacrifice is too great. You choose your goal, and you do anything to achieve it. I've always said, pursue your goal, no matter the path. Your mother didn't understand that. You clearly don't, either. No one does."

Alton Physician released Noah and hurried back to the panel on the beetle's side, swatting at the controls and switches there. His metal fingers made sparks as they struck the levers and dials.

"Every great thing I've done was the result of keeping my eye on only the goal. Could I create machines that were alive? Nothing else matters."

The engine above them stirred, and the wings began to kick up dust and dirt as they shivered to life. Noah wondered if it was possible his father had ever seen people as worthy of being helped. He wondered if his father had ever thought people fit in the world. It had probably never occurred to him.

"I'm going to save my friend now!" Noah shouted over the beating of the flying machine's wings.

"I was right to doubt you were the one. There's nothing special in you." Alton Physician didn't bother to turn around. "*You* could never be my assistant."

Noah's vision shrank to a small, angry circle. He rubbed at the spots where Physician had gripped him. "I didn't want to be your assistant." He stepped back and looked toward the entrance to the tower. He wanted to run down and help Winona, but what would he do when he got there? "You probably don't even know *how* to stop them or *why* they pay attention to you."

Alton let go of the controls he was working and spun angrily toward Noah. "I know more than you ever will! In my lab are canisters filled with the means to turn them all back to simple automatons. I choose not to use it! I embrace the future! They are more important than anything on this island or this world!"

Elijah stepped between Alton and Noah and put a finger to his lips as if hushing him. "I believe this is your moment of escape!"

Alton looked at Elijah in shock. "Escape? What escape?"

Elijah turned quickly and began to push levers before he could be stopped. The robot had studied Alton's movements and knew precisely what to do. The beating of the giant wings became erratic, the sound more terrible. It rose so loud that when Noah barked Elijah's name, not even he could hear it.

Noah ran toward the door, but glanced back one more time. Alton and the little robot struggled at the controls. *Elijah did everything my father commanded at first. Now he's struggling to give me a chance to save our friend.* Noah couldn't say what had caused the change, but he was relieved it had happened.

Elijah continued to grab at the control levers and Alton struggled with his robotic hands to pry them loose. The wings above them beat angrily. The robot caretaker raised a hand toward Noah and said something. It sounded liked he was asking Noah a question—maybe if he was okay?—but the boy couldn't hear over the sounds of the beetle's wings. They were beating too fast, their hum too great.

Noah hated that he would have to leave his friend

behind, but could see it was what Elijah wanted. Noah waved goodbye and ran from the platform back into the building.

The image in his head was the last thing he'd seen: Elijah calmly waving goodbye, and his father furiously fighting to regain control of one of his *children*, his eyes red and flashing, his robotic parts whirling madly.

Noah had come to the island with such hope, and his father had taken that hope and turned it into something terrible. He had put Winona in danger, and he'd lost Elijah. Nothing had gone right. As he raced, through room after room, taking all the shortcuts his father had shown him, he realized Marie had tried to save him from a moment like this and felt his anger peel away.

He tried not to keep the image of his father fighting Elijah in mind, but the only thing that cleared it away was reaching the lab. The room was as clean and white as they'd left it, and the swirling wall was in yet another configuration that looked like geometric patterns changing and rearranging in a vast void. It quickly reassembled itself into the eyelike image, and the clicking and twirling black pupil at the center focused on him, watching as he walked into the room. Shuddering, he looked away.

His eyes settled on the room's shelves and their contents,

and then Noah remembered what his father had yelled at him minutes earlier. *In my lab are canisters filled with the means to turn them all back to simple automatons.* Noah reached for one of the canisters, then ran toward the far door. He glanced back one more time over his shoulder. The wall was still watching him.

At the ground floor, he stood in the doorway scanning the clearing for Winona, the canister clutched to his chest. He could hear her shouting his name as octochine sirens rose and fell.

"Winona!" he screamed.

Just ahead, he spotted her darting between trees, but octochines circled her, and more were approaching from every direction. He shouted to her, waving his arms, and she ran at top speed toward him, an octochine on her heels.

Winona threw herself through the doorway. Her eyes were wide and she was covered in dirt and scratches. Her feet skidded and she looked ready to fly if only she had wings. The robot came to a clanking stop in front of the house. It loomed high above them, stumbling on its gigantic legs.

And with that stumble Noah knew which robot it was.

"Seven!" he shouted.

Seven honked back, but its eye stayed focused on Winona.

"What in the world is a *seven*?" she yelled.

As Noah took in her injuries, he felt a sinking guilt. How many times would she risk herself for him?

"It's friendly," he reassured her, but even as he said it, he wasn't sure if it was true. Seven blared its horn and other nearby octochines called back, speeding into the clearing, each pushing and honking in an attempt to get to the doorway. As the honks extended into long siren blares, the advance of the machines became more aggressive.

Seven remained at the front of the pack. Noah urged Winona to back away from the door, but even as he did, he could see that whatever had happened when the machine was repaired had only changed its attitude toward him. Seven kept trying to angle its eye around Noah, focusing on Winona.

When one of its legs poked at the doorway, both cried out.

Winona wavered, clearly wanting to find cover deeper into the house, but Noah grabbed her hand, and together the two slowly backed away from the doorway. "Stay behind me," Noah urged.

After a moment Winona yanked her hand free. "Stay behind you? You're nuts. We have to go!"

"Seven!" Noah shouted. "Stop them!" Seven staggered

back from the house, but another octochine's eye filled the open space, its siren blasting into the room. Suddenly Seven knocked the head away with a hollow, echoing clang. He couldn't do it alone, though. And Seven was alone. For every ocotochine he pushed back, two came up from behind. At last Seven was surrounded, then shoved to the side with angry swipes. The trees nearest the tower had all been toppled and crushed under many, many feet attached to many, many angry machines.

"We're trapped!" Winona screamed.

Noah stood his ground. "Trust me! I think I know what to do!" He held up the canister and turned the lid. It was hard to open, but at last it slid away from the rust holding it shut.

"What's that supposed to do?" Winona shouted.

"It should solve our problems," was the only explanation Noah had time for. Part of him mourned for Seven. Whatever was in the canister might change what it had become, and Noah had grown attached to the giant machine—once it had stopped trying to crush him. But he had no choice. He had to save Winona.

"Stand back!" he yelled, as he opened the canister.

Inside was nothing but dust. A gust of wind, and the soft gray ash rose out in a great puff, settling on Noah. He stepped back, his shirt filthy, and where his feet had been was outlined in the dust on the ground.

"*Stand back?*" Winona howled. "That's your plan? To make a mess?"

"My father said he had a solution," Noah muttered. He felt hollow inside. "I don't know why I thought it would be sitting on a shelf. Maybe I grabbed the wrong one?"

Winona rolled her eyes and looked like she was about to say more, but instead she shoved him hard to one side of the hallway. "Look out!"

An octochine leg reached in through the doorway, slamming down to smash a hole in the hallway floor. At last Noah could see she was right. Even if Seven didn't see him as a threat, it wouldn't be enough. Everything else on the island did. Even his father.

"You're right." The words caught in Noah's throat. He looked back at her and saw the panic on her face. "We need to get to the beach. Through the kitchen. There's a window."

Winona gave him a strange look. "How would you know?"

The answer made Noah's stomach churn. "I grew up in this house."

Winona raised her eyebrows, but there was no time for

him to explain. The octochines had grown tired of waiting. The one closest punched two of its legs through either
side of the door and ripped the frame from the house with
a shower of splinters and a crackling that sounded like a
thousand small explosions.

"*Run!*" Winona shouted as she fled into the kitchen.

For a moment, Noah couldn't move. The octochines'
calls and the grind of their gears was now matched in volume by the cracking of wood as they punched through
the front of the house. One of the octochines lowered its
head and hammered it against the second story with omi-
nous clangs. The wall above the door cracked as its head
smashed into the building. The air filled with the reek of
hot metal and oil churned from the spinning gears inside
the machine. Two legs speared through the new opening
and pierced the floor. The blaring octochine alarm filled
the tiny hall.

Taking in the destruction, something broke loose inside
Noah. He was suddenly very worried about Marie back in
Liberty. What might she be thinking as she sat all alone in
the house that grew larger at night? He hadn't realized how
much he could worry about her, even as he wanted to find
freedom.

Noah dropped the canister and turned, hurrying into

the kitchen. Winona already had the window open and was crawling out. "Come on!" she shouted. Behind them, more wooden beams groaned, and the house shook violently.

The pair tumbled onto the ground. Winona twisted to get herself free. "Hurry up, kid. They're not going to stop." She helped pull him to his feet and they ran into the trees.

Behind them came a tremendous crackling sound, almost like lightning tearing to the ground.

"Don't look back!" Winona called.

Noah did anyway, just in time to see an octochine rip through the rear wall of the house. It was stuck, but not for long.

"You're right!" he yelled. "Don't look back!"

Another siren joined the first, and another octochine started another hole in the back of the house. The crackling sound returned, and then an enormous pop.

Sirens blared all around as the octochines struggled to make it around and through the house. But there was another sound, deeper and occasionally interrupted by more snapping and popping. A creaking moan. Noah and Winona both watched, terrified, as the octochines hacked their way through the wood. The structure itself was shifting.

"They've broken the beams," Noah whispered. Elijah

was still up there. The thought took his breath away. He looked up at the twisting spiral of rooms rising up into the sky, topped by the platform and his father's humming, scavenging beetle. It was all beginning to sway—to tilt. "It's going to collapse!"

Winona started to back away. "Uh, collapse where?"

Here, Noah realized, and then grabbed her hand and took off farther into the tangle of forest.

They ran as quickly as they could. The air filled with the roar of shattering wooden beams and trunks under the weight of falling debris. Clouds of dust rose up, blocking the sun and making the path harder to see. For a moment, the noise was deafening, and then it was gone. In its place was a magnificent droning, and a terrible *whoosh*.

Winona gasped and pointed above them. "Look!"

Alongside the shards of the tower, the beetle struggled to stay aloft. Its wings buzzed, but it didn't have enough lift. It clung to what was left of the building, being dragged down along with the wreckage, until at last, it met ground with a startling crash. There was a terrible rending of metal as dirt and debris were kicked into the air, the ground shuddered, and Noah slammed into Winona.

"What was that thing?" she choked out.

Noah looked up to where the great tower had stood only

moments before. Bits of wood and vegetation fluttered down around them. He took a deep breath. "Just one of my father's children."

"Um, Noah? Speaking of your father. Is that . . . him?"

Noah followed Winona's finger and saw, far above, a figure plummeting toward them from the tops of the tallest trees, bouncing from one branch before crashing into another.

"Whoever that was falling, they just landed above us." Her voice was a whisper, as if she could soften the blow of landing from such a fall.

Noah spotted the figure high above them, but it was no longer plummeting. Instead, it leaped from limb to limb, scrambling down the trees. "Sir, you are in danger. The octochines are quite close."

Elijah jumped down in front of a gaping Winona and Noah. The fall had left a dent in the side of his face, but other than that and some small branches and leaves sticking out from his joints, Noah's oldest friend appeared unharmed.

"Elijah!" Noah exclaimed. "I'm so glad to see you!" He quickly wiped at his eyes before Winona could see.

"Well, I'm not!" Winona glowered. "This stupid machine pushed us off the ship!"

Elijah bowed his head. "Yes, miss. I am sorry, but it was the fastest way to reach our destination. Now we should make every effort to leave as soon as possible."

Winona gave Noah a skeptical look. "He brought us here, and now he wants to leave?"

Elijah's ticking sped up. "My clockworks were constructed so that in the event the spideratus message was discovered, I should bring the person responsible to the island at all costs. Now that those orders have been completed, I am able to return to my original programming, which is to keep Sir Noah safe from harm. That means departing from this island at our earliest convenience."

Winona shook her hands in frustration at Elijah. "What did he just say?"

Octochine sirens blared out from the other side of the debris pile.

Noah grabbed Winona's hand. "He said *run!*"

⚙ CHAPTER 14 ⚙

Noah's chest burned. The sun was setting, making it harder to navigate as he and Winona urged each other on. Noah was surprised to find he was glad she was there. But why *had* she come back? She could have kept herself safe. And they'd fought before he'd taken off to follow the octochine. Friendship with someone other than Elijah was turning out to be quite confusing.

His mechanical caretaker was also running, slightly ahead of them and to their left, but Noah could still see him. Elijah moved like a blur, shaking trees and bushes as he went. He made excited ticking noises and yelled "Run!" again and again. At first Noah couldn't understand what his old robot friend was doing, but as the octochines' sirens thinned behind them, he realized Elijah was making himself a distraction. Some of the octochines must have split off, heading in the wrong direction.

I've got to keep both of them safe, Noah thought as he struggled through the undergrowth. He was thrilled to have friends nearby, and terrified of losing either of them again.

As he witnessed the speed Elijah could maintain, and the ease with which he leaped over gulleys and scurried up rock face, Noah wondered at his robot friend's abilities—and his choices. Elijah had been programmed to deliver Noah to his father. He'd even pushed Noah and Winona into the ocean to do so. Yet, here he was, ensuring their safe escape. What program had commanded these new actions? And what program had commanded Winona to come back to help? What program commanded anyone?

The sirens still wailed behind them, and in the distance the din was echoed with the rumble of thunder. The idea of getting caught in a storm made Noah scramble even faster.

The ground beneath them became mushy, and the trees had wider leaves—sand underfoot and palm trees spreading around them. They were almost to the beach.

Noah burst through the tree line, nearly toppling Winona as the loose sand slid beneath their feet. Another siren wail and the menace of thunder kept him moving. But he couldn't help noting there was something strange about the thunder: it was too high pitched, and it didn't last long.

The daylight was fading faster now as trees crashed in the forest not too far away.

"I thought they were chasing your stupid robot!" Winona shouted. "How did they get ahead of us?"

Before Noah could reply that he had no idea, they rounded a thick stand of trees and saw at last what had drawn the machines to the beach.

A rowboat had been pushed ashore, and beside it stood sailors—Mister Steem, Lady Byrne, and Gentleman Nest—shouting encouragement as they took turns shooting at an octochine that had a tree growing from a large crack in its eggish head. The robot was creaky and slow and covered in rust. Its siren was muted as if filled with dirt and sand, but it was loud enough. The octochines in the woods responded as they came closer. They would be faster and less awkward, and would surely overwhelm the sailors and destroy their boat.

"Run, Noah!" Winona called, pulling him along, and somehow, they sped up.

They hollered as they approached the sailors—"Hello! Over here!"—stopping abruptly as the octochine pivoted its head toward them and then staggered in their direction, its siren blasting three times.

Noah felt as if he were moving at half speed, most of his effort just kicking sand behind him, but Winona locked her hand with his, driving him forward. Soon Elijah joined them, taking Noah's other hand and propelling them all across the sand. The sailors urged on the children racing across the hot beach, all the while continuing to fire shot after useless shot into the robot's back.

Mister Steem lowered his rifle and rushed to meet them. "Into the boat!" He swept Noah up gingerly with his hook arm and tossed him into the craft, where he landed with a crash that knocked the breath from him. He stood unsteadily in the rocking craft as Lady Byrne climbed after him, laughing as she fell in.

"I hate land," she said. She hopped up and pushed down on Noah's head, forcing him to sit. "Stay down, Young Noah. We'll be on the move soon."

She raised her rifle and took three quick shots before sitting down and grabbing an oar.

Noah could hear Mister Steem over the commotion on the beach. "Winona, you kept our guest alive and in one piece, I see. Well done." The next thing Noah knew, she sailed over the edge of the boat, no doubt aided by a lift from the first mate.

Elijah came last with no further comment from the crew. "We need to leave quickly," the robot caretaker said, ticking wildly.

Noah nodded, then glanced quickly at the forest and wondered if there was a chance his father had survived the tower's collapse.

Elijah saw where Noah was looking. "Doctor Physician was still atop the tower, I'm afraid."

"I figured," Noah mumbled, but he still had to force his gaze away. "Why didn't he want to help Winona? Or me? Why go down with the tower?"

Elijah tipped his head back to focus on the sky. His face had been tarnished and dented, but Noah was glad it was still the face of his friend. "As the tower shifted, I knew you would need me. I offered to help him down, but . . . he refused to leave."

Noah looked back at the octochine on the beach as Steem fired another shot. "What do you mean?"

"The tower was shaking, and he held on to the flying machine." Elijah kept his gaze skyward. "I said, 'Doctor Physician, let me help you.' He shook his head and tried to climb inside the aircraft."

"And then you jumped," finished Noah.

"Yes." Elijah's focus remained fixed above until the boat began to rock. He looked almost sad. Noah wondered if they'd both dreamed of Alton Physician rescuing them from their lonely lives.

"What will the octochines do now?" Noah wondered aloud as another wave of sirens came from the woods.

By then, Winona had finished gathering ropes and

preparing the boat to push off. "I hate everything about this island," she spat. Light from the setting sun hit her face and Noah could see the anger there. "The robots can rot here."

"I don't know if they will," Elijah said.

Winona glared at the robot caretaker. "What does that mean?"

"They can repair themselves in their factory, and they will be very interested in finding Doctor Physician." Elijah glanced from Winona to Noah. "If they can find him."

"Why is your robot talking about those monsters like they're ducklings looking for their mother?" Winona asked.

Noah said, "They imprinted on my father. Like he was their parent."

Winona shrugged. "And if they can't find him? Or what's left of him after that fall?"

Elijah's ticking sped up for the briefest moment. "I'm not sure what they'll do."

Noah watched water slosh at the bottom of the boat. Winona sat down beside him and said, "I'm sorry."

"For what?"

"For the 'what's left' comment. That was mean." She looked away.

Noah nodded. "It's okay. He was . . . not what I thought he'd be."

"But he was still your father," she said quietly. "And you were looking for him for a reason."

I'm no different from the robots, Noah thought. For now he wanted nothing more than to leave Singe and never return.

Gentleman Nest heaved the boat off the beach as Mister Steem continued shooting at the slowly advancing robot. It kept staggering to its right, unbalanced by the tree. Another ricochet hit it just above the eye.

"I can't get a decent shot!" the first mate yelled to no one in particular.

"We're ready, sir!" Gentleman Nest was already up to his waist in the waves.

Two more octochines broke through the tree line. More nimble, they advanced quickly. Mister Steem took two shots at the nearer one, striking it in the eye, which shattered. The robot fell forward, and thrashed in the sand.

Mister Steem turned and bounded into the water, grabbing on to the boat. "See?" he said as he pulled himself in. "I knew I wasn't a terrible shot."

Lady Byrne had locked both oars into their moorings and was rowing them away from the beach. Gentleman Nest pulled himself in with a squishy thud, bringing a good amount of seawater in with him. He sat up and grinned. "Glad to see you, Young Noah."

Noah grinned back. "Thanks."

Gentleman Nest gave a quick glance at Elijah, then handed them each a tin cup. "Now, earn your rescue and bail out this water."

This is how they made their way from the island: Byrne and Nest pulling on the oars hard enough to make them creak; Mister Steem standing aft, shouting at the crew to row harder; Noah tossing cupful after cupful of seawater over the side; Winona standing at the bow, scanning the horizon for the *Abbreviated*.

Elijah alone sat quietly, holding his tin cup, looking at the sky.

Here was why the others each took to their tasks with such urgency: half a dozen giant robotic octopuses were chasing them across the ocean. The octochines' long legs carried them quickly into the surf. Their pointed legs stabbed into the waves so quickly, there was little disturbance to the surface. In fact, the farther into the water they went, the more stable they became. And more confident. Even the one with the tree in its head.

"Get to the deep water," Mister Steem ordered. The rowers grunted as they continued to work the oars in perfect rhythm. "The tide's going out, and the wind's behind us. We might just outrun them!"

For a minute that felt more like an hour, it didn't look like they would. But after enough pulls of the oars, it became apparent the octochines simply couldn't keep up. The water was up to their eggish heads and slowed their progress, though they pressed forward, the roar of their sirens muted by the sea but there all the same. Their spotlight eyes stayed fixed on the dinghy even as the brine reached their lenses and began to block the view.

"You can stop bailing," Mister Steem told Noah in the sudden quiet. "There's no more water."

Noah looked down at his hands. He'd been scraping the tin cup along the wooden hull. Across the waves, he watched more octochines swarming onto the beach. Fighting through the surf at the front of the crowd of machines was Seven. Maybe it was some angry programmed drive to get to the sailors, to fight what it saw as intruders? Or maybe it was Noah, himself? If he could see Seven, could Seven see him? Seven had imprinted on Alton Physician once, and now Alton was likely gone. But Seven had also imprinted on Noah, and now Noah . . .

Exhaustion hit him suddenly, and the cup clattered to the bottom of the boat as it slipped from his fingers. The orange sky above him seemed to grow darker. He couldn't think anymore. He couldn't think about what Seven would want or do. He couldn't think about what the imprinting between them might mean.

"Hold on, son," said Mister Steem, helping Noah to settle more comfortably. "We'll be back to the *Abbreviated* shortly and then back to Liberty."

"No!" Noah struggled to sit up. "I can't go back!" He imagined his uncle ready to lock him up again.

Winona chuckled mirthlessly. "I nearly drowned for nothing?"

Elijah looked away from the sky, focusing on Mister

Steem. "Now that we have completed our trip to Singe, perhaps I could find some means of paying for passage somewhere else. Captain Moor need not worry that we will cheat him."

"Captain has bigger worries," the sailor said.

The waves lifted and lowered the small rowboat in a steady rhythm. On the next upward surge, they could all spot the *Abbreviated* on the horizon, the last glimmer of sun hitting the ship. The escapees and their rescuers squinted against the slanted light. Only Winona was sure of what she saw.

"Don't look at the ship," she urged. "Look at the light."

Noah did as she instructed, and now he saw it, too.

The *Abbreviated* floated calmly in the waters, and behind it, so large that its side reflected the setting sun like a mirror, sat the *Colossus*.

❋ CHAPTER 15 ❋

The rowboat approached the *Abbreviated* with caution, but no choice. Where else could they go? Behind them the beach swarmed with angry, violent machines, and beyond the *Abbreviated* loomed the *Colossus*.

But the battleship's forward guns weren't aimed at the *Abbreviated*. They didn't have to be. Everyone knew the massive battleship could remove the smaller vessel from the water at its leisure. As if to prove this point, one of the forward guns boomed, and on the beach behind them there was a crack like thunder before a great plume of sand rose into the air, sending the octochines scuttling back into the trees. Those in the water slowed their pursuit, possibly confused or concerned, or both. Who could say what thoughts turned in their gear-filled heads?

The machines scattered deeper into the trees as the

Colossus's barrage on the beach continued. A cloud of smoke hung over the island, and the sound of the machine's horns was now drowned out by the booms of the exploding shells.

Noah wondered if Seven had been scared off with the others. *It's probably for the best if all the robots forget about me, my father, and the city of Liberty.* "I hope they can stay here in peace," he murmured.

"Good riddance," Winona grumbled. Her gaze was fixed on the island, and she was clearly pleased to see the machines fleeing. But it was obvious they weren't seeing

the same thing when they looked at that shore. Noah saw the last proof of his father's genius, the place where he'd hidden himself away . . . and had probably died. Noah saw the dangerous mystery he'd once longed for. Now, the sight made him unbearably sad. Everything had changed. Every connection he'd hoped for had been severed, and he'd been forced to flee, back into the arms of a city that hated him.

The rowboat neared the *Abbreviated*, and lines were cast to pull them in. From the water, it appeared nothing unusual was happening on deck. Crew members threw ropes and called out happily upon seeing all members of the rescue party safe. Noah and Winona were welcomed aboard with pats on the back. Winona, especially, was given a hero's welcome. There were questions about her injuries, but she brushed away all concern.

"I wouldn't have needed rescuing at all if someone's stupid alarm clock hadn't pushed me from the ship."

Noah sighed. "He's not an alarm clock."

Elijah pulled himself aboard without help, ignored by the crew. They hadn't particularly cared for him before, and now that they were being forced back to Liberty, he might as well not exist. For a robot, he looked wrung out. His clothes were filthy from walking across the ocean floor, seaweed and salt had dried to his limbs, and leaves stuck from his mechanical joints. He settled himself on deck without complaint.

Noah was a bit overwhelmed at first, seeing nothing but smiles and the glow of the setting sun, but as he became more accustomed to the clamor, and the crew went back to their duties at the orders of Mister Steem, Noah noticed that the smiles were forced and the questions quick and muted. He followed Steem and Winona to the pilothouse.

There they found Captain Moor being harassed by the commander of the *Colossus*. Six men in mechanical suits stood in a ring around the captains. They were so massive, Noah wondered how they'd ever gotten through the doorway.

"And a man fitting your description claimed to be my first mate," said the *Colossus*'s commander. "I find this curious, as my first mate is not quite as tall as you, and also a woman."

Moor glanced at Noah and Winona. His relief at seeing them was obvious in his small smile, but he continued to address the officer. "I wouldn't know anything about that."

"I'm sure."

"But if she's shorter than me, she's lucky," added Moor helpfully. "I'm always hitting my head on the doorways."

The *Colossus*'s commander was not amused. "You will make best possible speed back to Liberty."

"That won't be too fast, considering the hole in our side."

"Best possible speed," repeated the commander firmly. "These fine soldiers will be staying here to ensure things go smoothly. And if there's any change in your course, I'll not hesitate to give your ship a hole in her other side to match. Remember, I have free reign to do what I want with smugglers and their vessels. The only order the governor has been clear about is that I return the boy to him unharmed."

With the discussion over, the commander gave some final orders to his soldiers. They stood in a line on deck watching the crew, their unmoving metal faces making them look for all the world like statues. When they did move, it was a lumbering sort of gait, accompanied by a horrible grinding. Noah recalled the hours, days, and weeks of work he'd spent on the various parts of mechanical armor. Now, seeing what it was intended for and how it was meant to work, he couldn't help imagining how to improve it. This was yet another way that Marie's secrets had made everything worse: he could have built something useful, instead of the poorly conceived contraptions awkwardly strapped to people unsure of how to use them.

The *Colossus*'s commander looked down at Noah and scowled. "Is this the one that caused all the trouble?"

Captain Moor shot Noah an apologetic look. "This is my passenger, Noah."

"*Passenger*. Well, when we reach Liberty, he will find himself a prisoner once more."

Noah doubted he would like the answer he was bound to receive, but still he asked, "May I stay on the *Abbreviated*?"

"May you? I wouldn't let you on my ship if this one was sinking." The commander laughed cruelly, and a couple of his soldiers joined in. Then, turning back to Captain Moor, he added, "Make sure that doesn't happen. I'd hate to have to explain to the governor why his nephew is at the bottom of the ocean."

The *Colossus*'s commander chuckled all the way to the small craft that would take him back to his ship.

Once he was gone, the soldiers took up positions around the *Abbreviated*. One stood menacingly by the pilothouse, two disappeared below deck, and the remainder walked the deck, keeping a wary eye on the now-captive crew. Captain Moor and the others watched for a moment before he gave some orders to Mister Steem. The first mate nodded, then departed to carry them out. The ship had to be prepared for its return to Liberty. The damage to her side needed to be seen to, and the crew needed to keep its focus. Mister Steem would make it so.

Moor then turned to Winona and smiled. "You made me proud. Kept our passenger alive, and yourself as well. Remind me to promote you."

"Yessir," she answered. There was a flush of color in her cheeks, but she kept her chin up as she smiled back at the captain.

"Our young hero," Moor said, focusing his attention on Noah. "You may be from Liberty, but you live neck-deep in trouble, don't you?"

Noah gaped at the man, unsure how to respond, but when he felt Winona's sharp elbow in his ribs, and then caught her smiling, he realized the captain was only teasing. "Yessir," he finally replied.

"I am glad of your return, young Noah. And I'm sorry for the danger you've weathered. I should have been more cautious." Moor looked ashamed. "You stick with Winona. She's kept you safe so far, so I'll weigh her down with that again. And now, you'd best get below deck."

"Yessir." Noah moved to exit the pilothouse when Winona grabbed his hand. She glanced at the captain, then widened her eyes to indicate Noah should do the same. The man regarded both of them, a small, sad smile on his lips. "I wish our voyage had been better run. I'm sorry for my part in dooming us. No sign of your father, then?"

Winona began to answer, but Noah cut her off. "My father isn't on the island."

Though confused, Winona said nothing. She tried to catch Noah's eye, but he kept his focus firmly on the ground. Still, he was thankful she stayed quiet.

Elijah's ticking sped up. "Doctor Physician has . . . gone."

Captain Moor focused on some point out the window, and Noah followed his gaze. The island of Singe sat low in the ocean, smoke curling above it. The towers of the ruined city weren't visible—not from so far away—and the beach was little more than a white line. The *Colossus* continued to fire volley after volley of shells, but it was impossible to see what they fired at, if anything. No octochines could be seen from this distance, if they were even still on the beach. "I don't know if the governor will think that a good thing or not," Moor finally said.

Noah had only met his uncle once, but he felt sure in saying, "Probably not."

"Why?" Winona asked.

Noah and Elijah exchanged a look. "My uncle wanted my father to . . . suffer. Now he won't have the satisfaction."

"I think you're right," said Moor with that same sad smile. "Your uncle likes everyone to know he's in charge, especially those who've 'wronged' him. My cabin." The captain pointed to the door. "Stay there until we reach Liberty. I'm afraid it won't take long."

They were silent as they entered the captain's quarters. Winona waited until the hatch was shut, then she grabbed Noah by his tattered shirt. "Why did you tell the captain you didn't find your father?"

Noah shrugged. "I don't know."

"You *don't know? Don't know!*" Winona sputtered. "The captain trusts me! Do you know what this could mean when he finds out? He expects me to tell him about what I see. You basically made me lie to him."

Noah didn't want to know what the lie could mean for Winona. He barely knew what it meant for himself. But he knew this much: Alton Physician had turned out not to be the monster that the city thought him, but neither was he the misunderstood genius nor the caring father Noah had hoped to find. He was a man more interested in himself and his own curiosity than he was in others and if what he did was dangerous. And Noah knew one other thing:

it had been *his* father. *His.* That brief visit was all he had of him, and now it was over, and everything was far worse than when he'd started.

Noah's exhaustion felt like someone had filled him with sand and rocks. The details of what he'd seen over the past four days swirled in his tired head, and right in that moment, Noah couldn't bear to think about any of it. He could barely stand. "It wasn't entirely a lie," he mumbled.

"It wasn't entirely a truth, either," said Elijah, sitting on the edge of a bunk in one corner of the cabin.

"Be quiet, Elijah."

The robot obeyed, turning to watch the dying light outside the window.

"You can't just pretend it didn't happen!" Winona crossed the small room, stopping just in front of Noah. "Elijah might have to do what you say, but I don't." Her cheeks were red, and she spoke through gritted teeth. "You lied, Noah. You lied, and I let you, but that's over now. When we get to Liberty, there are going to be questions, and I *will* answer them, even if you won't. It's your choice. Tell the truth, or I'll call you out in front of everyone."

"Why does it matter to you?" Noah asked, louder than he'd intended. "It's my father we're talking about!"

"Because it affects everyone!" Winona stomped to the hatch and took hold of the handle, but didn't open it. "Liberty," she said, her voice a hiss, "and the governor and your father. They're all as bad as the Homeland Empire."

"The Homeland Empire was much more aggressive than Liberty," Elijah interjected. "But Noah's uncle—"

"Be quiet, Elijah!" Noah and Winona shouted in unison

Once more, his caretaker stopped talking. In fact, it looked as though he might never move again.

"You're being unfair," Noah said. "My uncle wanted to protect the city, and in his own way my father *tried* to help. He wasn't very good at it, but—"

"The robots went berserk and killed people." Winona face was quivering with anger. "They destroyed families. In Liberty, and in other places, too. In the islands near here. They killed my parents."

Her voice cracked, and Noah stepped toward her without thinking. "I'm sorry."

"*Sorry* doesn't fix anything." She was silent for a long time. "Your father hid himself away, but the danger remained. He might be dead, and the machines went . . . crazy with panic. We have no idea what they might do now."

Noah squirmed, suddenly unsure where to put his arms.

"There might be a way," he finally said. "The robots don't attack if they're imprinted on someone. If I had time, I might be able to find a solution."

"No!" Winona looked directly at him, holding him with her glare. "No more waiting for solutions to come. No more pretending you and your family and your city don't affect the rest of us. We tell everyone everything when we get to Liberty. The people need to know the governor didn't fight off the robots. They need to know your father might have been in control of them, but he's gone. And they need to know now!"

Her fists were clenched. She looked away, and Noah felt hot tears building up in his own eyes. "Winona, I . . ."

She took a deep breath, then let go of the hatch. She'd been ready to leave, but now she simply looked tired. "I get it. There's so much happening, and it's hard to know what to do. But we've got to do what's best for *everyone*."

He nodded. "I will. I promise."

In addition to the bunk where Elijah was still sitting, there was a small sofa off to one side. As Noah lowered himself to the seat, exhaustion immediately wrapped around him. Winona collapsed onto the bunk. Noah, like Elijah, gazed out the porthole, watching the sky turn dark purple. The *Colossus* had stopped shelling the beach, and the engine's vibrations told him the *Abbreviated* had set course back to Liberty.

"I'm sorry," Noah said after a few minutes as the waves lapped against the ship's hull.

Winona's eyes were closed, but he could see she wasn't asleep. "I know."

"Why did you come after me? On the island?"

She opened her eyes slowly, focusing on the ceiling. "Because I realized if your father was on that island, you'd do anything to find him, and if I had even a one-in-a-million chance to find either of my parents alive, I'd do the same. And I knew you'd need the help. You may be annoying, Noah, but you're still a pretty okay kid."

"How interesting." Elijah leaned forward and studied Winona's face. "I knew he would need help as well when I jumped from the platform as the tower collapsed."

This made Noah smile, though he could see that Winona wasn't pleased with the comparison.

She rolled away and pulled a blanket over herself. "We should rest."

At first, the silence between them was tense and uncomfortable, but after a few minutes, Noah's weariness took over, and the silence simply became the sound of two very exhausted people drifting off to sleep.

⚙ CHAPTER 16 ⚙

Daylight was slanting steeply through the porthole when Noah awoke. The sun was bright in the sky, the ship quiet, its engine a low rumble as the ocean lapped against the sides. There was another sound, too. One that meant they were near land: gulls. They shrieked overhead, as if warning the *Abbreviated* away.

Noah sat up and listened for a moment. The return to Liberty had taken all night. If only it had taken longer.

Elijah was seated in a chair as Noah sat up on the sofa. Winona was still asleep, but she began to stir as Noah stood.

"We're going to dock soon," Elijah said. "I can see land. And buildings on the land. And behind the buildings are the hills, and a forest, lots of clouds—"

"Shut him up," Winona grumbled. She wouldn't look at Elijah, and barely glanced at Noah.

Noah watched the dark strip of land turn into harsh lines rising above the water: the buildings and streets of Liberty; the soot-black factory; the house on the hill rising like a frozen tornado, its jumble of rooms no different from the dozen toppling towers on Singe.

He kept his eyes locked on the buildings on the horizon and watched the little details grow into an angry city. Inside his chest was a hard, jagged feeling as he remembered how the tower on the island had tumbled down.

There was a knock at the door, and then Mister Steem ducked low into the room. He smiled, but it was hesitant. "Begging your pardon, young comrades. We're coming into Free Harbor, and Liberty awaits. Captain asks for your presence on deck."

The *Abbreviated* pulled into the slip, which had been vacated by the *Colossus*. The warship was anchored in the harbor, but at an angle, like a door that would close only after the smaller ship had passed. Noah and Winona made their way to the bow, Elijah following patiently behind them.

The day already felt uncomfortable and the smell of rotting fish and seaweed from the shore promised worse.

On the pier, twenty mechanized soldiers stood in a line behind Governor Stone. Noah felt as if he had never seen the city before. Like it was a stranger, filled with other strangers.

Winona stood silently at his side. Though he'd only known her a few days, she understood him better than any of the people related to him.

"I'm afraid," he whispered.

She shielded her eyes to shade her face and studied his. "Of what?"

"Of seeing my uncle. And Marie. I mean, my . . . mother."

Noah regretted the word as soon as it left his mouth. He recalled what Winona had said about her own family, killed by machines his father had built.

"You'll be okay," she said. "There are worse things to face."

Behind the soldiers, dozens, perhaps even a hundred citizens had gathered. More streamed down the main street, joining the crowd. It was still early, but word of the *Abbreviated*'s return had spread quickly. On the docks people pointed at him, while small children threw rocks at the ship before being chased off.

Behind the crowd sat the factory. A group of goggled workers milled about near the entrance, and from the darkness of the open doorway appeared a thin, black-draped figure: Marie. When she saw the ship, she ran toward the docks faster than Noah had ever seen her move. He took a deep breath. He wanted nothing more than for her to tell him it was time to go to home, and that everything would be safe and quiet, just as it had always been.

But she wouldn't be able to say that. He knew that not only had he gone out into the world, he'd brought the world back with him. Once, the house had been his entire world, but now it would be a small, empty prison. Now that he'd seen how vast the world really was beyond the house's walls, he wouldn't be able to forget.

His heart sank as two soldiers stepped out behind Marie. The factory was still running—the governor needed his army—but Marie was paying the price for Noah's escape. She might not be under arrest, but she was not exactly free, either.

As soon as the gangplank was lowered, more soldiers joined those already aboard. The crew clustered together on the main deck, arms raised. No one was saying they were arrested—everyone already knew.

Winona took hold of Noah's hand and pulled him to the center of the group, and he realized she was trying to hide him. Even now, facing her own detention, she was still concerned for him first.

Noah was suddenly, embarrassingly aware that he was blushing.

The crowd on the dock quieted as Governor Stone stepped forward and boarded the *Abbreviated*. Somehow, he looked taller than Noah remembered. The governor spread his arms wide as if to take hold of the entire crew, the ship, and the sea itself. He looked like the statue built in his likeness, only larger and darker and more imposing. "You should all be locked away in heavy chains until no one remembers your names," he boomed.

Captain Moor stood in front of his crew. Though his hands were raised above his head, like the others, he had that same small smile on his face. "Governor, sir, if you please. This was all a . . . misunderstanding."

Stone shook a fist at the captain. "You broke a prisoner out of jail!"

"He's a child, sir."

"And you colluded with a mechanical. You planned and collaborated with it against the security of Liberty."

Moor glanced over at the Elijah, who was ticking pleasantly. "Also a child?"

The crew laughed. There were even a few snickers from the crowd on the docks. Elijah looked around, curious to see what the joke might be.

The governor remained stone-faced. "You mock, but our beautiful city was nearly destroyed by *things* like this." He pointed an accusing finger at Elijah. "You have the audacity to mock our pain and our history."

Moor shrugged. "I've never been much of a fan of history, sir. There's far too much of it."

Governor Stone lurched forward, and for a moment, Noah thought his uncle might strike the captain. Instead he pulled at his mustache and eyed the sailors. And then he became unexpectedly calm. There was a threat in his silence. It reminded Noah of the feral cats he'd watched stalking birds outside his windows through his telescope. "Bring me my nephew."

More than a few of the sailors repeated the word *nephew*, scanning the deck as if a stowaway might emerge at any moment. Noah felt Winona's eyes on him, and he glanced her way. She knew. What's more, she was afraid, and the fear he saw in her eyes was not for herself or the crew, but for him. He gave her a small, hopefully reassuring, nod, and then stepped forward.

Governor Stone held out a hand. "You thought you could join your father," he said, his voice surprisingly soft.

Noah felt the ship sway beneath him. "Yes."

"You thought to join him, maybe help him. But *I* got

you back. My *Colossus* has returned you, and now I will keep you from ever seeing your father again." Stone shook his head, and Noah was surprised to see that there was real sadness there. "I never wanted to have to lock you up. I wanted to trust you. But I will do what I must for Liberty."

"It doesn't matter," Noah said. "My father is gone."

For a long moment, Governor Stone's face appeared frozen. Then he blinked several times, as if blinded by the sun. "What?"

Noah tried to find Marie in the crowd, but all he could see was a sea of strangers. He turned back to the governor. "Alton Physician's contraptions caused a collapse. He was . . . lost in the wreckage." As the words left his mouth, he understood something his father had never grasped: actions have consequences. His father approached curiosity and scientific exploration as if the outcomes would be forever self-contained. He willfully ignored how those choices could change—or harm—the world around him, or even himself. And in the end, his own curiosity had destroyed him.

I could never do that.

Noah heard cheers from the crowd and saw some smiles. Inside, he felt empty and angry. He hoped those people never had to feel as he did. He hoped they would never dream of finding a missing part of themselves, only to discover it was a part that would never, ever fit.

Governor Stone squeezed his fist tight and shook it as if he were trying to crush something inside it and cursed the name of Alton Physician, directing his oaths to the sky. The crowd had gone quiet. Soldiers on deck stood as silent as statues, their masks staring stupidly at their governor. The crew of the *Abbreviated* huddled together even closer.

"You should have suffered, Alton! You should have rotted, old and alone!" Even some on the dock appeared shocked at the intensity of the governor's anger.

At last Stone composed himself. He looked tired and sad, but as he bent to speak directly to Noah, his voice still trembled with rage. "Did you know he laughed when I told him he'd be exiled to Singe? Ask your mother, boy. She was there. Your father looked up at that wretched volcano, and he *laughed*. 'Just me and my factory,' he said. 'Just as I always wanted.' And his monsters, I told him. No one would dare set foot on that island with those mechanical monsters running along its beaches. And still, he laughed! He laughed, and he didn't even bid goodbye to your mother. My poor sister, Marie."

Stone stopped speaking abruptly, dazed, looking around as if just awakening.

"I don't know if they're monsters."

"What?"

Noah coughed to clear his throat. "There may be a way to keep the robots from hurting anyone. I changed one. Maybe—"

Noah wasn't given the chance. Stone's laughter silenced him, and it was not a pleasant sound.

"You're as misguided your father, boy. You went to find him—to *help* him—and now that he's gone, you suddenly imagine you have all the answers. No," the governor said, slowly shaking his head. "You have aided an enemy of Liberty, and that won't be forgotten."

"Nicholas! Please." Noah and Stone turned to see Marie, who had climbed the gangplank and now stood at the edge of the deck. Governor Stone's face softened for a moment before tightening into a fierce scowl. It was as if he wanted to be angry, and was looking for a target.

"Alton may have escaped his punishment, but his crimes remain. Those monsters walk the earth, and you fools endanger *all my efforts*. I won't have you go back and try to *fix* them. It cannot be done. I would know. I chased them off once.

"You!" he continued, directing his ire at the crew of the *Abbreviated*. "You have broken a prisoner out of jail and given aid to Liberty's enemies. You're under arrest."

"Hold on." Captain Moor held up a hand. "You can't hold my crew for my choices."

"I can, and I will! Take them away!"

Governor Stone's fury has risen to levels that scare even his own men, Noah thought. The governor looked ready to grab the nearest officer, and several actually seemed to pull away. He regained his composure enough to place a shaking hand on the shoulder of a nervous guard.

"Lock them up. And seize their ship," Stone ordered, his voice rumbling like thunder.

Everything seemed to happen at once. Soldiers shoved the sailors toward the gangplank, but the crew pushed back, and someone threw a punch, striking a soldier square in the nose. Shouting and screaming filled the air. And in the chaos, Winona grabbed Noah's hand again and tried to pull him toward the gangplank.

On the docks, citizens started to shout, throwing vegetables and then rocks at the ship, soldiers, and crew. A soldier kicked at the back of Winona's legs, knocking her to her knees, and she lost hold of Noah's hand. Another soldier grabbed her, dragging her back.

"Leave her alone!" Noah shouted. The soldiers ignored him.

There was a clatter of breaking glass, and Noah saw Pilot dragged across the deck by his collar and hair.

Noah stood beside the pilothouse in the middle of all the chaos, unsure what to do, until a figure approached him and called his name. He looked up into the face of Marie; she had been crying, and although her eyes were now dry, her hands shook.

"He was there," said Noah, his voice sounding small, even to him. "And he didn't want to help. He didn't want to help Liberty. He didn't want . . . me."

Marie, without a word, dropped to her knees and wrapped him in a hug. Noah couldn't remember the last time he'd hugged his mother, but now, folded in her arms, he felt warm and tired. All he wanted was to go home—his real home, the drafty old house that grew at night—and sleep for a week.

"I'm sorry I ran away." His voice, muffled by her embrace, was still hard to make out over the screaming and scuffling around them.

Marie put one hand on his shoulder, and wiped sweat from her face with the other. Usually she seemed weighed down with her thoughts, but she looked at him now with relief. She'd worried about him, Noah realized. Even missed him. And there was something else. Something in her eye, a sidelong glance that hinted at something more.

"I owe you a thousand apologies." She said this quietly so that only Noah could hear. Around them, Stone roared orders, the crew taunted soldiers, and the crowd continued its shouting. "I should have fought my brother harder. You didn't deserve to be a prisoner—his, or mine. I'm sorry, Noah." Marie squeezed him hard. "In spite of everything I knew, I still hoped you might find what you were seeking. I hoped your father had changed." She took a deep breath, then released Noah and stood. "We need to get you far from here. It's not safe." Suddenly, she seemed back to her old, no-nonsense self. She waved for Noah to follow her, and they made their way through the grunting throng of struggling sailors and soldiers. They dodged punches and curses, and swayed with the ship that seemed to reel from the fighting. As Marie reached the gangplank and was now in clear view, the crowd began to boo and scream insults at her.

"It's them!" someone yelled. "It's the mad doctor's family! They're bringing the machines back!"

The crowd continued to jeer as Marie and Noah made their way down the gangplank, but Marie refused to shrink from them. She stared back at the people blocking the way until they moved aside, and though the grumbling and shouting continued around them, the pair was able to move through the crowd without harm.

And then the mob went silent. Noah turned to see four soldiers carrying a long wooden plank. Elijah had been lashed atop it with ropes winding from neck to ankle, like a cocoon. Several strands ran across his face and into his mouth so that he could neither turn his head nor move his jaw, though the visible cogs and gears left no doubt what he was. Noah realized they had never seen a mechanical creation like him unless it was striking out at them. Yet, here was what they feared most right in front of them.

The crowd continued watching in silent awe as the soldiers lifted Elijah over their heads, trying to keep their balance as they descended from the ship. Governor Stone followed close behind, and then came Captain Moor, Mister Steem, and the rest of the crew of the *Abbreviated*, all now under military escort.

At the head of the gangplank, Governor Stone stopped and raised his hand in the air. Noah could make out the statue of him in the distance, modeled in nearly the same stance, and wondered if the statue had been built to mimic the man, or if the man now mimicked the statue.

"Citizens." The governor's voice was deep and booming. "Citizens of Liberty. We've known danger before, but

never has it seemed so close or so familiar. As you can see, we have captured the most recent threat to our fair city. This *contraption . . . this insidious machine . . .* kidnapped one of our own—a child. But now the child is returned." The governor pointed at Noah, who tried to shrink back, but not before the crowd turned to ogle him. He felt a hand on his shoulder and knew Marie was right there.

"But the threat has not passed," the governor continued. "We know what it looks like now. We will recognize it." Elijah's eyes followed the governor as he paused to pace the gangplank. The robot caretaker's face was impassive as ever, but in the silence, Noah could hear his ticking speed up, doubling its pace when Elijah's eyes found him in the crowd.

"He looks just like the mad doctor!" shouted an old woman standing near the front of the crowd, one bony finger pointed up at the immobile Elijah. "He looks just like him!"

"He does!" someone else agreed. "The mad doctor's sent a spy to Liberty!"

"He's not!" Noah cried. "He's my—"

Marie pressed a hand across his mouth. "Say nothing," she whispered urgently. "Your uncle may be a fanatic, but he is doing one thing right. He's keeping you out of it."

Noah took in the mob and saw everyone nodding. He heard more murmurs that Elijah looked just like the doctor, but they seemed to have forgotten about Marie and him. Still, one thing continued to trouble him.

"Who do they mean?" he asked. *Shouldn't they mean me?*

Marie frowned, then leaned close, and whispered, "Your father. Elijah looks like your father did as a child."

Noah couldn't help feeling a touch of jealousy. Elijah really was the one closest to his father. And yet, how could he feel envy at the very moment that the similarity was cause for the hatred being directed toward Elijah?

"The people want someone to blame," Marie murmured, "so let them blame him."

Noah swallowed hard and focused back on Elijah. The robot's eyes were fixed on Noah. The grumbling of the crowd had grown louder, and Noah could no longer hear Elijah's ticking.

"Friends," Governor Stone boomed. "No one knows better than I how you have suffered." He walked through the mob until he stood in front of Noah and Marie. And though he didn't so much as glance at them, Noah sensed that his uncle was giving them cover. Marie must have come to the same conclusion, because she began to back away pulling Noah with her. Gently, she guided him toward the factory doors where workers still milled, their grimy goggles and filthy coveralls making them seem a part of the sooty building.

"No one remembers better than I how you, dear people of Liberty, rose up to defend yourselves," the governor continued. "The Homeland Empire couldn't hold you in its grasp. The robot revolt couldn't knock you down. And this . . . pitiful . . . attempt to send a spy into our midst only demonstrates our readiness."

For a split second, the governor looked over at Marie. Noah saw something in their brief exchange, as if they'd had a secret conversation. For all his uncle's ferocious bluster, he still put one thing first: a sense of duty to his sister. His family.

"Nothing will stop us from continuing our preparations, my friends!" the governor bellowed. "No one will flee. No one will shirk their duty."

Cheers and applause erupted from the crowd as they surged around their leader.

And suddenly Noah understood. Governor Stone was twisting the truth, using some of it—what was useful—while discarding the rest, all to keep the people of Liberty on the path he had chosen for them. Marie knew this—had always known this. And now Noah knew, too.

It's just as Winona described. Secrets and lies to hide responsibility.

"I am moved daily by you, my friends," Stone called as he reached out to shake hands with those closest to him. There were smiles now, anger turning to renewed commitment and pride as Noah's uncle rallied the city to his side with lies. The boy might even have been impressed if he didn't know those lies came at the price of Elijah's freedom, and that of his new friends, the *Abbreviated*'s crew. Especially Winona.

"I am moved, my friends," the governor repeated. "Moved to action. Moved to prepare. Moved to fight. And nothing . . ."

His words trailed off there, one hand still firmly clutching a dockworker's. Governor Stone was a tall man, standing a full head above most of those around him. And like the statue honoring him, Stone looked out over Free Harbor. But the man did not look courageous and devoted. Shock, confusion, even fear had settled over his features.

Noah and the others on the docks followed the governor's gaze to the mist hanging above the wharf. At first, no one was sure what they saw. Spray off the water caught the sun, making a rainbow mist too thick to see through clearly.

But through the glow something was coming into focus.

Dark egg shapes rose from the water. When the first alarm horn called out, Noah almost didn't recognize it, but then others replied, harmonizing.

As the first screams broke from the crowd, Marie turned, glad to find Forewoman Issa standing at the factory door. "The governor will need his army," she said. "The robots have come home."

CHAPTER 17

The horn blasts rose in volume, drowning out the screams of the people fleeing the docks. Marie shouted orders at the factory workers, but it was nearly impossible for those seeing the robots not to panic. Men and women ran in every direction, and the sounds of tools crashing and glass breaking echoed from every corner of the factory. Forewoman Issa pushed Noah ahead of her as they tried to keep up with Marie.

"Where are we going?" Noah asked, but his words were lost in the chaos.

They raced to the back of the factory. If this had been the one on the island, it would have been toward the volcano. Instead, Noah took in a large turbine connected to two enormous boilers. Heat radiated from the twin tanks, and blue flames licked from gaps in the metal frames beneath them. Four filthy workers were shoveling coal into gaping furnaces. The air was thick and hard to breathe. The turbine was nearly as tall as the ceiling, and Noah could feel static in the air, but he was surprised by how quiet the machine was, emitting only a high-pitched whine.

His eyes traveled from the boilers and turbine, along the cables that ran across the floor and up the walls, separating into smaller lines that connected to the rows of workstations. This was the source of electricity for the factory. This was why its lights burned brighter than the entire city.

But not all the cables ran up. One, thick as a tree trunk, had been laid through a great hole in the floor.

Nearby, Marie stood at a control panel. The number of dials and switches was beyond guessing.

"You have your own electricity," Noah marveled as Marie threw switches. She was like a musician before her instrument.

"Your father had his genius. I have mine."

Noah felt the floor vibrate. "What is that?"

"Your mother's genius at work," Issa said. "And the reason I want to learn everything she can teach me." The forewoman pulled Noah toward a wall that, upon closer inspection, actually turned out to be filthy black windows. She rubbed soot from the glass, then pointed outside. "Watch the warehouse doors."

Noah could barely see through the grimy glass. To the right, he spied wide warehouse doors in the lower foundation of the building and a section of the wharf that stretched to meet them. The wooden path wound around to the front of the building. Beyond the narrow strip was a view of the rocks that littered the shore.

"What's in the warehouse?" Noah asked.

"What I've been making this entire time," Marie shouted. "My brother's army."

She threw a switch, and there was a shower of blue sparks.

Noah could still hear the horns and screams, but they sounded far away. A new sound drowned the others out. An alarm. A repeated clanging bell coming from atop the factory.

Then came the beat of marching feet. The pounding was in his ears and in the floor. It was coming from the building, itself.

Row after row of figures marched from the warehouse beneath the factory. The sound of their footsteps rattled the windows, and through the filthy, distorted, old glass, they looked like shadows.

Noah counted ten, twenty, thirty, and more—ten in each row—row after row passing through the wide doors. Women and men in mechanized armor. Their cast-iron faces, warped in the window glass, looked more like masks of sorrow than courage. They moved quickly, with purpose. More and more soldiers rushed toward the building to climb into their own armored suits, but nothing would come of this march except mourning.

Forewoman Issa turned to Marie. "The machines. Why are they back? Why now?"

"Alton is gone," Marie answered, and Noah thought he saw a touch of sadness in her face. "He was like a lure to his creations. At the height of their uprising, they attacked anyone but him. With him gone, they must be searching for him, or reverting to old programming."

Noah thought Marie's explanation sounded mostly right, but something about it bothered him. He'd watched his father's end. He expected the machines to have searched the wreckage, perhaps finding his father's remains, or if not that, that they would have been consumed by their search of Singe, hoping to find their "father" again. So, why *had* they come back to Liberty?

"This won't work," Noah said.

Issa looked at him strangely. "What?"

"The octochines are so large, and so . . . scared." He'd meant to say *angry*, but realized only after the word popped out that *scared* seemed much more accurate.

Marie chewed at her lip. "I'd forgotten their size. They

are . . ." She gave Issa a nervous glance, and tried to smile at Noah. "With luck, it will be enough."

Noah shook his head, watching the waves of mechanized soldiers. "It's not just their size. The machines attack because they don't understand. They need to be calmed."

Issa thew up her hands. "You're talking about them like they're children."

"Alton always called them that," Marie mused. "He had some kind of influence over them. Without him . . ." She trailed off, then gently turned Noah to face her. "Tell me, how did they behave on the island? Did they stay away from you?"

"No. The opposite. The octochines always chased after us, unless my father was there. Except, I wasn't bothered by—"

Then it hit him. The answer to what had been nagging him. He shuddered, and Marie took hold of his shoulders. "What's wrong?"

"I know why they're back." His voice was a whisper. "It's me."

Seven.

Quickly, he explained how Seven had imprinted on him, how his father had compared it to a child imprinting on a parent, and that Seven had been calm, even happy, to be around him.

"But it didn't make Seven safe around Winona," he explained. "Seven still went after her. It's like they can only learn to trust one person at a time."

"I still don't understand what this has to do with them coming back to the city," Issa said.

"Me." Noah took a deep, shuddering breath. "They came back because of me. Seven was on the beach. It saw me leaving the island. And since it couldn't find my father, it followed me. And the others must have followed Seven." Noah could hear more screams outside, and his voice trembled. "I did this."

"No," Marie said fiercely. "You didn't do this, Noah. Your father did." She focused on her departing army. "We did."

The last of the soldiers had exited building, and now the sounds of battle rang out. There were occasional shouts and screams, but mostly crashing and the octochines' sirens filled the air.

Issa covered her ears. "Those monsters sure put up quite a racket."

"Not always." Noah scratched his head. "When they're calm, they almost sound like they're talking." Issa gave him a skeptical look. "No, really! If only there were some way to send them a message. . . . Something to let them know they shouldn't be afraid."

"Oh my." A smile stretched across Marie's face, and she leaned down to kiss Noah's cheek. "There just might be."

The three of them clanked their way down a flight of metal steps into a subbasement below the factory. Noah, pressed between Marie and Issa, felt lost in the dark until Marie stopped and opened another door. There was a vast empty space ahead, and a rectangle of light at the far end. It took Noah a moment to recognize they were in the now-empty warehouse where the mechanized soldier armor had been kept. Shelves with large wooden boxes and spare parts lined the walls. Marie crossed to one of the crates and scanned the printing on the side. "This one," she said. "Issa, help me open it."

Forewoman Issa found a hammer, and together, she and Noah's mother pried open the lid, splintering the unpainted wood. Outside, the horns blasted, and Noah heard the governor shouting orders at his mechanical army. "Line up!" he bellowed. "Line the wharf!"

"Noah! Over here." Marie and Issa had the crate open. Inside was a mechanical man. A robot with Elijah's face, but . . . not. This face was older. Marie was tugging at its coveralls, opening the panel in its chest. Issa stood beside her watching, confusion etched across her face.

"What are we doing?"

Marie grunted as she tried to lift the mechanical man. "Perhaps we can adjust the clockworks in this contraption to send the message we need."

"And what message is that?" Issa asked.

Marie closed her eyes. "Calm down? You're safe?"

"How about just 'Follow me,'" Issa suggested. "And then we send them back to that stupid island."

Marie laughed as she searched through her tools. "That might also work. It doesn't hurt that this thing looks like their maker."

And with that, Noah finally saw what he'd been grasping at: the mechanical man lying in the crate looked like Alton Physician. The metal face had been cast to look just like the father he'd met on Singe, but it was younger, and without scars or dirt or lens contraptions masking its eyes. There were no additional fingers or enhanced robotic legs. This machine simply resembled a young man with hopeful eyes.

As Noah considered the face, he felt a flash of anger. This was the face of a man oblivious to everyone around him, who'd pushed away his own family, even his own son. This was the face of a man who, in his arrogance, had nearly destroyed a city. His father, the genius. His father, the destroyer. His father, with his horrible curiosity about *what would happen*. Noah's anger grew, as if Alton Physician had been responsible for locking him away from the world—which, in a sense he had.

Above them, the building shook and octochine horns blasted out angry stutters. Dust and grit showered down from the rafters, and Noah coughed as he rubbed dirt from his eyes.

Focused on her task, Marie removed an inner panel from the machine man. As he watched her work, Noah was suddenly overcome with guilt. Alton Physician was his father, but it was Marie who had raised him. It had been Marie who stayed behind, who had worked to build the city's true defenses. Who Noah had always called by her first name, instead of what she was: *his mother.*

Marie—his mother—now had the robot's chest open. Gears as small as fingernails locked together. Springs coiled and uncoiled. Axles and hinges and counterweights, all in their places, clean, unused, and still. This contraption had never run, but that wasn't the problem. Noah could understand every piece of the machinery. Looking at it, he understood how each collection of gears would drive a part of the whole. It was complex, sophisticated, but too simple. It lacked the mystery of what had been in even some of his simplest contraptions. It lacked the interior complexity of the octochine. It lacked the soul of Elijah.

"This won't work," he said.

Marie's hand froze. "It has to." She resumed her work, but slower.

Noah wanted to explain, but didn't know how. He couldn't explain any more than he could explain how he knew that the octochines were special or what made Elijah different from this collection of clockworks. He'd worked on the interior of his friend, and he'd seen the intricacy of Elijah's inner workings. This robot lacked all that. He could see that this machine was built to do what it was told, but it needed to be able to communicate with other machines that had been built to do what they wanted.

"It won't know what to say or how to say it," Noah finally said. With enough time, Noah knew he could eventually build what they needed from the parts lying before him, but there was no time.

More screams sounded from the factory above, drowned out by a horn blast, and an explosion sent debris crashing all around them.

"The octochines are inside the factory." Issa groaned.

Heavy steps thudded above them, sending the lights flickering. Marie grunted as she dropped the pliers she'd been using to try to get inside the mechanical man's chest. Noah snatched them up. "My hands are smaller. Let me."

He worked the tool, finding the wires Marie had been trying to connect. Gears fell into place quickly, but Noah knew it still wasn't right.

His mother watched him work, agreeing with every choice he made. "Good," she said. "That's it." She smiled at him, and he felt a strange mix of excitement and dread. Her praise made his heart swell, but he knew it was going to be for nothing. Though he hoped he was wrong, he knew he wasn't.

Overhead, a series of crashes shook the ceiling, and the screaming abruptly stopped. An octochine's horn blasted, and then what sounded like a dozen pairs of feet ran toward the noise.

Marie closed the panel and pulled at the arm of the robot. "Help me get it out of the crate." She and Issa pulled the figure up to a sitting position, and then Marie took the pliers back and inserted them in the robot's ear. She twisted, and the soft clicking of a clock tick-tocked to life. The mechanical man looked at each of them in turn. Its eyes were black and lifeless, and Noah's heart sank.

"Get out of the crate," Marie said.

The machine pushed from the wooden box, then stood before her, waiting.

Issa pulled at its head and looked into the visible machinery at the side of its neck. "It seems to hear us."

The governor's voice came from a distance, magnified by loudspeakers. He was giving short commands, most of which sounded contradictory. "Line up at the dock," he demanded, and moments later, "Surround the jail," then, "Run to the marketplace."

The robotic man before them continued to stand and just stare blankly ahead. "I once envisioned these as the machines that would help us build and defend Liberty, Noah," Marie explained "But your uncle didn't find them *impressive*. And your father, well, he had . . . other plans. I was ordered to halt production. To destroy them all." She gestured at the rows of shelves behind them. Stack upon stack of crates. "But I'd invested too much time to just throw them into the sea."

Noah wondered why she had made them look like his father. *Because she loved him. She loved and respected him, even as he failed the city.* Then he remembered: Elijah also resembled Alton Physician, but younger. Which meant Marie must have built Elijah, too. Which meant . . .

My father only modified Elijah. Alton had helped Marie build the caretaker robot's inner mechanisms, and while doing so, he'd hidden his secret message, ensuring that

Elijah would have what the octochines had: a will, a self.

Noah reached into his pocket and felt the golden gear he'd hidden there. The one piece that hadn't fit when he'd repaired Elijah now made sense. This was Elijah's rebellion from Marie, planted by Alton. Noah played it between his fingers. It had been added to impose Alton's control over Marie's. Now that it was removed, Noah had completed what neither his father nor his mother had achieved. Marie had made Elijah a problem solver, but always under her control. Alton Physician had given Elijah a way to override that control, a way to make independent choices. Noah had given Elijah a willingness to do what neither of his parents had envisioned. Elijah was willing to sacrifice himself to help. He had the ability to think of others first.

Elijah helps us because he wants to.

Alton had locked that ability behind secret commands, but once the extra gear was removed, he was free. That was what made him different.

As Marie walked toward the open doorway, chunks of plaster fell from the ceiling. The sounds of glass breaking had been replaced by the snapping of wood and falling bricks. Marie covered her mouth, trying not to breathe in the dust. "Robot," she called, "come with me."

The mechanical man immediately moved toward her, ignoring the bits of the ceiling falling around it. "Greetings, madam. How can I help?" the robot said flatly. There was no curiosity there, only gears that guided behavior.

Marie leaned in, and nearly shouted into the ear of the robot. "You have to calm the attacking machines. Tell them we're not going to hurt them. Then you will lead them back to the Singe."

The mechanical man looked at Marie, its lifeless eyes locked on hers. It was neither confused nor certain. It simply was.

It was worse than Noah feared. *We could have just as well changed the gears in a clock.*

A grinding sound came from the robot, and it shuddered. It opened its mouth as if to say something, but all that came was a high-pitched whine. Marie took a step back as the sound turned into a stuttering click, like a word was stuck in the robot's throat, and then into a solid crunch. There was a rattle of gears, and then silence.

"I think Noah was right," Issa said.

The robot looked around the room, as if for the first time. "Greetings, madam. How can I help?"

A huge thud from upstairs shook the warehouse, followed by what sounded like anvils being thrown against the walls. They all coughed as the air filled with more smoke and dust.

"Robot! Do you understand?" said Marie, her voice cracking. She shook the robot's arm. "Tell the octochines to stop attacking!"

The robot opened its mouth to respond, but before it could say anything the ceiling collapsed. A raging octochine fell through the hole, a dozen tiny figures clinging desperately to its legs and head. It thrashed about on its back, its legs taking out more of the ceiling. Wooden beams and planks rained down. Noah coughed, struggling to breathe through the new cloud of dust. Someone was shouting, but he couldn't make out the words. Then Issa was in front of him, shaking him.

"We have to go!" the forewoman called into his ringing ears, before trying to pull him after her.

"Where's Marie?" Noah yelled back, refusing to budge. "Where's my mother?"

"She wants you safe! That's all she's ever wanted, and she'll kill me if I let something happen to you!" The forewoman focused on the stairs, and then back on the octochine tearing itself from the rubble. Shelves and crates, which had neatly lined the wall, had been caught up in the collapse. She pointed toward the jumble. "We can hide under there!"

She led him toward the wall, making a cautious circle around the octochine, which continued blasting its horn and thrashing. As they drew nearer, Noah could see the octochine hadn't been fighting off factory workers. The figures that had fallen with it were soldiers in Marie's mechanized suits, and more of them were now leaping down from above, their faces unmoving masks of sadness, but their bravery unmistakable. The governor's army swarmed the mechanical monster, forcing their way toward the spots where its gears were visible. They hammered their fists against its metal plates and kicked at its eye, pulled the panels off its head, and as they exposed the inner workings of the gears and cables, they attacked the insides. A terrible grinding rose up as they forced debris—bricks and metal and grit—into the octochine's gears, jamming and fracturing them. The machine's loud horn blast faded to choking. All its legs pushed against the floor as it tried to stand, but as it did, even more mechanical-armored fighters jumped down to force it into submission. The octochine was now covered with soldiers, and when its horn blasted for the final time, a high-pitched squeal, Noah thought it sounded like the creature was in pain. There was a metallic whine, a snapping sound, and then the octochine moved no more.

The soldiers examined the machine a moment, then rushed through the open doorway, eager to return to the fight.

"Help us!" Issa shouted. One of the soldiers turned, studying them for a moment. The metal mask looked sad. The person beneath it said nothing. Then the soldier joined the others rushing back to battle.

Noah and Issa crawled along the wall, around debris, toward the wide doorway and the spot where Marie had been standing. They had just cleared a large section of collapsed ceiling, when Issa put out a hand to hold Noah back. "I see her! Wait here a moment."

But Noah couldn't wait. He scrambled after the forewoman, then froze. Marie was partially trapped beneath metal beams and wreckage.

"Mother!" he shouted.

Marie's head was bleeding, and her legs were pinned beneath rubble. They were all closer to the giant robotic octopus than was probably safe, but Noah had no sense of his surroundings. He saw only Marie. He tried to lift the beam pinned across her legs, but it wouldn't budge. Issa joined him, but even with both of them working together, they couldn't shift the metal.

"Mother!" Noah shouted again, his throat hoarse.

Marie's eyes fluttered open, and she moaned. "Noah? What happened?"

"Be still, Marie," said Issa. "We have to get you free."

Noah looked around frantically for help, but they were alone in the devastated subbasement. There was only the fallen octochine, and all around them, shattered cases. The ceiling's collapse had crushed the crates, and the mechanical men inside had tumbled out. Dozens of figures with his father's face lay amid the rubble, still and stunned-looking.

Noah understood what needed to be done.

He found the pliers still in Marie's hand. Even in her groggy state, her grip was tight. When he tried to take the tool, she hesitated before releasing it. "I'll fix this," he promised, giving her hand a gentle squeeze. She relaxed.

He went quickly to the nearest mechanical man and searched for the switch he'd seen Marie use to activate the first. He found it in the robot's ear, and with a twist of the pliers, it started to tick. Then he moved to the next robot lying in the rubble. After that one, there was another, and another. Noah didn't pause to examine any of them, to see the face he both knew and didn't know at all. He activated them, one at a time, until he could find no more.

Only then did he look up.

Several dozen robot men now stood stiffly in the sub-basement. In one eerie motion, they all regarded Noah with their lifeless black eyes. Then slowly they began to gather around him. The robots all resembled his father, but they also did not. *They'll listen.* They all resembled Elijah, but they also did not. *They don't have his heart.*

"Now," commanded Noah, "help her." He pointed at Marie, still pinned under the debris, grimacing in pain. Issa held her hand, watching the robots uneasily. As one, the mechanical men turned their lifeless eyes to Marie, then back to the boy addressing them.

"Help her!" repeated Noah, louder. This time, the robots obeyed.

Marie was trapped by a massive beam. There was plenty of room along either side, and each mechanical man worked to find a handhold. They didn't work together, but still they mimicked one another. As each lifted, and others joined, there was first a snap, and then a shudder, and finally the beam was in the air.

Issa and Noah rushed to pull Marie out from beneath the metal and stone. She cried out in pain, and Issa held her hand murmuring words of reassurance. Meanwhile, their task complete, the robots dropped the beam back to the floor with a heavy thud, then returned their attention to Noah. They had no desire, he saw, other than to do what they were told.

"Go fight the octochines," Noah ordered them. "Stop them however you can. Use whatever you have to."

This time, the robots didn't hesitate. They walked briskly to the door, and out into the light. He watched, glad to see them go.

Noah, Marie, and Issa were once again alone. The sound of someone crying drifted down from the factory. The horn blasts sounded more distant.

The attack had moved deeper into the city.

Marie was still clearly in pain, and Noah looked around for anything that might help his mother. Then, in a dark corner, he spotted a glimmer, light glancing off metal. Somehow, one of the mechanical men had stayed behind.

"Come here," Noah said. At first there was no response. "Come here!" he repeated, angrily.

The robot stepped slowly from the shadows. As it came closer, Noah realized this was the one his mother had tried to reprogram to speak to the octochines. Part of its expressionless face had been damaged, revealing the metal skeleton beneath, and as it limped forward, Noah could hear the sound of gears grinding.

Marie tried to stand, but she slipped back to the floor.

Her head was bleeding. "We have to send it out in front of the robots," she said. "We have to see if it can calm the octochines."

Noah shook his head. "If it was going to work, it would have already."

"You can't be so sure," protested Issa.

But Noah was. He couldn't explain to the others how he had seen the robots on Singe change whenever they were near his father. And he couldn't explain how instantly Seven had responded to him.

"We need to leave," he said instead. "We have to get to safety. Robot, pick her up."

"No, Robot," said Marie as the mechanical man approached her. "Go to the governor. Calm the attack. Lead the robots back to the island."

The robot had bent down to pick up Marie, but now it stopped. Awkwardly, gears grinding noisily, it stood and turned to the door.

"No," Noah insisted. "Stay here."

"Go!" said Marie firmly.

The robot stood caught between them, looking from one to the other as it tried to process the correct command. It was simple and unthinking. There was nothing in it that would ever be able to calm the octochines.

"Don't you see? It's not even as smart as they are," he finally said. "It can't do anything for them."

Before Marie or Issa could respond, there was a terrifying crunch, and a spray of metal erupted into the air behind him. Shards and springs rained down around them, and the horn of the fallen octochine blasted out triumphantly. Its gears had evidently managed to grind the broken metal and rocks, spitting them out, and its legs suddenly swept out over the floor at its enemies.

Issa leaped at Noah, knocking him to the ground, and the robot's leg passed over both of them harmlessly. But the robotic Alton wasn't so lucky. Caught by the heavy iron of the octochine's leg, it was swept into the air. Its gears and springs clattered and crashed to the floor as the powerful octochine tore the metal man in half.

The octochine tried to push itself up again, but its legs slipped across the floor, and it slammed back, letting out one short blast of its horn, followed by a loud grinding, and then a toll like a bell as something inside snapped. The giant machine struggled; its legs twitched, then it was still.

Noah carefully crawled to his mother's side. In the attack, Marie had been showered by the gears and inner workings of the destroyed robot, but thankfully, she seemed no more harmed than before. She wiped oil from her face and let out a sound that seemed halfway between a sigh and a sob. "That's it. There's nothing to do now."

Nearby, the upper half of the robot was somehow still functional. It kept trying to stand, but as it had no legs, it could only push itself upright. Its face showed the same expressionless acceptance as before.

"It was never going to work," said Noah softly.

"Still, it was our only chance. Now . . ." Marie's eyes fluttered, and she laid her head back on the floor.

As Noah watched, his mother gave up her last hope. He had wanted so badly to find his father, to see the brilliance of his work, to fill the gnawing need in his heart. Instead, he'd brought back something terrible. He'd hurt people.

He sniffed. "This is my fault."

"No." Issa looked from Marie back to the boy. "She was right about you."

"Right about what?"

"As brilliant as your father, she always said. But without his arrogance."

Noah didn't believe her, but he also didn't have the energy to argue.

Outside, there was a mighty rumble—perhaps the sound of a building collapsing. The floor shook, and above them, the rafters groaned.

"Your father did this" Issa insisted. "Not you. He made these monsters. Not you."

"But I brought them back here."

"You don't know that."

The sirens roared again outside.

"I do."

Noah watched the half robot pull itself toward the door on its hands. Even nearly destroyed, it was still trying to follow the last command it had received: Marie had told it to go stop the robot invasion. It would keep trying until it was utterly broken. *Just like the robots from the island.* They would continue to attack, trying to remake the city into something perfect and empty. They'd continue to panic at the sight of people. Unless they could be destroyed . . . or convinced that they were safe.

"Seven!" shouted Noah.

Issa looked at him blankly. "*Seven* what?"

"I need some tools." Noah quickly explained about his encounter with the injured octochine, and how the machine had imprinted on him. "If I find Seven, maybe I can make it talk to the others. Maybe it can be our messenger."

Issa nodded, then stood, picking her way through the rubble back to the workbench. Noah stayed beside Marie, holding her hand. "I'll make this right," he said.

Issa returned with a set of tools. She held them out to him, but her face was grim. "How on earth are you going to get close enough to one of those machines to work on it?"

"I'll get help. Stay here with Ma—my mother." Then, Noah jumped to his feet and ran toward the exit.

Issa laughed. "And where are you going to find *help*?"

Noah grinned back at her over his shoulder. "The jail."

⚙ CHAPTER 18 ⚙

Noah ran through the battlefield that was the city of Liberty. Most of the army lay injured across the wharf. Their impassive, mournful faces emitted the moans of the wounded soldiers inside. Some didn't move. Scores of destroyed robots, both octochines and Marie's army, lay broken. A few still struggled to crawl across the docks.

In the distance Noah could see an octochine staggering across the wharf, half a dozen of Marie's recently released robot men clinging to its back, kicking and hitting—anything to slow its progress. Its deep horn blasted as it tried to get its bearings, despite its shattered eye.

Fires had broken out across the wharf, and several ships were burning, sinking below the water in clouds of steam and smoke. Noah could see the *Colossus* sitting listlessly in the harbor, its guns silent. To fire on the attacking machines, he realized, would mean firing into Liberty. He was relieved to see the oddly shaped *Abbreviated*, somehow still in one piece, moored at the dock, as undamaged as Noah had ever known it. Without anyone aboard, the octochines must have had no interest it.

Noah was surprised how quiet his surroundings had become. The shouts and screaming now came from up the hill, deeper in the city. Noah could see flames flickering there as well. The sky to the east was growing dark, and the sky to the west was blotted out by black smoke. Everything seemed made of shadow.

Noah raced toward the wide-open arms of Governor Stone. The massive statue stood in the dark smoke and fading light, staring, as ever, toward the ocean. Behind it, the city it was meant to protect, burned.

The doorway to the jail stood open. Inside, the space was dim, and strange voices echoed in the halls. Noah felt his way toward the cellblock, his fingers shaking against the cold stone wall. He found the metal door, then turned the lock with a loud *click*. The whispered voices abruptly stopped. He turned the lock again and the door clanked open.

The cellblock was lit with a single lantern on the floor. Inside the cell Noah had once occupied, he spied Elijah, still tied to the plank of wood. In the other cell, crammed in like feathers in a pillow, were Captain Moor and the crew of the *Abbreviated*.

"Look, friends! It's Young Noah!" called out Mister Steem, waving his wooden arm.

Gentleman Nest nodded at the boy, quietly humming a tune, while Pilot cleaned something from beneath his nails with a stick and then examined it. Winona waved, flashing Noah a small smile. She seemed happy to see him—which was a relief, since he felt the same way.

Mister Steem smiled down at him. "Tell me you're here to rescue us."

"I am. But I also need your help."

Captain Moor tapped the bars between them, as if counting them one by one, and said, "Son, I think you have that backward."

"I'll get you out of here, and then . . ." Noah's voice trailed off. Even to him, *We need to capture one of the giant machines that's destroying the city and reprogram it* sounded crazy.

After a few moments, Captain Moor asked, "What do you need, Young Noah?"

Noah swallowed. "I'll get you out of here . . ."

"And then?"

"I'll need your help in . . . making something."

"You're leaving out the parts that are scary!" Mister Steem said. "We are used to being scared, Young Noah. Tell us."

Noah swallowed again. He had to spit out his plan or he'd choke on it. "I'll change one of the octochines. Get it to imprint on me. And then . . ." He suspected they wouldn't like this part. "Then we'll lure the robots back to Singe."

The crew took it rather well: they simply blinked at Noah as if he'd just spoken in a language they couldn't understand.

Winona was the one who broke the silence with a low whistle. "And how do we do that?" she asked.

Before Noah could reply, Lady Byrne said, "How do we do it? More like, how is this our problem?" A chorus of other crew members grumbled in agreement.

Captain Moor quieted everyone with a look. "You all may recall Noah saved our Winona. Fact is, they've traded saving each other back and forth, but I'm still inclined to say we owe him. *I* owe him." He gave Noah a hard look. "How he plans to do this task is his affair. But at least we will all be getting to the ship and can make a quick exit if things go crooked."

"And until that happens," Mister Steem added, "no complaints." He leveled a stern eye at Lady Byrne.

She stared straight back, quiet but not ashamed.

Noah focused his attention on Winona. She was shaking her head, but still smiled at him. Suddenly, his plan didn't sound quite so impossible.

"All right," said Moor. "We'll help. But first, you'll have to get us out of here."

Noah surveyed the room. There were no keys to be seen. "I'll check in the hall," he said, but when he turned toward the door, he froze.

Standing in the doorway was his uncle, Governor Stone.

The man seemed even taller than before. His black coat was now covered in dust. A small trickle of blood ran from a cut above his eye, making him look ready to crack open. He glowered, taking in each smuggler, and then Noah. When he took a breath, it was with a deep rattling wheeze. He coughed and spat blood onto the stones.

"I've tried to do one thing," he said, his voice hoarse. "Just one thing: protect this city." He stepped forward, his head knocking into the dark light bulb hanging from the ceiling. The light flickered on as he hit it and started it swinging. His shadow lurched from wall to wall, shrinking then shooting up. "Everything I've done has been for

Liberty. It needed protection. The citizens demanded a strong leader. . . . I had to be—I *was* strong. I was *right*. I was a hero. *I was everything they needed.*"

He stepped forward again, and Noah noticed that he was limping. The light swung behind him, and his face was lost in darkness.

"He's gone mad," said Pilot.

Noah was inclined to agree. He backed away from his uncle, and as he did, he noticed the man was clutching something in his hand. Something long and thin and glittering silver.

The governor kept his eyes fixed on a point somewhere above Noah. "But I can't do it anymore. It's too much."

"Mister Governor, sir," said Captain Moor. "Perhaps you and I could—"

"Silence." Stone moved quickly for such a big man, and he was suddenly looming over Noah. He seized his nephew's arm with one great hand. In the other was that thin silver line.

Is it a blade? Noah wondered. He looked up, terrified, into the bloodied face of his uncle. *He knows. He knows Seven followed me here. He knows I brought the robots back.*

"Tell me, Noah," rumbled Stone. "I heard your plan. Do you *truly* believe you can change the machines?

Even just one? Be honest with me. *I will know if you lie.*"

Mister Steem reached through the bars, though he couldn't reach the man. "Let him go, sir."

Stone gripped Noah harder, ignoring the smugglers. "*Can you?*"

Noah nodded. "Yes. I think so." *If we can find Seven. And if we can trap him. And if I can complete the work. And if . . . if . . .*

The governor's hold slipped. "Then your plan is the best one we have to save the city." He held up the glittering silver object and pointed it at the cell door. It was the key. "You lot will have to help him. There are no soldiers to spare. They're fighting or hurt or . . ." He fell silent.

Governor Stone wasted no time unlocking the cell, and the smugglers quickly slipped through the opening. Off to the side, Captain Moor conferred with Noah's uncle, while Mister Steem and the others searched the jail for weapons. Outside, the roving searchlight of an octochine passed over the windows, while sirens wailed in the distance, with an occasional response from close by. The call was far too close for Noah's comfort.

He took the key from his uncle, and entered Elijah's cell. Bending over his old friend, he managed to loosen the ropes over Elijah's mouth.

"You should have left the city," Elijah scolded. "The octochines are dangerous when they get . . . excited." His ticking was fast and uneven.

"I can't." Noah's hands shook as he tried to loosen the other knots. There were so many. "This is my fault," he whispered.

Elijah's ticking grew louder. "I don't understand how you arrived at that conclusion."

Noah's hands froze. He looked around to make sure no one was listening. "The octochines followed me back, Elijah. It's my fault."

Winona pushed into the cell, and focused her attention on a particularly tricky knot. Noah watched her work and quietly whispered, "Thank you. I know you don't . . . like him."

Winona pulled a tangle of ropes away and Elijah began to move freely. "Don't remind me, kid." Her reassuring wink was exactly what he needed at that moment.

Elijah looked from Noah to Winona, and his ticking slowed. "Sir, you think you brought them here, and so this is your fault. But I am the one who took you to Singe, so it is my fault. I am to blame."

Winona smirked. "That's one way of looking at it."

"No," Noah insisted. "You only did that because you were programmed to. You had no choice."

"This is true," said Elijah. "So it is the fault of my programmer. It is Doctor Physician's fault."

Noah gaped at Elijah. "It can't be that simple," he finally said.

"Why not?" Elijah, now free, shook away the last ropes and stood.

The smugglers and governor were busy looking out windows, shouting suggestions, and complaining about the lack of useful weapons in the jail.

"Why not?" Elijah asked again. "I followed the chain of events from you to your father. Alton Physician built the attacking robots. He programmed me to take you to him. He refused to help us change the robots. He is to blame. It is his fault, so therefore he should be the one to save Liberty."

Noah didn't have an answer, but Winona did: "I have a feeling that Noah thinks he's the one to save Liberty."

"Saving people is right," Elijah agreed. "I wonder if the octochines know that. Has anyone told them?"

Captain Moor suddenly hissed and everyone quieted. "One of those machines is outside."

The thudding of octochine footsteps had become so familiar, Noah hadn't even noticed the noise. Now he felt how constant and close it really was.

Elijah leaned in to whisper, but said at his normal volume, "I have to get you to safety."

Noah cringed. "That's the plan."

"Shhh!" Winona hissed.

"We can make a run for it," Mister Steem said quietly. "Get to the *Abbreviated*. She might run."

Governor Stone nodded. "My soldiers didn't touch her, but I'll have to get a signal to the *Colossus* so she doesn't blow you from the water if you do reach her."

"That would be helpful." Captain Moor chuckled. "First things first. Let's all be clear on what we're doing. Step one—"

Before he could continue, a long metal leg crashed through a nearby window and hooked the edge of the rock. Everyone watched as the stones cracked, and then the wall collapsed, leaving a jagged hole. Through the opening pushed the giant eggish body of the robot, its eye beaming light into the cell and onto their group. Its horn blasted, and they all scrambled for cover.

"Sir." Elijah grabbed Noah's arm. "Come with me. It is not safe here."

"No, you come with me!" He pulled Elijah toward the exit. Half the crew was already through the door and had stumbled to the lower floor of the jail. The robot stabbed at the bars with two of its legs as its face filled the widening hole.

"Go!" shouted the governor. "Find the octochine you can use and fix this mess!"

Gentleman Nest joined the governor, and together they lifted broken stones from the cell floor, hurling them at the robot's eye. The octochine's siren screamed back in reply.

Before Noah could wonder how his uncle and the sailors would get out, a large hand clamped over his shoulder and yanked him out the door. "Come with me, lad." Mister Steem pulled Noah, who pulled Elijah after him, down the dark stairs. At the jail entrance, Winona waited with Pilot.

"Byrne's already flown to the ship." Pilot had looked ancient when Noah had seen him behind the *Abbreviated's* wheel. He looked still older now. "A few of the others went with her."

Mister Steem nodded. "Good. They'll know to make her ready in case we need to flee. You join them."

"Aye," said Pilot.

Mister Steem looked down at Noah. "Now, about your lovely plan. What do you need?"

Noah described Seven to Steem. "I need to be alone

with it. No one else can be around. Seven will lash out if anyone but me is nearby."

Steem rubbed at his head with his one large hand. "And you say this robot is like the others, but with seven legs instead of eight."

"Yes."

"And it has a kind of funny walk," added Winona. "Like a limp."

Steem grimaced and looked back to the ship. "Well then, I think we may end up just fleeing, I'm sorry to say."

"What! Why?" Noah cried.

"Well, there's good news, and then there's bad news," Steem said carefully. "The good news is I know where that machine of yours is."

"What's the bad news?" Winona asked.

Steem sighed. "That's the robot attacking the jail."

From behind them came a tremendous crash, followed by shouting.

Elijah tapped Noah on the shoulder. "Yes, that is bad news. Good news and more good news would have been better. I would prefer to keep you safe. I think we should flee."

Noah took a breath. "No," he said. "We need to try."

Elijah's ticking sped up faster and faster. From the sound of his gears he was nearly in a panic.

Mister Steem wasn't ticking, but he, too, was thinking

through their situation. "Well, we have the beast right here. You need it alone?"

"Yes," said Noah.

Mister Steem shook his head. "I wish we'd thought of that earlier. We could have left you to do the work there."

"Not with a building falling on him," Winona said, and Steem shrugged.

"Then you all get to the ship," he said. "Follow Pilot and Winona. Wait there. I'll try to lure that thing down to the dock. When you see it following me, you come running."

Noah shook his head at the man. "But you could be killed!"

"I'll lure it down and jump into the water as soon as you arrive. It's the only way. These people need our help."

Elijah's ticking grew even faster. "These people need to be helped."

Noah nodded, but he couldn't believe the risk Mister Steem was taking. He saw the fear in the man's eyes. He wasn't from Liberty, and he'd only just met Noah, yet he was willing to do this dangerous thing simply because it was the right thing to do.

"Okay," Noah said after a moment. "I'll wait aboard the ship for you to lure it away."

Winona jumped forward and gave Mister Steem a hug. "Don't get . . ." She couldn't finish her sentence, and Noah couldn't blame her. Saying *killed* seemed to make it more likely somehow.

Pilot and Winona both ran. Noah took Elijah's hand again, and followed. His robot caretaker's ticking had reached what seemed an impossible speed, and the mechanical boy appeared almost frozen. Noah hoped nothing was mechanically wrong. He couldn't take another loss, especially not Elijah.

As they rounded the fallen statue, Noah looked back at the jail. Mister Steem had been right. The robot smashing at the side of the building (and now more than half-way inside) was Seven. Its missing leg and staggered gait were obvious. Noah wished the robot would respond to his orders now, but he knew it wouldn't—not with the others there. *It needs to feel safe. It needs to be alone with me, and only me, and then I can fix this.*

Seven strained to push all the way into the jail. The hole it had created was wide and high, big enough for its head to fit through, along with three of its legs, but it was off-balance.

On the ground, just out of range of the writhing legs of the machine, stood the brave Mister Steem. Hitting one of the legs with a metal bar again and again, he hollered, "Down here! I'll take you apart, monster!"

Noah was sure this was a mistake, but he was doubly

sure when he heard Elijah say, "He ought not do that." Noah tore his eyes from the scene for a moment. "It isn't safe," Elijah added helpfully, before staggering. His ticking had become a constant hum.

Mister Steem continued to strike out at Seven's leg. At last, the lopsided octochine pulled itself away from the building, directing its eye back on the first mate. The beam of light narrowed to focus on the giant of a man, who looked so small compared to the massive robot.

"Come on," called Winona. "He'll be okay. He knows what he's doing." But from the way her voice cracked, Noah wasn't sure she believed that.

Noah, Elijah, and Winona ran the rest of the way to the ship, trying not to look back. When they reached the *Abbreviated*, they found it dark and silent. The lights remained unlit. The engine wasn't running. The only smoke near the smokestack had been blown there from the city's fires.

"What in blazes?" said Winona.

A whistled melody tweeted above them. "Power's a little spotty," Gentleman Nest called down. "Watch yer step. We nearly fell in."

Winona led the way, and Noah and Elijah made their way up the gangplank together.

On deck, inky figures drifted in the darkness. The city

was transforming into a kind of gross beauty as fires sprang up and searchlights swept across the skies, the octochines' horns and sirens echoing off the cliffs. Far above it all sat what looked like an oddly shaped star. Noah narrowed his eyes, trying to figure out the strange glow, and it took him a moment to recognize the house—his home—its haphazard rooms caught in the lights of fast-moving octopus machines.

Noah and Elijah were ushered to a spot along the rail, where they could see octochines approaching the harbor. The jail was nothing but rubble, and Seven was chasing sailors directly toward the *Abbreviated*. Captain Moor and Mister Steem led the pack, and sailors were already climbing the gangplank.

"Ahoy!" Captain Moor called from the dock. "Steem's injured!"

Noah and the sailors rushed to help. Below them, Moor was supporting Mister Steem who held his good arm wrapped across his body. There was blood everywhere.

"Get him aboard!" Moor yelled. "Winona, loose the ropes!"

She was running back across the deck. "Already done!"

"Pilot, get us away!"

Pilot's bell rang out in reply.

"No!" Noah shouted. "We can't leave!" He turned to

Elijah for help, but the robot boy only gazed back at him, his clockworks inside still running at incredible speed.

Mister Steem and Captain Moor fell to the deck. Steem groaned as his mates tried to roll him over.

"That metal monster swiped him," Moor explained as he helped his crew turn the big man over, so his injured arm could be seen.

"Oh heaven," said Lady Byrne. "The bone's been shattered."

Captain Moor was shaking. "Do what you can." For an instant, the captain caught Noah's eye, but then he quickly looked away as if he'd chosen not to see the boy. Instead, Moor grabbed hold of the nearest railing and forced himself to his feet. "Pilot! Let's go!"

The bell rang again, followed by a groan, and then the deck shuddering. The crankshaft was turning. The propellers were engaged. Slowly, the ship pulled away from the dock.

"Thank the deep waters," muttered Captain Moor.

"No, we can't go!" Noah shouted again. "The city can still be saved!"

Captain Moor scrambled forward to take hold of Noah's hands. "I wish it could, lad. I truly do. But look around you. We must go!"

Suddenly, the entire ship shook, sending everyone stumbling across the deck. From the water, a long metal tentacle shot straight up and splashed water across the bow. It fell toward them like a tree, crashing down and wrapping itself over the ship. A horn blast rang through the air, and then the ship tilted. The crew clutched to anything they could reach as the *Abbreviated* listed wildly toward the dock. An octochine head rose from the water into view, and two more legs reached out to smash at the pilothouse and the bow. Railings collapsed and glass shattered, though in the dark, it was impossible to see if Pilot had been inside or not.

Noah saw the glimmer reflected in the eye of the octochine. It was shiny and still looked new. This was Seven. Seven was tearing the ship apart.

The robot blasted its horn again. The captain looked toward Noah and though he couldn't see his eyes, the boy was sure the captain was telling him, *Your plan won't work.*

"Abandon ship!" shouted Moor.

Sailors started to jump from the deck. Moor pulled at Mister Steem, and even with Winona's help, dragging the giant man appeared a struggle. Captain Moor shouted something to Noah, but the boy couldn't hear it over the chaos on deck and Seven's deafening siren.

And then a hand took hold of Noah's and squeezed.

Noah turned as his caretaker leaned in close. The maddening ticking stopped—only for an instant—before resuming at a slower, steadier pace.

"The people need to be helped," Elijah said. "You need to be saved."

Noah nodded. The world around him went silent. All except for Elijah's voice.

"The octochines don't know this. They don't know people should be helped. They need to be told."

Noah listened to the ticking of his caretaker. Of his friend. Suddenly, he knew what was coming, but he didn't want to hear it.

"I can tell them. But they cannot hear me."

Noah's throat felt tight, and his eyes burned. He looked around the deck. Captain Moor was shouting orders as he attempted to lift Steem into the boat. Winona was trying to help him, but she looked small and terrified. Out past the rail, running down the dock alongside the ship, Governor Stone had a rock in each hand. He screamed as he hurled them at Seven. He would never save the *Abbreviated* alone, but he was still trying.

"Mister Noah."

Noah refused to look at Elijah, though he knew what

his friend meant. His father's designs followed a direct line from goal to completion. The robots were designed to build and protect a city, but they lacked any care or concern for the citizens of that city. They rolled over people because his father had rolled over the people. But Elijah had been built from Marie's designs, and she had built him to see the whole of the world around him. She'd designed Elijah not to simply complete a goal, but to understand why it was worth completing.

"I need you to help me tell them," Elijah continued. "You can make it so they hear me."

"But if I do that, you'll have to go with them." Noah's throat felt even tighter.

"I will." Elijah looked around. "It's a shame I have to go. I think the city is rather nice to look at."

There was a rumble as another building near the docks collapsed, and a series of horns blasted as if the octochines were celebrating.

"I don't want you to go."

"Neither do I, but things must be made better. You're very good at making things better than they are, sir. Do that now."

Noah looked at the gears spinning at the back of his friend's head. Without meaning to, he started planning for what changes would be needed to allow Elijah to calm the octochines. He hated himself for knowing how to change his friend into a lure. "Elijah, I don't want to be alone."

"But you have Marie." The little robot patted Noah's shoulder. "Marie is your mother."

"I know." Noah looked at Elijah sadly. "She's yours, too."

Elijah opened his jacket and shirt, and then he unhinged the panel on the front of his chest. Inside were the gears and springs, the whirling cogs and tumblers, and from it all, came a deafening *tick-tick-tick*.

"I'm going to miss you, Elijah."

Elijah's ticking slowed to a crawl. "And I will always be thinking about you, little brother."

Noah found the gears he needed. A few things would need to be moved, some parts placed in different places to create the song that would be the lure. The octochines and spideratuses spoke in honks and horns; Elijah would speak to them in a siren call made by the gears inside him. As his gears ran, a constant song would call out—a song of Elijah's choosing. No human would hear it. They didn't need to. Elijah would speak to robots, and Noah knew better than anyone what the caretaker would say: *You'll be safe. You are safe. Stay with me.*

Elijah pointed at the gears in his own chest. "Our father helped make these." He pointed out at the octochine. "And he made these. They will be safe. I will be safe."

"I hope so," Noah said. There were small switches and springs in every part of Elijah, and he had to disconnect many to rearrange the parts. He was breaking to rebuild, and he wouldn't let himself think about what might happen if this plan didn't work, or if he destroyed Elijah in the process.

At last, the small wheels inside the robot boy's chest began to turn. Noah could feel them humming. For a moment, he could almost hear the song Elijah had inside him. He paused, then pushed the panel in Elijah's chest shut. His fingers hurt and were bleeding. He'd had no choice but to remove the gears and springs with his bare hands. Inside, Elijah was a new design—Noah's design. And now Elijah would be able to do what neither his father nor mother nor uncle could: soothe the terrible machines and keep the city safe.

The ship tilted and shook. Sirens wailed as something hammered at the hull, and the sailors screamed.

Elijah looked at Noah. "I should go now?"

Noah took a gasping breath. "Yes. But first, let them know they don't need to be afraid."

"Yes." Elijah looked at the city and said, "I will tell them."

A symphony of sirens erupted right behind Noah. He didn't turn to look, but could feel the ship tilt toward the sound. It was obvious that several octochine had gripped the boat and were pulling it toward them. Another moment and it would capsize. Another moment and he'd be back in the ocean along with the entire crew, the ship turning over on top of them.

And then the sirens stopped.

The ship righted itself, gently rocking back and forth. The hammering stopped. After a few moments, the sailors stopped screaming.

Except for the churning of engine and the lapping of the ocean, all was quiet.

"I think it's safe now," said Elijah. "I should go now?"

"Yes," said Noah. "I think you should."

✺ CHAPTER 19 ✺

The wind had changed. It blew from inland, pulling the burning city's smoke out over the water like a blanket. The cliff tops could no longer be seen in the haze, and the hilltop was gone. The impossible house that had grown larger at night was hidden by smoke.

The *Abbreviated*'s crew stood on deck, leaning against the rails, watching the robots wander down the main avenue, leaving the city.

Octochines moved in unwavering paths toward the ship. The factory had been knocked to the ground. Noah took a deep breath and tried not to think about where Marie might be. *She has to be safe*, he thought. She was with Issa and that half robot in the basement. *The collapse can't have hurt them*. He didn't know what he would do if it had.

Noah found the captain standing beside the gangplank,

staring into Seven's eye, which was nearly at deck level. The octochine looked blankly back at the captain.

Noah touched the man's shoulder. "Captain?"

Moor glanced back. His jaw was tight as he ground his teeth. "This thing nearly killed Steem. Now it just . . . stands here?"

"It's waiting."

"Waiting for what?"

"To go home," said Elijah.

Moor took in Noah and Elijah, then peered up into the smoke drifting from shore. In that moment, it didn't look like smoke—just a black curtain with no stars.

"You did this?"

Noah nodded.

"We take your caretaker and you to the island?" Moor said.

"Yes."

"And then leave it there?"

Noah had to take a breath before he answered. "Yes."

"And we never go back. We leave it and them there to rot."

Not to rot, Noah thought. *Please, no.* "Yes."

Moor nodded, then waved at what was left of the pilot-house, making a motion with his hand, like stirring a pot.

Though the wheelhouse was now without roof or windows, Pilot sat there with the wind in his hair and a smile on his face. A moment later, the ship started pulling away from the dock, the vibrations from the engine a little uncertain, but its speed steady.

The crew barely exchanged words as they went about their work. Mister Steem had been carried below by two crewmen, while Winona had taken over coordinating the various activities that needed to be done. She was at least ten years younger than most of the other sailors, and some were old enough to be her parents, yet they all nodded when she spoke and did as she asked.

When the captain was ready to disappear below to check on his first mate, he approached Winona. Taking her elbow, he rattled off a long string of commands, and as he turned away, Noah heard him say, "You're in charge, Lady Winona."

Winona said, "Aye," and gave a salute the captain didn't see. When she turned back to her duties, she saw Noah and Elijah watching her and flashed them a small smile, but it was not an invitation to talk. She was working. *She* was in charge. She turned away, calling commands to the sailors, and they fell to their tasks with more than focus.

Noah and Elijah walked to the stern of the ship as the

Abbreviated made a slow clockwise circle. Behind them, the city still glowed with fires, though fewer than before. And between the blaze and the ship lumbered dozens of robotic octochines. Lit from behind, they looked like a mass of legs beneath bobbing black blotches, all detail lost. Behind them, the air wavered from the heat.

It seemed impossible there were so many. And they were all so quiet. No more sirens, no bleating horns. Only the sounds of gears and footfalls on the dock, and then the sloshing of water. Noah spied the one with the tree growing from its head in the distance. And nearby staggered Seven, splashing in the water.

The machines were no longer afraid. They had chased a ship from the island and attacked Liberty, all because they had nothing to assure them they were safe. But now they had Elijah. The calm of the octochines at the docks spread out across the city to each of the machines.

Noah watched it all, and as he did, a sad realization surfaced: his father had had the solution the entire time, and he'd chosen instead to see what might happen.

Noah took a deep, shaky breath, then blew it out. His father had started this. His mother's son had been then one to end it.

The *Abbreviated* waited in the harbor. The crew joined

Noah and Elijah at the rail, watching the tide of robots pull itself to the ocean. Noah looked back to the wheelhouse. The captain stood beside Pilot, both men gazing out at the city. Noah hadn't told him to make sure the robots all heard the call, but somehow the captain knew. He'd waited. He would give them time to gather before he had Pilot begin their journey. There was no danger now. Elijah was calling them home.

In the water beside them sat the black iron hump of Seven. It waited. It watched. There was no emotion on its face. There never had been. There never could be.

When they began to move at last, the crew stayed silent for a time. They stood there until the light from the burning city was far enough away and the waters deep enough that the robots following were unseen. Then, one by one, they returned to chores and then from chores to cabins to sleep. The last to go was Winona. She came to Noah's side with a lantern and a blanket. Just one, for Noah. Elijah wasn't cold. He never was. The gears spinning at the back of his head caught the lantern light. His ticking was steady and slow.

"You did good, kid." She wrapped the blanket around Noah's shoulders, and for just a small second, she hugged him. "So did you, Mister Elijah." She reached out to pat the robot's iron face. In the night air and with the mist from the ocean, Elijah's face was wet with condensation. It streamed down his cheeks. He looked at Winona with the only expression he had.

"My Noah did all the work." He touched his own chest, now hidden beneath his shirt and jacket, and it looked to Noah as if his oldest friend was heartbroken.

Winona grinned. "Yeah, he's a real hero. But he never would have made it without me." She slapped playfully at his shoulder. "Stupid kid."

"Bossy," Noah replied with the best smile he could muster.

She left, and then Noah and Elijah were alone. Noah raised the lantern to see Elijah's face in the dark. His eyes were locked on Noah's, his face as calm as ever.

"What will you do?" asked Noah.

Elijah tilted his head and ticked for a moment. "I'll keep them safe," he said.

Noah nodded. The city would be safe now. He thought how he'd need to convince the people of that. What could he say to his mother or uncle so they'd believe it was so? Nothing, probably. They would always look at the ocean and wonder what walked across its rocky bottom.

Noah noticed that Elijah's focus was no longer on him,

but the ocean. And somehow, the robot's face looked different. Determined? Focused? But how? Elijah's expression couldn't change. But something else about him had.

Keep them safe, Elijah had said. But he hadn't meant the people of the city.

"You mean the robots."

Elijah nodded. "I know so much more than I did before."

"What do you know?"

Elijah looked back at Noah. "They were so . . . scared."

Marie's design of Elijah was genius. The caretaker would care for his father's machines. He would be the voice of understanding they needed. Elijah was sending a signal to the robots. Noah realized only now, the robots were sending one back.

"Our father really was a genius," Elijah said.

Noah didn't know how to respond. So many had been hurt and killed because of that "genius." His father was not only a genius—he was what he did. So was his mother.

So was he.

"So is our mother," Elijah continued. He put a hand on his own chest and looked down into the water.

Noah pulled the blanket around himself and settled back against the railing. He watched his former caretaker. This was what his mother had intended and what his father never imagined, he realized. The evolution his father had looked for wasn't in his machines alone. It was in Elijah. And it was in Noah's hands. And in Marie's words. Being near Alton Physician had calmed the robots nearby, but only just. He had known what they were made of, but he hadn't heard them. He had never even tried.

Noah looked at Elijah, and Elijah looked out at the dark water. There was nothing to be seen there. The city was far behind them. The smoke had cleared, and above them were a thousand stars, but in the ship's wake, there was only the sounds of an ocean.

Nothing I can see, Noah thought to himself. Perhaps Elijah could see what he couldn't.

They reached the island a little after dawn. Clouds shifted from behind the volcano, looking like arms reaching out to hug the ocean. Noah watched the landscape, but in his head all he saw was the city and the fires and the collapsed factory. He worried about his mother.

The sailors kept their distance. When Captain Moor came on deck, he walked to the back of the stern, looking exhausted and filthy with ash and oil. Noah thought he must have been working with the engineers to repair the engine through the night. The hole in the side of the ship was leaking seawater into the engine room, and it was a battle to keep the engine from flooding.

Moor approached with his hat in his hands. "We're here," he said, almost apologetic. Noah looked past him toward the island. It was still a good distance away. "I won't take my ship any closer. It's deep enough here that those things can't reach us."

Elijah stood. "They won't touch your ship, Captain."

"No, they won't," Moor replied. "I won't give them the chance. We'll send you off in the dinghy." Without another word, he turned and walked away.

"Let's go," Noah said after a moment. He and Elijah walked to the crewmen who were lowering the dinghy into the water.

Nest and Byrne were already inside, whistling something to themselves as they looked out over the ocean. The clouds made the light gray and pale.

"All aboard," called Winona, offering Noah a hand to help him onto the rope ladder. He hesitated.

His heart was beating too fast in his chest. "I can't go back." He felt as though he was abandoning Elijah. And farther inland was the place his father had crashed into the forest. Even after everything his father had done, he felt the ache of that loss. He wanted to know the man was safe, and he knew he never would. "I can't go."

Winona simply nodded. "I understand."

Noah wondered if this was why she lived aboard a ship. Had she left her pain behind when her parents had died? Was sailing on the ocean her way of staying ahead of the sadness?

Elijah didn't appear to care. His expression was the calm and focused one he had gained since becoming the lure. *Not the lure*, Noah thought. *Something more. The guide.*

"Be careful," Noah said, stepping aside. "The island can be dangerous."

"We will be fine," said Elijah. "This is their home. And now it is mine."

The robot boy climbed onto the ladder without help. As he descended, Noah watched. Below his friend, he saw the dinghy, and below the dinghy, the gently swirling ocean. Just beneath the surface, countless black shapes moved back and forth. They were distorted by the water, but it was obvious they weren't fish. The octochines waited for their guide.

Noah looked again at the island. Its beaches were teeming with spideratuses. They had heard Elijah coming, and they had come to greet him. Crawling on and over one another, they waited.

Captain Moor shouted to the two sailors in the dinghy. "As soon as he can get out safely, you turn round. Stay clear of those things."

The oarmates readied themselves. Winona pushed them away from the side of the ship, and they were off. Noah waited for Elijah to look back—to search for him—but as he drifted away, the small caretaker's gaze never left the island. He stared straight ahead, kneeling at the front of the dinghy as Gentleman Nest began to sing:

> "I was the ship,
> And you were the anchor.
> I was adrift,
> And you held me to shore.
> But winds upon waves,
> They took me a-sailing,
> And now a home
> I have one no more."

As the dinghy moved farther, the singing became less clear.

"I'm sure he'll miss you, in his own way." The voice was deep, but weak, scratchy from exhaustion. Mister Steem stood behind Noah. His wooden arm was missing and his other was wrapped in bandages. A spot of blood soaked through. Noah tried not to stare, but he couldn't help but notice the arm looked odd. Too short. Mister Steem had lost his other hand. His face was pale, and he held his chin high, but his eyes were dark and full of sadness.

Noah didn't know what to say, so he replied, instead, to the man's comment about Elijah. "I don't know that he *can* miss me."

"He was your caretaker. For a long time. He'll think of you."

Noah didn't explain that that wasn't how machines worked. Elijah had changed. Noah had altered his purpose. He was no longer a caretaker. He was something else now.

Winona slipped next to Noah, and they stood at the railing watching the dinghy approach the shore. The tops of the octochines rose from the ocean behind it. Noah expected their terrible sirens to rise up, but there were none. With each step toward shore, the robots grew taller. A dozen of them. Two dozen. More. The dinghy reached the shore, and the giant robots surrounded it, their eyes focused on Elijah.

"Byrne and Nest need to get out of there," said Mister Steem uneasily.

Noah was less worried. "They'll be fine."

"Not with those beasts." Mister Steem pulled the bloody new stump close to his chest.

Noah watched Elijah climb from the boat and walk ashore. The robots looked down at the dinghy and the two small sailors inside. There was a small horn wail from one of the octochines. It rose up, higher pitched at the end, like a question mark. It was Seven, Noah realized. It was saying goodbye.

None of the octochines moved.

Elijah stood on the beach. He waved, then started toward the tree line. One by one, the octochines and spideratuses followed. The sounds of them crashing through the trees and the seagulls calling to them were the new sounds of the island.

Mister Steem continued to hold his arm tight to his chest, but breathed a sigh of relief when the last of the robots walked away from the dinghy.

"I'm sorry about your hand," Noah said.

Mister Steem tried to smile. "No need for you to be sorry. You didn't do this."

Noah wondered if that was true. "I . . ." He didn't know what to say.

"The one who did this is the monster who made those beasts."

My father, thought Noah. He'd tried so hard to bring back proof that his father was a misunderstood genius, and instead, he'd discovered that Alton Physician was closer to being the monster everyone thought him to be. His disappearance on the island had seemed like a sign of some great truth: if he were a villain, he would have exacted revenge on the city. And perhaps he had. Slow, plodding, and terrible. *Monster* was the word.

The dinghy was halfway back when the sound of Nest's singing reached the *Abbreviated*'s deck. It was the same tune as before, but Noah didn't care to hear how it ended. He left Mister Steem and Winona at the rail, and crossed to the stairs to escape below deck.

❈ CHAPTER 20 ❈

The *Abbreviated* returned to the city along with a storm that had started as a halo over Singe. The clouds caught up to the ship an hour after the island had disappeared below the horizon. It was an angry storm, one that seemed intent on tipping them. Pilot kept the ship pointed to the wind, but the waves were too much for Noah, and even some of the crew. He spent most of the journey half asleep, half sick, lying on a bunk in the captain's quarters. When Winona checked on him, she looked nearly as green as he felt.

The sun was rising as the *Abbreviated* limped into Liberty's harbor. The trip back was slow due to the foul weather and the damaged ship. Everyone was exhausted despite the extra time they'd had to rest. Captain Moor and Winona stood with Noah at the rail, and the captain let out a breath and smiled. "Thank the deep waters. Our engine is barely working, and the hole in our side leaks like my boots. We'll make it to the city, but this ship won't make it much farther." He looked down at Noah. "At least you'll be home."

Home. Noah knew an empty house waited to trap him inside, alone. Elijah was gone. His father had never been there. And his mother . . . He didn't want to think about what might have happened to her.

And then there was his uncle, the governor, who was likely furious at the destruction of his precious city. There was a possibility that Nicholas Stone was Noah's only living relative now. If so, Noah might fall under his care. What would that be like? he wondered. How terrible would it be? Would he be forced to work for Stone, like his mother had, in the factory, preparing for another attack? An attack Noah knew would never come.

Moor shook Noah by the shoulder. "Why so glum? You're home! And you've bled on the ship now," he said, eyeing the cuts on Noah's hands, cuts from working on Elijah. "That makes you one of us."

Though the captain looked ready to collapse, he held himself up against the rail. *He's holding on until we reach the harbor.*

"We don't have to return to Liberty," Noah said.

Captain Moor and Winona both glanced over at him, surprised.

"I mean, if you think we ought to go someplace else, then we should. We could keep going. I know my uncle wasn't . . . friendly to you before. We could go . . ." Noah didn't know where. *Anywhere*. "And I could be a part of . . . I could be one of . . ."

"A part of the crew?" Winona smiled at Noah, though she made certain to mask it before she turned her attention to the captain. "It would be nice to have him around, but I'm not sure we need a kid on board."

"Hey!" Noah protested.

"It's dangerous," she said. "I just don't want you to be . . . you know . . . scared."

Noah did know. "You don't need to worry about me."

She gave him a look that said she did.

Captain Moor put a hand on Noah's shoulder. "Lad, I meant it when I said you were a part of this crew. I'm not the only one to think so. But circumstances are against us. We float now, but even with your genius, my short ship is sinking. If the *Colossus* doesn't tow us to harbor, we'll be swimming there. And once we hit the shore, Governor Stone and the *Colossus's* cannons will call the shots. I'll count myself lucky if he doesn't sink us just so he can charge for the rescue."

Noah looked out over the water. If he didn't hold the rail tight, his hands would shake. "I understand."

Moor squeezed his shoulder. "Don't know that you do. If the leak were smaller, the repairs more permanent, the city farther away, the *Colossus* smaller. If we were in just a little less danger, I'd sail away to our next job, you'd be my engineer's assistant, and that would be that."

Noah blew out a shaky breath as he and Moor and Winona watched the *Colossus* approach.

Soon enough the sun was up, the lines secured, and the *Abbreviated* was safely towed into Freedom Harbor, practically dragging on the bottom by the time it was tied to a slip and secured to the dock.

Governor Stone stood on the docks beside the ship. A half dozen of his mechanized soldiers stood nearby. Behind them, workers wandered across the streets, slowly beginning the process of clearing wreckage. Somewhere beneath ruin lay their city.

The governor waved a hand, motioning the sailors to lower the plank. "Down!" he shouted. "Down, down now. Bring my nephew. Now. Now!"

Nephew, Noah thought. It was almost funny. He had

met the man only days earlier, the man who had been part of keeping him hidden away from the world, and now he called himself family. Noah prepared himself to be taken into custody again. The jail had been destroyed, but he was sure the soldiers had a place set aside for him with a strong lock and a heavy door.

Governor Stone was still shouting from the dock. "Noah!" he cried. "Bring him here!"

Captain Moor knelt before the boy. "You take as much time as you need." His face looked ready to crack around his eyes. "No one leaves ship without the captain's permission. And no one comes aboard, either."

Winona stood beside him. "I'm ready when you are," she said.

Noah was confused. "Where are you going?"

She grinned. "You think I'm going to let you walk down into all that noise by yourself? Captain put me in charge of you, and I'm not leaving your side until I know you're safe, kid."

Noah laughed and let out a sigh. Elijah may have been gone, but someone was still watching out for him. Still, it felt wrong somehow. As kind as it was that Winona wanted to help, Noah knew it couldn't be her job.

"It's all right," he said. "I'm ready. You stay here."

"You're sure?" Winona looked over the rail at the governor. "That man makes more noise than Seven ever did."

Noah nodded. "Yes, I'm sure."

They hugged goodbye. Noah had also only known Winona for a few days, but it now felt as if he was leaving another piece of himself behind. First Elijah, now Winona and Captain Moor. He spotted Mister Steem in the doorway to what was left of Pilot's wheelhouse. Pilot was behind the wheel, as ever. The crowd of faces on deck included Lady Byrne and Gentleman Nest. Noah tried not to focus on any of them. Leaving was already difficult enough without seeing each sailor watching. He had just reached the gangplank when Gentleman Nest started to sing:

> "'Hey, hey,' said the rock to the boat on the sea.
> 'I can float better than you.'
> 'I was there when the oceans were not.
> I do all you cannot do.'
>
> 'Ho, ho,' said the boat to the rock on the shore.
> 'If you try, I'll scoop up your bones.
> For you're hard, and you're dumb,
>   and stubborn as dirt.
> If you swim, you'll just sink like a Stone.'"

The sailors cheered at the last line, and Noah laughed. As he descended the plank, he decided he wouldn't let his uncle see how upset he was. He wiped his eyes and stepped onto the dock.

Before him stood his uncle, Governor Nicholas Stone.

And the man looked exhausted and broken.

Governor Stone fell to his knees before Noah, taking hold of his sleeve as if it were a rope that would save him from drowning. "Did it work?" he asked. "Please, did it work?"

Stone's eyes were bloodshot, with dark rings beneath. His hand shook against Noah's arm.

"Yes, they're back on Singe."

Stone mouthed the beginning of another question, but he couldn't make himself speak it. His voice cracked and his eyes darted to the side. Noah thought he knew what the man wanted to know.

"They won't be back."

His uncle's face broke into a smile. He laughed, but it sounded hollow. There was no true joy or emotion behind it. "Good," he croaked. "Good!" He wiped at his face and forced his shaking hand to his side. "Just as I thought," he said in the booming voice Noah had expected. It was the voice of the man from their first meeting, but it still cracked a bit.

He's barely holding himself together, Noah realized. How long had his uncle been this way? How long had he played at being the strong leader, all while falling apart inside?

"As I hoped, your contraption worked, and we are rid of the monstrous robots." Governor Stone smiled broadly, though Noah noticed his lips quivered, and waved a hand, making certain all the mechanized soldiers heard. "They won't come back? You're sure?"

"Yes," said Noah. He was suddenly aware that his mother wasn't on the docks. "Governor . . . uncle . . . my mother . . ."

The governor's eyes filled with tears, but his face broke into a smile. "How could I not have said so the moment you arrived?" His voice was cracking as he spoke in a hush. "She's injured, but waiting for you at home."

Noah felt the ground beneath him sway, and he took a deep breath. A hand steadied him from behind.

Captain Moor stood at the bottom of the plank and held Noah's shoulder. He gave the governor an odd look. "Mister Governor, sir. Your nephew is quite the hero. The robots followed us to Singe and stayed behind as if pleased to be home." Moor's smile was uneasy. He, too, had noticed the governor's strange behavior.

Governor Stone coughed and looked at the captain blearily. "What? Yes, yes, he . . . he's a hero, yes . . ." He took a shaky breath and leaned forward. "The Homeland Empire," he whispered harshly, clamping one giant hand on Captain Moor's shoulder. "Did you see any of the Homeland Empire's vessels on the horizon? This would be the time they would strike. When we are vulnerable. When we are . . . hurting. . . ."

Captain Moor and the governor both looked exhausted, but where Moor looked like he simply needed to rest, Noah's uncle looked ready to collapse.

"Sir, we saw no one. Not one ship was spotted and—"

"It's only a matter of time," the governor said. "We must prepare. They will know we are weak. Alton might even go to them. He—"

Captain Moor put up a hand. "The time to prepare will come. Right now, the city—you—need to rest and heal."

Governor Stone looked at the captain and nodded. "Heal?" His voice was soft, as if rest was a secret, but one just out of his reach. "Yes, we must rest. . . . We . . ."

"Begging your pardon, Governor, sir," Moor began. "Am I . . . that is, is my crew . . . ?"

The governor eyed Moor as if seeing him for the first time. "Are you what, Captain?"

Moor looked at his feet and smiled. "*Under arrest* is the easiest way to phrase it."

Noah's uncle waved the idea away. "I'm tired, not daft. I know what you did for this city. Still, I would rather a ship of smugglers be on someone else's waters. So find other waters."

He turned to walk away but Moor chased after him, tugging at his sleeve. "Begging another pardon, sir, but as your nephew can confirm—"

"They're sinking," said Noah. "They need time for repairs."

His uncle stood himself up to his full height. "The city needs repairs. There is nothing I can do. There is nowhere for them to stay, and the city must repair itself before it can even think of helping . . ."

"Smugglers," Noah finished. His uncle didn't even want to say the word again.

"We just need a safe place to bed," Captain Moor explained, and we can do the repairs ourselves. A few weeks is all I ask."

The governor shook his head. "Look around you, Captain. There are no rooms. Where would your crew stay when the city can barely find shelter for itself."

Noah closed his eyes. He was tired of hearing the men argue. He was tired and desperate to see Marie. Behind his exhausted eyes, he saw the city and Singe again. They blurred together as before. And his father's face, the plummeting airship, the waves of the ocean. It was all too much. And above it all rose the teetering spiral of the growing house. Empty and echoing and now silent without a robot to build it.

Noah opened his eyes and pulled at his uncle's sleeve. "I might have a solution."

Noah and his uncle talked very little on their way to the house. They walked past the statue of Nicholas—now facedown, embedded in the rotting wharf—and the rubble of the jail. The signs of where octochines had created new entrances were a terrible reminder of their size and power.

The city streets were covered in ruin. As they reached the market street, Noah could see the front of nearly every store was gone. They navigated a street of broken bricks, passing shopkeepers in their excavated stores, their families lurking behind them. All eyes were on Noah and the governor as they passed. A few fingers pointed in their direction, accompanied by whispers.

It's worse than before, Noah thought. Worse than when he and Marie had been taunted. The silent accusations had stung more than the singing had. He was certain he was the target of everyone's anger.

An older woman—her white apron smeared with ash—stepped from a nearly destroyed butcher shop and stopped in their path. "Well done, Governor. Well done." She made a show of clapping, but she sounded angry. "Our friend and protector! Hurrah!"

Others came forward and a ring formed around Noah, his uncle, and the woman. Half the people sneered at Governor Stone, nodding along with the woman's jeers. The other half looked angry, but embarrassed. They didn't seem to agree, but their lives were in ruins, and they saw no reason to rise to the governor's defense.

But no one paid any attention to Noah. It was his uncle that drew them forward, and his failures, alone, that had stirred their anger.

"Come on, child," Stone said to his nephew. "Let's get you to that house and your mother."

Noah's heart raced. His mother was at home.

The pair left the city, passing through the woods in silence. Governor Stone—Uncle Nicholas—led the way. Noah had only come this way once, and the path wasn't familiar.

At last, through the trees, he spotted the towering funnel spiraling into the sky.

The house was unharmed, but many of the trees

surrounding it had broken branches. Some had even been pushed over. Noah glanced back the way they had come, and realized that the path through the woods was no longer a hidden one. It was a wide gaping route straight through. The octochines had found their first home.

Whether they knew it as such, or they had simply wandered up the hill during the battle, it was impossible to know. Maybe they recognized the awkward tumble of rooms rising high above them, like the multiple towers on the island. Noah thought that might change with Elijah guiding them now. He would help them understand what it meant to have a home. They would not wander aimlessly. He reached into his pocket and felt the golden gear there. It was the last thing he had from Elijah. In a way, it was from his father as well.

Inside, the house was just as it had always been. Only, it seemed smaller now. He took in the stuck clock, and the stairs leading to the second floor, and felt as if he were looking at them from above, like looking at a toy model.

"She's upstairs," said Uncle Nicholas, and began to climb. The man's weight made the stairs pop and groan. And it was only then that Noah realized the strangeness of the silence. Since he'd shut down the spideratus, the house would grow no higher. There would be no more banging and slamming and crashing.

Outside Marie's room, sunlight spilled through nearby windows. Uncle Nicholas blocked the light with his body as he stepped aside and waved for Noah to enter.

As he passed the threshold, he couldn't recall ever having been inside before. He knew he must have, as he'd spent all his days here, but everything in the room looked new to him. There was a desk to one side with an ornate silver mirror hanging above it. There was a black, wooden dresser. And there was a bed with four metal posts. Sitting beside the bed, in an uncomfortable-looking wooden chair, was Forewoman Issa, her face smothered with exhaustion. And in the bed was Marie.

Noah's mother.

Noah released a breath and Issa looked up. "She's sleeping. But she seems to be improving."

Marie's head was bandaged, and there was a spot of blood, but she looked peaceful. More peaceful than Noah had ever seen her.

"I saw the collapse," he said. "I thought she might be . . ."

Issa patted his shoulder. "No, we got out. The robot and I managed to pull her free."

"Even as damaged as it was?"

Issa smiled. "Your mother made devoted machines."

Uncle Nicholas stood at the foot of Marie's bed. His shadow lay across her like a blanket, and his own face was serious and dark. "Wake her."

"She needs her sleep," Issa insisted, avoiding his eye.

"She asked me to notify her the moment I had word of Noah. You don't have to like me, but you ought to respect her wishes."

Issa glared up at the man. "I've respected her from the moment she let me take hold of a wrench in her factory. Since when have *you* respected her wishes?" She collected herself and then gently shook Marie's shoulder.

Noah's mother opened her eyes and looked around the room as if unsure where she was. That is until her eyes fell on Noah. She smiled weakly. "Come here," she whispered.

Noah did as she asked, and they held each other in a tight hug. After a long time, she let Noah go and looked at him. There were tears in her eyes. "You did it?"

"Yes," Noah said. "But Elijah . . ."

"He was destroyed?" Marie watched Noah's face, and then understanding swept over her own. "Oh, Noah. I'm sorry."

One day, Noah might tell her how he did it, and he

might tell her how it felt to have to make the changes to his oldest friend. His brother. But for now, the words wouldn't rise up, and he didn't force them.

Marie looked at her brother. Nicholas shifted uncomfortably under her gaze. Despite the low light, the red of his cheeks was obvious. "As you asked, sister. He's home, safe and sound."

"He was brought home by the same ship?"

"The smugglers brought him home, yes."

Marie took a deep breath. "I would like to meet the captain. To thank him."

Uncle Nicholas gave a lopsided grin. "That will likely happen sooner than you expect. I'll let Noah explain. In the meantime"—he walked to the door—"I'll leave you to recuperate for as long as this silence lasts."

"I want you to tell Noah what you told me," Marie said before he could step into the hall. "He deserves to hear it from you."

The big man suddenly looked frightened, his eyes searching the walls and ceiling. Finally, he looked down at Noah. "I told your mother I was wrong to force your father's punishment onto you. I . . . I won't make that mistake again."

Noah saw his powerful uncle was on the verge of

collapse. Part of him pitied the man. Part of him thought he deserved what he got. He wondered if there would be a day when he could both understand and forgive his uncle. Today, he didn't think he could do either.

"When you begin the rebuilding process," Marie said, "let us know what needs to be done."

Nicholas stared at her blankly. His governorship was over. Noah knew this, too. He'd seen how the people in the city responded to him now. He watched as his uncle chewed on the truth, then swallowed it back. "I will."

Without another word, Nicholas Stone left, the sounds of his footsteps growing more distant. They heard the front door crash open, but not close.

Issa stood. "I'll step downstairs for a moment. You take care of your mother."

Noah and Marie were left looking at each other in the quiet room. Marie rubbed at her temple. Whatever was damaged would take time to heal, but when it had, she would return to the city. She would rebuild. She would prepare. And she would need his help. She looked at him and took his hand. "I'm so tired," she said. "But more than that, I'm so sorry."

She squeezed and he squeezed back.

"It's okay, Mother." The word seemed to clank in his

mouth. "Mom." He blushed. It still felt unfamiliar. But it was better than calling her Marie.

For some reason she started to cry harder even though she was smiling. "Don't forgive me too quickly." She shut her eyes again and wiped at her face. "This was never your fault."

Lurking inside Noah was a feeling that echoed what he'd felt for his uncle. There was understanding at the edges, but at its core, ticking away like a perfect machine, was anger and distrust. He wanted Marie to be Mom, but it would take time to change the machine of his heart.

"You should rest," he said. "I'll be here when you wake up."

She gave his hand another squeeze and raised it to her lips to give it a kiss. Her eyes were still closed, but she looked brighter and far happier than Noah could remember. "I know you will."

Noah gave her a kiss on her cheek. She tried to pat his face, but she was tired and her hand missed, waving the air. She laid it down and then turned her head away. Her breathing was slow and steady. She was already asleep.

Noah stood by her bed for a minute and listened to the steady rhythm. *We'll talk when she wakes.* About what exactly, he didn't know, but he knew it would be important. Things for the city, and for them. He felt a rush of energy build inside him. He knew he was tired and hungry, but he also felt as if he just couldn't sit still. He gave his mother another kiss on the cheek and then left the room.

She would wake and heal. And when she was ready, she would find him waiting, ready to help. And she would find that the house had grown larger as she slept. Not physically, but in spirit. It would have to. It was about to be full of guests without a home.

No, not guests, Noah thought. *Family.*

They were already arriving. He could hear them making their way through the trees and up the path to the front door. Noah stood at the top of the stairs and looked down at the stunned face of Issa. Hearing the approaching shouts and laughter, complaints and songs, she'd gone to the door to investigate. It was a cacophony. She looked up at Noah.

"My uncle agreed," he said as he came down the stairs. "They have nowhere else to go."

Noah and Issa stood side by side as Captain Moor led his crew up the winding path.

The captain smiled wickedly at Issa. "Begging your pardon, miss. Is the master of the house home?"

Issa silently pointed at Noah.

Moor smiled and saluted. "Permission to come aboard, your honor?"

"Aye, Captain." Noah grinned. "Welcome home."

Captain Moor grinned and stepped into the house. Noah thought he saw the man stagger a bit, now that he was on dry land. "Pilot!" Moor called over his shoulder. "Set up an observation deck at the highest point. I want to be able to keep an eye on my ship. That harbor is full of scoundrels."

Pilot winked at Noah as he came through into the entryway. "Aye, and I'll find a spot that can see into some of the richer houses, as well."

Mister Steem's bandages still looked too painful a reminder of his new loss as he passed through into the house. Noah nodded up at him, already imagining a contraption that might solve some of the first mate's troubles.

Winona was next, and Noah was so happy to see her, he couldn't keep from laughing. "Lady Winona," he said, sweeping into a bow.

She punched his shoulder. "Watch yourself, kid."

"Yes, boss."

She laughed at that.

Gentleman Nest and Lady Byrne, the chief engineer and her crew, the other sailors, they all pushed past Noah and Issa.

The forewoman was still stunned. She looked from

Noah to the line of sailors and then up the stairs. "Well, you do have room."

And they did. The house had grown so large every night for no reason, but now every part of it needed to be even larger.

The sailors carried boxes of gear, clothing, and equipment. The *Abbreviated* was in danger of sinking, and everything they owned had to be stowed until they made her shipshape again. Until then they would be at home in Noah's home.

The house had once been filled with the hammering and sawing, the banging and clanging of growing ever larger. Now, it was the boom of footsteps and the thud of dropped crates that smelled of seawater. And above it all, the warbling song of Gentleman Nest. Noah had told Winona about his life in the house, and she must have told Nest, for Noah somehow recognized the song.

He smiled as the rooms above began to echo with the thrashing and crashing of a family turning a house into a home. He might not have known it, but his heart had been set on that goal, and now he found he was on that path.

He climbed up after them. To help. To be there in the crowd of them, and to hear the later verses of Gentleman Nest's somehow-familiar song.

*"There are rules to living in a house that grows
   at night,
And this boy knew them all.
When there's crashing and smashing
   and banging and clanging,
Rules echo from every wall."*

✸ACKNOWLEDGMENTS✸

This book couldn't have happened without the support of many people. Initially, it was with family and friends that I found the support to even start this journey. My everlasting love and gratitude to Sarah for constant encouragement, and Aidan for being the inspiration for the entire world that lives in this book. Thanks to my parents, to my brother Matthew, Frank, and especially early reader/supporter Brooks.

The book grew with the support of my wonderful editor Alison Weiss, my supportive publisher Bethany Buck, my open-minded agent at Writers House Alec Shane, and illustrator extraordinaire Graham Carter. It has benefitted and grown with the support of copy editors, marketing and publicity and other teams and assistants that work in support of Pixel+Ink's authors and readers. My thanks to each and every one.

And lastly, in the words of Gentleman Nest, I'd be sunk as a stone if I didn't thank the most important of all: You. The one holding this book. The one reading these words. Thank you for taking the time to breathe life into this story. I only carry half the weight. You carried the other half. And you did it beautifully.